When the Moon Was Ours

Also by Anna-Marie McLemore

The Weight of Feathers

When the Moon Was Ours

Anna-Marie McLemore

THOMAS DUNNE BOOKS
St. Martin's Griffin ⋈ New York

THOMAS DUNNE BOOKS.
An imprint of St. Martin's Press.

WHEN THE MOON WAS OURS. Copyright © 2016 by Anna-Marie McLemore.
All rights reserved. Printed in the United States of America. For information,
address St. Martin's Press, 175 Fifth Avenue, New York, N.Y. 10010.

www.thomasdunnebooks.com
www.stmartins.com

The Library of Congress Cataloging-in-Publication Data is available upon request.

ISBN 978-1-250-05866-9 (hardcover)
ISBN 978-1-4668-7324-7 (e-book)

Our books may be purchased in bulk for promotional, educational, or business use.
Please contact your local bookseller or the Macmillan Corporate and
Premium Sales Department at 1-800-221-7945, extension 5442, or by e-mail
at MacmillanSpecialMarkets@macmillan.com.

First Edition: October 2016

10 9 8 7 6 5 4 3 2

To the boys who get called girls,
the girls who get called boys,
and those who live outside these words.
To those called names,
and those searching for names of their own.
To those who live on the edges,
and in the spaces in between.
I wish for you every light in the sky.

Acknowledgments

)

While this book is very much a work of fiction, I wouldn't have felt safe writing a story that draws on so many aspects of my identity if it weren't for many wonderful people I have the privilege of knowing and working with. I'm tremendously thankful for all of them. I'll name a few here.

Taylor Martindale Kean, who I wanted to work with the first time we met, who I've been grateful to work with ever since, and who is an incredible advocate for diversity in literature. Stefanie Von Borstel and Adriana Dominguez, for their help with my Spanish, and everyone at Full Circle Literary for creating a place where diverse authors and stories are welcome.

Kat Brzozowski, for her guidance and wisdom with this book, and for her energy, humor, and spirit. Lisa Pompilio, for another gorgeous cover that captures the spirit of two characters and their world. The team at Thomas Dunne Books/St. Martin's Press: Tom Dunne, Michelle Cashman, Brittani Hilles, Marie Estrada, Karen

Masnica, Brant Janeway, Lisa Davis, and Romanie Rout; Talia Sherer, Anne Speith, and Peter Janssen at Macmillan Library; and everyone else who turned this story into a book.

The writers who offered their insights: Mackenzi Lee, for the candor and the camaraderie across three thousand miles. Kelly Loy Gilbert, for her invaluable thoughts no matter what stage a manuscript is at. Aisha Saeed, for helping make this story's grounding more authentic and its magic more accessible. Shveta Thakrar, for her advice on helping these characters' heritages shine through, and for being a sister in fairy tales.

Robin Talley, who through her books and her friendship makes me braver and a little less afraid to write queer characters.

Nadia Hashimi and Jenny Nordberg, whose work first introduced me to the cultural and societal context of bacha posh.

My mother, who taught me to be a hopeless romantic. My father, for raising me to believe there was nothing being a girl could stop me from doing. My family, who makes me proud of the people and places I come from.

My husband, for his grace and patience in all things and, in particular, with all my questions about his life as a transgender boy.

Readers, for giving books lives of their own.

Maybe I need you the way that big moon needs
    that open sea.
Maybe I didn't even know I was here 'til I saw you
    holding me.

—*Andrea Gibson*

When the Moon Was Ours

sea of clouds

)

As far as he knew, she had come from the water. But even about that, he couldn't be sure.

It didn't matter how many nights they'd met on the untilled land between their houses; the last farm didn't rotate its crops, and stripped the soil until nothing but wild grasses would grow. It didn't matter how many stories he and Miel had told each other when they could not sleep, him passing on his mother's fables of moon bears that aided lost travelers, Miel making up tales about his moon lamps falling in love with stars. Sam didn't know any more than anyone else about where she'd come from before he found her in the brush field. She seemed to have been made of water one minute and the next, became a girl.

Someday, he and Miel would be nothing but a fairy tale. When they were gone from this town, no one would remember the exact brown of Miel's eyes, or the way she spiced recado rojo with cloves, or even that Sam and his mother were Pakistani. At best, they would remember a dark-eyed girl, and a boy whose family had come from somewhere else. They would remember only that Miel and Sam had been called Honey and Moon, a girl and a boy woven into the folklore of this place.

This is the story that mothers would tell their children:

There was once a very old water tower. Rust had turned its metal such a deep orange that the whole tank looked like a pumpkin, an enormous copy of the fruit that grew in the fields where it cast its shadow. No one tended this water tower anymore, not since a few strikes from a summer of lightning storms left it leaning to one side as though it were tired and slouching. Years ago, they had filled it from the river, but now rust and minerals choked the pipes. When they opened the valve at the base of the tower, nothing more than a few drops trickled out. The bolts and sheeting looked weak enough that one autumn windstorm might crumble the whole thing.

So the town decided that they would build a new water tower, and that the old one would come down. But the only way to drain it would be to tip it over like a cup. They would have to be ready for the whole tower to crash to the ground, all that rusted metal, those thousands of gallons of dirty, rushing water spilling out over the land.

For the fall, they chose the side of the tower where a field of brush was so dry, a single spark would catch and light it all. All that water, they thought, might bring a little green. From that field, they dug up wildflowers, chicory and Indian paintbrush and larkspur, replanting them alongside the road, so they would not be drowned or smashed. They feared that if they were not kind to the beautiful things that grew wild, their own farms would wither and die.

Children ran through the brush fields, chasing away squirrels and young deer so that when the water tower came down, they would not be crushed. Among these children was a boy called Moon because he was always painting lunar seas and shadows onto glass and paper and anything he could make glow. Moon knew to keep his steps and his voice gentle, so he would not startle the rabbits, but would stir them to bound back toward their burrows.

When the animals and the wildflowers were gone from the brush field, the men of the town took their axes and hammers and mallets to the base of the water tower, until it fell like a tree. It arced toward the ground, its fall slow, as though it were leaning forward to touch its own shadow. When it hit, the rusted top broke off, and all that water rushed out.

For a minute the water, brown as a forgotten cup of tea, hid the brush that looked like pale wheat stubble. But when it slid and spread out over the field, flattening the brittle stalks, soaking into the dry ground, everyone watching made out the shape of a small body.

A girl huddled in the wet brush, her hair stuck to her face, her eyes wide and round as amber marbles. She had on a thin nightgown, which must have once been white, now stained cream by the water. But she covered herself with her arms, cowering like she was naked and looking at everyone like they were all baring their teeth.

At first a few of the mothers shrieked, wondering whose child had been left in the water tower's path. But then they realized that they did not know this girl. She was not their daughter, or the daughter of any of the mothers in town.

No one would come near her. The ring of those who had come to see the tower taken down widened a little more the longer they watched her. Each minute they put a little more space between her and them, more afraid of this small girl than of so much falling water and rusted metal. And she stared at them, seeming to meet all their eyes at once, her look both vicious and frightened.

But the boy called Moon came forward and knelt in front of her. He took off his jacket and put it on her. Talked to her in a voice soft enough that no one else could hear it.

Everyone drew back, expecting her to bite him or to slash her fingernails across his face. But she looked at him, and listened to him, his words stripping the feral look out of her eyes.

After that day, anyone who had not been at the water tower thought she was the same as any other child, little different from the boy she was always with. But if they looked closely, they could see the hem of her skirt, always a little damp, never quite drying no matter how much the sun warmed it.

This would be the story, a neat distillation of what had happened. It would weed out all the things that did not fit. It would not mention how Miel, soaking wet and smelling of rust, screamed into her hands with everyone watching. *Because* everyone was watching, and she wanted to soak into the ground like the spilled water and vanish. How Sam crouched in front of her saying, "Okay, okay," keeping his words slow and level so she would know what he meant. *You can stop screaming; I hear you, I understand.* And because she believed him, that he heard her, and understood, she did stop.

It would leave out the part about the Bonner sisters. The four of them, from eight-year-old Chloe to three-year-old Peyton, had been there to see the water tower come down, all of them lined up so their hair looked like a forest of autumn trees. Peyton had been holding a small gray pumpkin that, in that light, looked almost blue. She had it cradled in one arm, and with the other hand was petting it like a bird. When she'd taken a step toward Miel, clutching that pumpkin, Miel's screaming turned raw and broken, and Peyton startled back to her sisters.

Once Sam knew about Miel's fear of pumpkins, he understood, how Peyton treating it like it was alive made Miel afraid not only of Peyton but of all of them. But that part would never make it into the story.

This version would also strip away the part about Sam trying to take Miel home like she was a stray cat. His mother's calm conviction as she diced potatoes that they would find a place for this girl. And she was right. In less time than it took the saag aloo to finish cooking, Aracely, the woman who had seemed to Sam as much like an aunt as a neighbor, appeared at their door saying she might have space in her rented house for this girl made of water.

It would not mention how Miel's hair had barely dried when the first green leaf of a rose stem broke through her small wrist. That was a different story, strange and bloody and glinting with the silver of scissor blades. A story for older children, ones who did not fear their own nightmares.

And this version of the story would scramble the order of events. No one but Sam had heard what Miel was screaming into her hands. *I lost the moon,* she had said, sobbing against her fingers. *I lost the moon.*

He never asked her what she meant. Even then, he knew better. Her feeling that the moon had slipped from her grasp seemed locked in a place so far inside her that to reach it would be to break her open. But this was why Sam painted shadows and lunar seas on paper and metal and glass, copying the shadows of *mare imbrium* and *oceanus procellarum*—to give her back the moon. He had painted dark skies and bright moons on flat paper since he was old enough to hold a brush, old enough to look through the library's astronomy atlases. But it wasn't until this girl spilled out of the water tower, sobbing over her lost moon, that Sam began painting so many copies of the brightest light in the night sky.

He would never let it seem lost to her again.

Moon had become his name to this town because of her. Because of her, this town had christened him. Without her, he had been nameless. He had not been Samir or Sam. He had been no one. They knew his name no more than they knew who this girl had been before she was water.

lake of autumn

)

They'd touched each other every day since they were small. She'd put her palm to his forehead when she thought he had a fever. He'd set tiny gold star stickers on her skin on summer days, and at night had peeled them off, leaving pale constellations on her sun-darkened body.

She'd seen the brown of her hand against the brown of his when they were children, and holding hands meant nothing more than that she liked how warm his palm was in the night air, or that he wanted to pull her to see something she had missed. A meteor shower or a vine of double-flower morning glories, so blue they looked dyed.

All these things reminded her of his moons, and his moons reminded her of all these things. He'd hung a string of them between her house and his, some as small as her cupped palms, others big enough to fill her arms. They brightened the earth and wild grass. They were tucked into trees, each giving off a ring of light just wide enough to meet the next, so she never walked in the dark. One held a trace of the same gold as those foil star stickers. Another echoed the blue of those morning glories Sam could find even in the dark. Another was the pure, soft white of the frost flowers he showed her on winter mornings, curls of ice that looked like tulips and peonies.

The one she passed under now was the color of a rose that had grown from her wrist when she and Sam were in ninth grade. She remembered it because, in the hall at school, her sleeve had slipped back, and the rose accidentally brushed the elbow of a girl who recoiled, yelling, "Watch where you're going."

That same afternoon, when the girl's boyfriend broke up with her, she'd blamed Miel and that brush of petals. She cornered Miel in the girls' bathroom, and looked like she was about to backhand her when Sam came up behind her and said, "Oh, I wouldn't do that if I were you." His voice had been so level, more full of advice than a threat, that the girl had actually turned around. "You know the last girl who did that turned into a potted plant, right?" he said, and he sold it with such caution and certainty that the girl believed it. She sank into all the rumors about Miel and Aracely, and she backed away.

If Miel hadn't known Sam was her friend before, she knew after that. That was the first and last time he ever went into the girls' room by choice.

Miel could chart their history by these moons, lighting the path between the violet house where she lived with Aracely and the bright-tiled roof of Sam's house.

The closer she got to him, the more she felt it in her roses, like a moon pulling on a sea. Since she was small, the roses had grown from her skin, each bursting through the opening on her wrist that never healed. One grew, and she destroyed it, and another grew, and she destroyed it. But now she hesitated before cutting them, or pushing them underwater so the river's current carried them away. Because for the past few months, they'd responded to Sam. The more time she spent around him, the more her wrist felt heavy and sore. He caught her holding her forearm during school, and stole bags of crunchy, fluffy ice from the chemistry lab for her to put against her sleeve.

If she thought of him too much, her roses grew deeper and brighter; the one on her wrist was now as dark pink as her favorite lipstick.

Tonight, he was waiting behind his house, hands in his pockets. His stance showed neither impatience nor boredom. She always wondered if he saw her from his window, or if he just came outside early, and didn't mind waiting.

"I stole something from work today," he said. The moons gave enough light to let her see he was holding his tongue against his back teeth, proud of his own guilt.

"You what?" she asked.

"Don't worry," he said. "I'll bring it back. I just wanted you to see it. Come on."

Inside, he showed her the brush he used to pollinate each pumpkin blossom by hand.

They only opened for one day, Sam had told her when he started at the Bonners' farm. An explanation for the slow, careful work of taking pollen from each anther and brushing it onto each flower's stigma. That small act made a blossom become a pumpkin. The Bonners gave Sam this task because they thought his skill with brushes covered in paint would translate to brushes coated in pollen.

But Miel had never seen one of the brushes before. Now Sam flicked the oat-colored bristles first against her forearm and then against her rose. For those few seconds, the tiny birthmarks on her arm were grains of pollen, and her rose was the corolla of a pumpkin blossom.

The bristles made her flinch, like the petals growing from her wrist had as much sensation as her fingers. They didn't. Yes, pulling on the stem would hurt her. Knocking the flower head against a kitchen table stung the opening her roses grew from. But the petals themselves were like her hair, rooted in her, but not the same kind of alive as her skin.

For that moment though, of those bristles skimming over that lipstick-colored rose, the sense that those petals could feel as much as her lips or her fingers shimmered through her.

Her eyes flashed up to his.

His eyes were a little more open than they always were, the brown clearer.

The brush and his fingers stilled on her skin.

He hadn't meant it like that. She knew that. She could tell by that startled look.

This wasn't his fingers tracing her back and shoulders, finding stars. This wasn't her checking the flush of his forehead and then leading him home in the middle of a school day. This was a thing that turned into his mouth on hers. This was the pollination brush he'd forgotten to set down, still in his hands as he held her, bristles feathering against her neck. This was the breaking of the strange nervousness that had grown between them over the past few months, a hesitancy to touch that would vanish one day and reappear the next.

She felt the shape of pumpkin blossoms glowing on her skin, waiting for Sam's fingers.

The understanding settled on her that it was Sam, not that wooden-hilted brush, that held the magic of turning a vine-laced field into a thousand pumpkins.

Now Miel's body felt like soft, papery petals. She kissed him back, pushing him toward the stairs, him stumbling up them without turning around. Even with his eyes shut, taking the stairs by muscle memory, he was careful not to crush her rose. She reached for his belt and the top button of his jeans, and he let her. He slid his hand under her shirt, and she let him.

He let her, she let him, and then they were in his bed. The smell of paint made the air in his room bitter, sharp. A tarp covered the floor, his brushes and paints and the makings of half-finished lights scattered in a way that looked disordered to her but made sense to him.

Light from the moons spilled a layer of milky lilac over the floor. They were covered in the blue-green of his bedroom walls, and the smell of spices from his mother's kitchen that soaked into his hair and came off onto his sheets. Orange flower. Green cardamom. Pomegranate molasses. It was so sharp and vivid on him that it made her bite the back of his neck. He startled, then settled into the soft pressure of her teeth, and set his fingers against her harder.

He didn't take off his shirt. She didn't try to take it off him. He never took off his shirt for the same reason he worked on the Bonners' farm. Their school let his work weeding the fields and cutting vines stand in for the PE requirement he'd put off since ninth grade. He couldn't meet it any other way, not if it meant changing for class or team practice in a locker room.

His skin smelled like warm water, not taking on the scent of his soap. She ran her fingers over the faint scarring that shadowed his jawline, from acne he had both grown into and out of early.

The petals of her rose skimmed his neck—she did that on purpose—and then along the inside of his thigh—she did that without meaning to. He shivered, but didn't draw back. Even when her touching him made her rose petals flick against his body, she kept a little distance between him and her wrist so the thorns wouldn't scratch him.

When he traced her skin, the thought of everything he told her about the moon skimmed across her, about the lunar seas and bays. *Mare nubium* and *mare undarum*, the sea of clouds and the sea of waves. *Lacus autumni* and *sinus iridum*, the lake of autumn and the bay of rainbows. The features he painted with brushes and with his bare fingers.

His hands were so sure, the pressure of his fingers so gradual and steady, that she couldn't help thinking of his family, years ago. Their fields of crocuses. Their quick, delicate work of picking the saffron threads from the center of those purple flowers. She wondered if this was a thing that lived in his blood and in his fingers. A craft that started as finding wisps of red among violet petals, and that, through years and generations, became the skill of finding, easily and without hesitation, what he was looking for.

The one thing that marred it all, that made it anything shy of perfect, was the Bonner sisters. Las gringas bonitas. Those pale girls, pretty and perfect. One stray thought, and those threads of saffron turned to the red of their braids and curls. Just that single, unwanted thought, and the gradient of their hair swirled through Miel like fall leaves.

The Bonner girls hadn't felt far from Miel since the first time she saw them at the water tower. She let Sam think it was just that Peyton had been holding that pumpkin she treated like a pet. But it was more than the pumpkin. The water had barely cleared from Miel's eyes when she saw the moon, caught between last quarter and full, disappear behind their heads. Even against the not-yet-dark sky, it lit up the red and gold and orange of their hair. From where Miel stood, her eyes feeling new, blurring everything, it looked like the moon had vanished into them, like they'd absorbed it. They had taken all its light. And Miel kept screaming, wanting to warn the boy standing in front of her that the moon was a thing that could be lost.

Now the Bonner sisters were older, and beautiful, their eyes a fierce and fearless kind of open. Together, they were as imposing as an unmapped forest. Some called them witches, for how many hearts they'd broken. Some said they had hidden, in the woods, a stained glass coffin that acted like a chrysalis, turning each girl who slept in it as beautiful as every Bonner girl before her. But ever since Chloe had left town, they were no longer the Bonner sisters. It was just Lian, and Ivy, and Peyton drifting through their father's fields. Sometimes Miel saw Lian in the grocery store, picking out yellow apples, or Peyton riding her bike at the edge of town.

Miel had never understood why, with the four of them around, Sam would ever choose her. Miel was a handful of foil stars, but they were the fire that made constellations. Her hair was the dark, damp earth under their family's farm, and they were curling vines and scrolled pumpkins.

But the Bonner sisters weren't the ones who'd met Sam a thousand times in the open land between their houses. They hadn't shown him the slight differences in blues and browns of Araucana and Wyandotte chickens' eggs. And maybe these things had made Miel look different to Sam. Maybe the time he'd helped her shear a pair of jeans, the knees worn through, into cutoffs, made him overlook the fact that jeans fit her a little different in a thigh than they did the Bonner sisters. Or maybe the deep, bright colors of her roses distracted him from how her nails were almost never polished.

Maybe the day she'd helped him paint his room the color of the ocean his father was born near, that afternoon when she'd gotten that deep blue-green all over the front of her, made Sam forget that she did not stretch out a shirt like the Bonner sisters. Except for Peyton, the youngest, the Bonner sisters filled their bras like batter poured into a cake pan.

If those things made Miel look different to Sam, if that was why he was under her now, she didn't mind. Because she saw him as something different than anyone else did too. She had seen him naked. Almost naked. And she understood that with his clothes off, he was the same as he was with them on.

new sea

)

*O*ne day, they would be no more than that fairy tale. They would be two children named Honey and Moon, folded into the stories whispered through this town.

But tonight they were not those children. Tonight, they were Sam and Miel, and he was pulling her on top of him and then under him. The way she moved against him made him feel the sharp presence of everything he had between his legs and, for just that minute, a forgetting, of everything he didn't.

He thought he knew her body. He was so sure that he could have drawn it, mapped it as easily as the lunar seas he could paint without looking at a map of the moon. But under his hands, against his own body, she was both safe and unfamiliar. She was a world unknown. She was a place whose darkness held not fear, but the promise of stars.

Even against him, she was a locked world, sealed off. Even with how she let him put his hand anywhere he tried to, even with how she took his hand and put it where he was too shy to go, she had so many secrets. He'd given her every one he had, from why he never took off his shirt, to the truth of how badly his mother had wanted a child, and the cold bargain she'd made to get one.

Miel still had thousands of secrets, small and shimmering. She held them tight in her hands, and he had nothing left that he had not given up.

bay of harmony

)

*T*he day after Miel slept with Sam was the day Chloe Bonner came back.

That morning Miel came downstairs and found Aracely in the
kitchen, putting on coffee and yawning at a morning so new it was
still silver.

Miel set three cups she'd collected from her room in the kitchen
sink. Lately Aracely had had it with Miel leaving forgotten cups of
tea on counters and tables. She'd find one and say, *Will you put this in
the sink already? I feel like I'm living in a coffeehouse.*

Even in her nightgown, without her makeup on, Aracely was a
slice of color against the window. Her hair was as bright as the fruit
of a nectarine. The brown of her skin looked like raw gold stripped
from quartz. And she stood tall enough that she looked like she could
meet the gaze of the sky out on the horizon.

The stories said that Aracely had appeared one summer along
with a hundred thousand butterflies. The butterflies covered the

town like bright gold scales, powdered wings shivering in the breezes. And when, early that autumn, they all flitted away, there was Aracely, this strange, tall young woman with skin like those iridescent wings.

Of course, that was years before Miel fell out of the water tower, before the water had given her back. So she never saw that cloud of wings.

Aracely handed Miel a spoon of honey, thick and deep as amber.

"Fireweed," Aracely said, pulling her hair back into a loose bun. Her fingernails, painted the color of achiote seeds, stood brick-red against the pale gold. "Just got it from that place on the edge of town."

Aracely knew how much Miel liked honey, how she ate it straight, every kind Aracely brought home. This woman who acted as something between a sister and mother to Miel knew every food and spice she liked and disliked. She knew that windstorms gave her nightmares, and that the light of Sam's moons let her sleep.

But Miel didn't know how to tell Aracely about what had happened with Sam. About sneaking out of his house before his mother came home. About the soreness in Miel's body that felt like a thing to hold on to instead of wait out.

Of course there were some things Aracely did not know. Sometimes, she seemed about to ask Miel something. Maybe about who Miel had been before she spilled out of the water tower, or if she had ever belonged to anyone else before she belonged to Aracely. But Aracely would always open her mouth, pause, and then close it again and turn back to the sink or the stove. Aracely knew, without being told, the things Miel did not want to talk about.

Now Miel couldn't even meet Aracely's eyes. Aracely's work was curing lovesickness. It was her gift to know when a heart was overrun with wanting someone. When it came to Aracely, this town alternated between gratitude and blame. At night, they came to her, asking her help for their worn-out hearts. During the day, they whispered that she was a witch, or blamed her for the powdery blight bleaching out an orchard's harvest, or held her responsible for the storm that might rain out that year's lighting of the pumpkin lanterns.

They gave her the same inconsistency they might give a lover, adoration at night, disavowal in the morning. How indebted they were to her meant they offered her either scorn or respect, depending on the time of day and how many people were watching.

Miel had learned to live with the self-conscious feeling that Aracely could sense the weight of her heart. This morning, she was sure if she let Aracely look at her for too long, she'd know. The fact that Aracely liked Sam made it worse. Miel imagined Aracely thinking of them more like brother and sister, recoiling at the idea of Miel digging her fingers into Sam's back.

Aracely poured coffee into heavy mugs, and Miel flushed and looked down. She'd never noticed that the color of these cups, blue-green as eucalyptus, was only a little off from Sam's bedroom walls.

"She's back," Aracely said. She half-sang the words, drawing out each syllable until it was almost a trill.

Miel licked the honey off the spoon. It tasted a little like tea, the flavor from the stalks of pink flowers that dotted scarred land after a fire. "Who?" she asked.

"La última bruja."

Miel gave Aracely a laugh. This was one of a thousand reasons Miel loved Aracely. So often, Aracely was called a bruja herself, a witch, and still she didn't flinch at calling someone else the word.

Miel's smile vanished the second she realized who Aracely meant.

Aracely was trying to make a joke of it, sipping her coffee like this was any other morning gossip. She was all charm and assurance. It was what made her so good at curing lovesickness. Less skilled curanderas left their patients stricken with susto, a fright so deep they wandered the woods startled and blind. But Aracely never left a lovesick man or woman sobbing on the wooden table. She placed her palms on their shoulders, whispering to them, so they barely noticed the lovesickness leaving their bodies.

Miel knew Aracely's voice better than those men and women. She heard each catch and hitch. It wasn't that Aracely was afraid of the Bonner girls. Aracely wasn't afraid of anything; she had pity for Miel's fear of water but little patience for her fear of pumpkins. Each fall, on the night that half the town came out to set carved, glowing pumpkins floating on the river, Miel hid in her room, and Aracely stood outside the door saying, "Oh, for God's sake, they're fruits not hornets. Get out here."

But even Aracely was wary of the fire-haired girls. She'd always thought their nervous mother and father pulled them from school less because of what happened with Chloe, and more because if they taught them at home, it was less obvious that the girls had no friends but one another. That they never invited anyone over. That they flirted with boys on crowded streets but that even those boys were not their friends, would not last the next frost or blossom that marked a new season.

Miel left the spoon on the counter and went back upstairs.

"Don't do it," Aracely called up.

Miel heard the smile in her voice, but that smile didn't veil the warning.

"I mean it," Aracely said. "Don't do it. You'll just torture yourself."

Miel listened.

She listened until about four that afternoon, when she stood at the edge of the Bonners' farm trying to keep away the echo of Aracely's words.

If Mr. or Mrs. Bonner saw her, she could always say she was there to see Sam. She could say he was going to show her how he used the pollination brushes.

No. Something else. Not the pollination brushes.

Miel kept her distance from the vines. No matter Aracely's reassurances that they were just fruit, Miel still feared pumpkins the way other girls feared spiders or grass snakes.

Then she saw the curtain of Chloe's hair, the softening light turning it peach.

The opening of Miel's rose grew from prickled and turned hot.

Chloe had graduated last year at nineteen, and had turned twenty while she was away. Twenty, that number that Miel always thought of as making someone, in some final way, an adult. Now Chloe swept across her family's side yard wearing cigarette jeans that would have looked out of style on anyone else, and a sweater thin enough to show the pink tone of her skin underneath. She'd grown out her hair. When she left last winter, it had fallen to her shoulders in uneven curls. Now it tumbled to her hip, the weight stretching it straight, so light it was almost blond.

She must have been wearing jeans that tight to show her flat stomach, to show that the thing everyone knew about had not happened.

When Chloe left, the Bonner sisters had lost just enough of their hold to let every other girl in town breathe. Their parents, as frightened of their own daughters as they were concerned for them, had pulled Lian, Ivy, and Peyton out of school, convinced they'd end up like Chloe. So the girls stayed in that house. They sat at the kitchen table with their mother's lesson plans. They peeked out of windows with white edging that stood crisp against the house's navy paint. Or they wandered through their father's fields, barefoot or in soft, worn slippers they borrowed from their mother but were too vain to own themselves.

Chloe wore no shoes. Her feet and her ankles, bare from her cropped jeans, were pale as Lumina pumpkins.

Miel dragged her gaze away from the corner of the farm where

Chloe stood, sure if she stared too long Chloe would know, and catch her looking. Her eyes swept over the fields, and found Sam. First his hair, like black ribbon curled with scissors. The harvest season had left him even darker, his forearms the brown of a Welsummer chicken's egg. He wore that color with the pride of knowing he'd inherited it from his grandmother, a woman Miel knew only from the few bright details he remembered enough to tell her.

The metal of his shears glinted in his hands. He was checking for vines that had started to die off—*going away*, he said they called it—and shells just beginning to harden.

For that moment, he could have been any boy. He could have been Roman Brantley, who once had a gaze so reckless teachers couldn't meet it. But he'd lost that look to Lian Bonner, to her hair that was so dark red it was almost auburn, to the bursts of freckles fanning her temples like wings. She still had his grandfather's hunting jacket, which Lian swore she'd give back if he ever asked. Of course he couldn't look her in the eye long enough to do it.

Or Wynn Yarrow, who broke up with his girlfriend of two years for Peyton. Peyton, the shortest and youngest of the Bonner sisters, with pumpkin-colored hair her mother barrel-curled every morning, and who everyone but him knew would never be interested. Wynn lost not only his girlfriend, but every friend who took her side.

Miel backed away from the edge of the pumpkin field, trying to vanish into the shadows before Sam saw her. The Bonner sisters, like everyone else in town, had seen her with Sam so many times that they noted it no more than seeing her alone. But if Miel came up to him now, he might slouch and blush in a way that traced a ribbon of cool air in the dusty heat. And when he did, Miel's smile might glint like a coin.

The Bonner girls would see it. It would draw them.

They would watch how Sam sometimes climbed trees to set his moons where the branches met and joined, but just as often threw a thin rope over a bough and pulled the moon up. They would notice how, when he had to climb trees to put in new candles or relight ones that had gone out, he did it without hurry. How, if a moon was fragile, he carried a wooden ladder from his mother's shed and leaned it against the trunk, so he wouldn't jostle the moon as he climbed.

They would realize how beautiful this odd boy was, how the moons he hung in the trees at night glowed like a bowl of stars. They would see how his painted lunar seas gave off different shades of light.

No boy was ever so interesting to them as when he was interesting to someone else.

Chloe turned, her braid running the length of her spine, rubber band hitting the small of her back as she followed the brick walkway. She took the stairs to the front porch, and the soles of her feet, dust-covered, flashed a little darker than her ankles. But even the defiance in how she whipped her braid through the air couldn't hide the way she held herself a little differently. Her stomach was flat but her hips had spread. She folded her arms, even thinner than when she'd left, like she was cold. She looked both fearless and young as any Bonner sister, but now the set to her shoulders gave her the proud but cautious look of being someone's mother.

But maybe that was just because Miel knew. Everyone knew. The thing Chloe had tried to keep secret had become its own little life. It had grown so big it refused to go unremarked on.

No matter how tight Chloe's jeans, people would look at her stomach and wonder if she was showing again. She may have been a porcelain figurine, repaired by the finest hands, but she had still cracked and broken. When anyone held her up to the light, the milky threads of where she'd been glued back together showed.

She'd never rule the Bonner girls again. Her reign would pass down to Ivy. Not Lian, even though Lian was the second-oldest. If anyone called Lian dim, the Bonner girls would have scratched them to bleeding with their unfiled, bright-polished nails, but that wouldn't mean they didn't agree.

Now that the Bonner girls were together again, they were a force as strong as the wind that ripped the leaves off maples and sycamores. They were every shade of orange and gold in an October forest. The life would come back into them, and every girl in town who loved any boy in town would take a little longer to fall asleep tonight.

If the Bonner girls knew Miel wanted to keep Sam, that she was not just a strange girl who was friends with a strange boy, they would realize how much fun it would be to take him. It was why they had never had any friends at school except one another. Whenever a girl wanted a boy, so did they. The second they sensed that Miel cared would be the second they decided he would be the next boy whose heart they broke. Not that they ever tried to break anything. They never meant to hurt anyone. They were children petting a cat too hard for no reason except that they liked the feel of its fur.

Together, they were similar enough to dazzle half the boys in this town, different enough that they'd intrigue Sam. And if he ever trusted them as much as he trusted Miel, they would ruin him. They would take everything from him without trying.

Miel's wrist prickled. She looked down at her rose. The pink of her favorite lipstick was draining out of the petals, giving way to red, and then orange, until every petal had turned to copper or amber or rust.

Las gringas bonitas, these four girls who'd made the moon disappear, were back.

lake of hatred

)

She had to kill it. She'd already waited too long, not wanting to slice away the rose she'd worn on her body the night she slept with Sam. And if she kept it on her body, the Bonner girls would know. They'd see the colors of each of their hair. The copper of Ivy's hair at the center, the soft orange and strawberry-blond of Peyton's and Chloe's, the almost-brown of Lian's at the edges.

If they were witches like the rumors said, they'd know. Even if they weren't, they would wonder why Miel's rose held their colors in its petals, and they would look at her, and then at Sam.

Miel paused, finding a break in the familiar silhouettes along the river.

Two shapes stood against the dark, close enough to Miel that she hid in a tree's shadow so they wouldn't see her. Her eyes adjusted to the dark, letting her see one feature at a time. A girl. A boy. Neither standing in enough light for her to recognize them.

But she could make out their posture, the girl's inclining forward.

Eager and flirtatious, her hands flitting in the space between them like birds. From where Miel stood, a tree branch obscured the girl's face, but the moon lit her hair enough to show the color. A veil of rich red that could only belong to a Bonner girl.

The boy's stance did not match the girl's. He did not lean forward. He did not try to touch her. There was no sense that he was making an attempt at persuading her. To let him kiss her, or to get her sisters to sneak out and see him and his friends, or anything at all.

He seemed bored, humoring her rather than being entranced by her. The way he held his shoulders, facing a little out, made him look like he would leave as soon as he could figure out a way that wasn't rude.

Miel knew this same scene. She'd seen it, when girls had tried flirting with Sam, who seemed as oblivious as he was indifferent. She'd been half of it, with other boys, to get back at Sam for—she flushed realizing this later—nothing more than being interesting to another girl.

But she'd never seen it with one of the Bonner girls. The Bonner girls had stolen boyfriends, enchanted reverends' sons, lured away boys who, before, never did anything without their mothers telling them to.

If a Bonner girl couldn't interest a boy she wanted, if she couldn't have anything she wanted, how could she keep her own last name?

Miel moved a little farther down the river, putting tree cover between her and those two shapes. She knelt alongside the river and stared down into the dark water, trying to make out a shape, any sign that something was down there. Fish. The glimmer of pondweed leaves. Or the river mermaids Sam told her stories about, so Miel would one day be unafraid to go in the river.

She wasn't ready. She was never ready; even when she was anxious to have the weight of the rose gone, she cringed before slicing the blades across the stem.

Rumors about her roses laced this town's gossip. Some said her roses could turn the hearts of those who had no desire. Others insisted their perfume, the soft brush of their petals, was enough to enchant the reticent, the frightened, the guarded.

One said Miel had given a pale pink rose, barely blushing, to one of Aracely's friends. A boy had done something so bad to her that she could not think of parting her lips to be kissed even years later, when another boy with hands as gentle as tulip tree leaves wanted to love her. Another said that last year, she'd given a rose to a farmhand who had fallen in love with an apple grower's daughter, but who could not see past how her eyes were the same green as his family's, a family that never let him forget his were brown.

But Aracely had cured them both, not Miel and her roses. Aracely had convinced that girl to love the boy with hands like tulip tree leaves. And the farmhand, he had come to Aracely, and so had the apple grower's daughter, wanting her heart rid of her love for a boy too shy to love her back. They had both wanted lovesickness cures, and Aracely had told them both to come at the same time. When they saw each other in Aracely's indigo room, when they both realized they were heartbroken enough to want the love torn from their rib cages, they touched each other with their hands and their mouths, and they forgot they wanted to be cured.

Aracely was all the magic and skill. Miel was just a body so restless petals burst from her skin. Aracely was all the beauty and goodness in their violet house. Miel was a girl stained with rusted water and the blood on her hands of two people whose names she could not speak.

The silver-plated scissors, both the strangest and the most useful gift Aracely had ever given her, whined when she opened them. She poised the scissors low, close to her skin, and snapped the blades shut. Pain shivered along her veins. It found her heart and her stomach and everything in her that was alive.

Blood seeped from the opening. Pain made Miel's fingers heavy. It weighted her to the ground. It hurt like a knife blade, pressing into her wrist so hard she felt it flash to her ribs.

She let the rose slip into the water, an offering to the mother who now lived on the wind but had died in this water. When the storms came, Miel could hear the murmur of her mother's voice beneath the shriek of the winds, like she was trying to whisper Miel back to sleep.

This was the only gift Miel could give her, the obedience of destroying the roses her mother had feared. She wanted to give her more, a fearlessness of water. But inside Miel was the small, echoing voice of the girl Sam had found, a girl whispering that she should not trust water she could not see to the bottom of.

She didn't remember her father as well as her mother. She knew he was a curandero, the kind skilled at treating wounds, with a talent for setting bones that gave him work as a huesero. And she remembered his hands, how gently he cut her roses away, and then covered the wound with a bandage. Sometimes she tried settling into the memory, but she knew him so little he was not really hers.

The petals vanished under the surface, and the water rippled like the hem of a dress. The moon refracted into a dozen sickles.

Even with as little as Miel remembered, she remembered the whispers about how children with roses growing from their skin would poison their own brothers, or steal the rings and rosaries from their family's graves. It didn't matter if the roses grew from their wrists, like Miel's, or from their ankles or backs. Every son or daughter in their family whose body made roses, they said, turned bitter and ungrateful.

Once their family made cakes with rosewater and cardamom. But that was before roses were things edged with the fear of new mothers. Young women worrying over their sons and daughters, looking for the first signs of green coming through their skin.

The river settled back into its slow current, and the soft rushing of the water carried the sound of muffled sobbing. It broke into small, stifled cries.

Miel startled, searching the sky and listening for the wind. When the wind came, she listened for her mother's voice, hoped she wouldn't hear her crying. The only thing she wanted more than she wanted Sam was for her mother to know that Miel forgave her. That she understood why she did what she did. That she knew her mother loved her.

But the sound wasn't coming from the sky. Or even from under the water. It pulled Miel's eyes down the length of the bank.

The dark outlined the figure of a girl, arms crossed, wind fluffing her hair.

The Bonner girl, though Miel still couldn't tell which one.

Miel got to her feet, pain spinning in her forearm.

"Are you okay?" she called, trying to keep her voice calm like Aracely's, soft and clear as the trickle of water over stones.

But the girl still jumped. Her gaze snapped toward Miel, and the moon turned her face as pale as its own surface.

Ivy Bonner. The ribbons of light off the river showed her features. Her cheeks shone wet. Hints of copper warmed the edges of her hair, even in the dark. Her nose sat between Chloe's, long and straight and proud like their father's, and Peyton's, short and upturned like their mother's.

Ivy nodded, dabbing her fingers over her cheeks. Miel was not important enough for Ivy to pretend she hadn't been crying.

That nod made Miel feel like she was intruding, like she'd been summoned and now was dismissed. She clutched the silver-plated scissors and turned her back to the river.

But Ivy took a few steps toward her. Not in a hurried way. But quickly enough that Miel stopped in her path.

"What are you doing out here?" Ivy asked, and in the same

moment glanced down at Miel's bare wrist, and the scissors. "Oh," she said.

Ivy lifted her eyes to Miel's again. This close, the salt and water drying on her cheeks looked like the thinnest frost.

"Does it hurt?" Ivy asked.

"What?" Miel asked, cringing at the uncertainty in her own voice.

"Cutting them," Ivy said.

To say *no* would seem like a kind of defiance Miel could never wear as well as Ivy or her sisters. To say *yes* was too much of an admission.

Miel nodded.

She hadn't been this close to Ivy since the Bonner sisters left school. And now, so close to her that she could smell the watery camellia scent of her soap, all Miel could think of was Clark Anderson, another of the boys lost to the Bonner sisters. Clark had thought a girl like Ivy, with her hair the color and shine of new pennies, could cure him of wanting to kiss John Sweden under the new water tower. He slept with Ivy in her bedroom in broad daylight, with Sam and the other workers on the farm below her window. And less than twelve hours later he was kissing John again, this time on the water tower ladder at midnight, where people could just recognize their shapes against the stars.

He disappeared from the town the next week. But unlike Chloe or the boy whose baby she had, no one knew where he'd gone.

The way Ivy kept blinking, stung by the salt of her own tears, made pity spread through Miel, until she had to give it words.

"He doesn't matter, you know," Miel said.

Ivy drew back. "What?"

Miel knew to be quiet, but she wanted to even out what she'd said, like smoothing the layer of cream on a tres leches cake.

"He's just a guy," Miel said. "Who cares?"

Ivy's eyes tensed and narrowed.

With that pinching of her eyelashes, Miel knew she'd made a mistake. Now Ivy knew Miel had seen. She would hold against Miel her witnessing this sign of the Bonner girls losing their power over this town's boys.

Ivy tilted her head, watching Miel's wrist. "Why do you kill them?" she asked, neither horrified nor concerned. More curious. More like she thought drowning those petals was a waste.

Miel sank into the relief of Ivy changing the subject, then realized this was something she wanted to talk about even less. She knew how everyone looked at her, at her roses. The rumor that, if a girl slipped one under a boy's pillow, if he breathed in the scent while he slept, she could make him fall in love with her. Or that, for even better effect, the petals could be sugared and baked into a vanilla cake or lavender alfajores, but only with the secret recipes used by the girls in the violet house.

For that second, her nervousness around Ivy, her feeling that she was her handmaid waiting for dismissal, softened. Miel might have been as strange to Ivy as the Bonner sisters were to her. She lived in a house as violet as blueberry cream. Roses grew from her wrist, and Aracely, this woman she lived with, invited lovesick men and women to lie down on her wooden table so she could cure their broken hearts.

If Aracely had been there, she would've told Miel to stop standing there, stop waiting for la bruja to give her instructions.

Miel tipped her head, a greeting and a good-bye.

But then her heart pinched. The Bonner sisters had rarely talked to anyone but one another and the boys they loved and wrecked. Lian had been quiet but friendly enough when she and Sam had to do a group presentation on the orographic effect; Sam wrote the report while Lian drew and colored in all the pictures. When Miel got her period a week early, Chloe had, without comment, slid her a tampon under the bathroom stall. They were neither rude nor warm; they just preferred one another's company to anyone else's.

Now maybe Ivy was lonely enough that she'd talk to anyone. Chloe had been gone for months. She'd missed Lian turning eighteen and Peyton turning fifteen. (Ivy, sixteen, wouldn't have her birthday until December.) Now that Chloe was back, Miel imagined everyone as formal and careful, so attentive to Chloe that she felt smothered and the rest of the sisters felt both jealous and grateful not to be her. Lian and Ivy and Peyton would have crowded together not to miss her, to make it less obvious that she was gone. Now they would all try to shuffle apart to make room for her.

Chloe had been sent away the same week she started to show. Her baby now lived with the aunt she had stayed with these past six months, and, likewise, the boy she'd been seeing was sent to live with relatives in a town so far away Miel had never heard of it. Her sisters must have both missed her and considered her a stranger. This tall young woman who was now a mother, who was angled in her arms and nose but soft in her hips and breasts.

"Ivy," Miel called out.

Ivy turned.

Miel was one of a hundred girls who would sleep better if the Bonner girls lost their peculiar power. But she couldn't help feeling a little sorry for Ivy.

"If you ever need anyone to talk to," Miel said.

Ivy paused, and then nodded, saving Miel from having to say the rest, and herself from having to hear it.

sea of islands

)

*H*is mother knew.

She'd stayed the night before at the Hodges'. Mr. and Mrs. Hodge were in the city until morning, so they'd asked her to watch their children. She'd probably told them bedtime stories about a brother and sister crossing a forest guided only by stars, or a girl learning the language of Kashmir stags and musk deer. Or one Sam had heard from his grandmother, the story of a girl named Laila and a boy called Majnun.

Now his mother stood in the doorway. As soon as she looked at him, he caught the slight lift of her chin, half a nod, that told him she understood.

She looked tired but not wearied, this morning's kohl drawn over the smudged echo of yesterday's eyeliner, so soft gray ringed her eyelashes. The kohl, and the way she painted it on, was one of the few traditions from their family she'd held to, that one from her mother's side. Her father, Sam's grandfather, had given her washed-out blue eyes that looked even paler the way she lined them.

Neither surprise nor disappointment crossed her face. Only a breath in, a steadying. As much as Sam wanted this to pass by without comment, he knew better.

Finally, she said, "Well, I hope you were both safe." She set down the red and blue tapestry bag she'd taken over to the Hodges'. "I'd hate for you to get that girl pregnant. Aracely would murder me."

He was supposed to laugh. He knew he was supposed to laugh. But he couldn't force out the sound.

He wished he were different. He wanted to laugh off her words, to say back, *Oh, very funny.* Short of the kind of miracles Aracely taught Miel out of her Bible, Sam wasn't getting anyone pregnant.

"And you trust her," his mother said, more checking than questioning.

Of course he trusted Miel. She knew everything that could wreck him, but acted like she didn't.

When he was eight, and she walked in on him changing, she didn't scream, or run down the hall. She just shut the door and left, and when he pulled on his jeans and his shirt and went after her, he found her sitting on the back steps. Her expression was so full of both wondering and recognition, as though she almost understood but not quite, that he sat down next to her and told her more than he'd ever planned to.

Now, she slipped him tampons at school because he couldn't risk carrying them in his bag. They had it timed so they passed each other while she was leaving the girls' bathroom and he was going into the boys', the two of them clasping hands just long enough for the handoff.

Once they'd worked out the system, they never spoke of it again, and she never brought it up. He never asked how she always knew when. He didn't have to. They'd spent enough time together that their bodies had pulled on each other, and they now bled at the same time, when the moon was a thin curve of light. If Miel had been anyone else, her knowing this, the steady rhythm of her knowing every month, would have been humiliating.

Sam braced himself, though for what he wasn't sure. Not a morality lecture. His mother had never cautioned him to wait until he was married. Agnostic, indifferent to the faiths of both her father's family and her mother's, she had barely tolerated Sam going along with Miel and Aracely to church and Sunday school. She allowed it only because she thought things would be easier for him if this town thought he was a *good Christian boy*, a phrase she never said without disdain edging her words. She'd made it clear that any God she believed in could not be contained within walls, certainly not inside the whitewashed clapboard of the local church.

But he was never supposed to sleep with a girl. This had been temporary, him living this way, with his breasts bound flat and his hair cut as short as his mother would let him. It was so he could take care of his mother, so there would be a man of the house even though his mother had no sons.

"Are you mad?" he asked, trying not to cringe and look down. His mother hated when he did that, which made him tend toward it even more.

"If you didn't hurt yourself or anyone else, it's not my place to be," she said.

Sometimes she said things like that, and he could almost see the pallor of frost on her words. *It's not my place to be disappointed,* she'd said when he was failing math three years ago. *It's your future, not mine.* And that made him feel even worse.

But it wasn't like that now. There wasn't the same posture of holding herself tall and straight, her expression still. Now her face looked soft with worry. Worse, pity.

"Are you upset?" he asked.

She put her fingers to her temple, shut her eyes, let out a long breath that turned into a sigh. "Sam," she said, the word sounding like wind, like a soft, sad song.

Whenever she said his name like that, it meant the same thing. That whether she or anyone else was upset wasn't the point. That, failing math grade or lost virginity, this was his life, and to her mind, he wasn't acting like it, not as long as his first question was *Are you mad?*

"Are you okay?" his mother asked.

"I think so," he said.

"Is she?"

"I think so."

He would grow out of this, he wanted to tell her. The same way he'd grown out of saying his favorite color was clear (*Why?* Miel had asked him. *Because everything clear is magic, because it's invisible,* he'd told her) and Miel had grown out of saying her favorite color was rainbow (*Why?* he'd asked her. *Because they all look prettier together,* she'd said, *and because I don't want to pick.*).

He would wait it out.

His grandmother had told him the name for these girls. She had brought it with her from Pakistan, and from stories she'd heard from across the border in Afghanistan. Bacha posh. Dressed as a boy. Girls whose parents decided that, until they were grown, they would be sons. Sam and his mother had lost his grandmother when he was so small he could barely remember the wrinkles of her face and whether the brown of her eyes was more gray or gold. But he remembered her voice. Her telling him that their family's saffron farm in Kashmir had been small, but for its size the most productive for a hundred miles. How it took a hundred thousand of those purple crocuses to yield less than a kilogram of saffron.

When his grandmother told him this, it was always with a current

of sadness beneath her pride. Their family had had to leave Kashmir to stay with distant relatives in Peshawar, abandoning their
bright fields. As things around them grew worse—that was how she
always put it, *things were getting worse*—trading the spice from their
fields became impossible. And when she got to that part of the story,
the part that left her heart bitter, she turned to stories that did not
pinch and bite, like the stories of these girls. Daughters who lived as
sons in families who had no sons. These girls spoke to boys and men
in the street. They escorted their sisters out. When Sam heard these
stories, he felt a clawing envy as strong as if he knew these girls by
name.

He had been four, his grandmother only a few months gone, when
he decided he could—he would—be one of these girls. He would
be a bacha posh. He would be the same kind of boy as those girls
who lived as sons.

But when those girls grew up, they became women. And maybe
their lives as wives and mothers at first felt cramped, narrow after
the wide, cleared roads of being boys. But whatever freedom they
missed was not because they wanted to be boys again. It was because
they wanted to be both women and unhindered.

That was his problem. Sam was sure of it. He couldn't be a girl.
But maybe if he waited out these years in boys' clothes and short
hair, he would grow up enough to want to be a woman. He would
wake up and this part of him would be gone, like rain and wind wearing down a hillside.

"You know, I never wanted a son or a daughter," she said.

"Mom," he said, trying to cut her off.

"I didn't think about it that way," she said, ignoring him. "I just
wanted a child."

Sam nodded. He'd heard the story before. How his father had
come from a family of fishermen in Campania, all of whom were
famous for catching a kind of red-mantled squid that came close

enough to the surface only during new moons. And how his father's lack of talent with that squid was the first of many things that made Sam come to be.

But she didn't go on with the story.

"Do you want to talk?" she asked.

Sam picked up the tapestry bag, to take it upstairs for her. "No."

bay of the center

)

iel picked up the phone thinking it was Sam. When he
got back from his shift at the Bonners' farm, he'd call
her, never starting with a greeting. He'd hear her answer and then
start with something like, "I just saw a woman jog past the hardware
store with two parakeets, one on each shoulder." Or, "The king of
hearts is the only one without a mustache. Ever notice that?"

She was one of the few people Sam would talk to on the phone,
afraid of how the line skewed his voice a little higher when he was
always working to keep it low.

But it wasn't Sam. It was Ivy. Asking Miel to come over.

Not asking. Just saying, "Come over."

Miel wondered if Ivy was calling on the ivory princess phone that
had once belonged to her grandmother. So old it had a rotary dial
and a silver base, that phone, according to Sam, was something
buyers always wanted to see when they came to negotiate pumpkin
prices. Carlie Zietlow, the girl Miel shared a desk with in math class,

said the Bonner girls took pictures of one another with it each time they dressed up, once before dances and now before the pumpkin lighting each October.

A week had gone by since Miel had seen Ivy at the river. She'd settled deep into the relief that Ivy had disregarded her offer, and had forgotten about it.

Now Ivy hung up, so softly the noise was a single, crisp click.

Ivy's voice stayed inside Miel's ear like the sound of the ocean caught in a shell. The words had sounded open, guileless, one girl asking another outside to play. But there was also the edge of something a little alluring, like the piloncillo sugar Aracely melted into hot chocolate. It made Miel cringe, thinking of every time Sam heard that voice as he bent down to the vines crossing the Bonners' fields.

But in those two words, Miel thought she caught a little of that same sadness. Ivy's voice matched that same blank, damp-cheeked look she'd had by the river. So she did what Ivy said.

If no one in this town had cared what happened to Miel, she would still be wild-eyed, hiding in the brush where the old water tower had fallen, or in Sam's house, his mother wondering what to do with her. It was the least Miel could do to go over, even if the Bonner sisters, the whole Bonner house, scared her. The Bonner sisters talked to so few people outside that house that Ivy's request seemed like something of an honor, and something dangerous to turn down.

Compared to the violet house Miel and Aracely lived in, with Aracely's blue-green cups and her kitchen table, yellow as a Meyer lemon, the Bonners' farmhouse looked so neat and tame. That navy paint made the white trim so bright. The shutters were hooked in place. The lace curtains in the windows looked age-softened, but Mrs. Bonner bleached them so often they never yellowed.

The door was open, only the screen shut. That seemed like an invitation to come in without ringing the bell.

The strangest thing about the house was their mother's mint-green refrigerator, an antique that, according to Aracely, she spent more money to repair than it would have cost to replace it. The rest was so much more muted, so ordinary, compared to the girls and even the farm. The kitchen counters were plain white tile. Linen dish towels, creased and folded, were stacked next to the sink. There was no orange like the girls' hair or the Cinderella pumpkins, flat and deep-ribbed. No deep green or gold or blue-gray like the few rare ones dotting the fields.

Miel's eyes moved over the first floor, until they landed on those four shades of red hair.

Las gringas bonitas. All four of them. The Bonner girls clustered around a wooden dining room. Round, no bigger than needed to fit the six Bonners, or at most, them and a couple of guests. As though Mr. and Mrs. Bonner assumed their daughters would never leave them, or that they would leave and never come back, never bring their husbands and children for Thanksgiving or Christmas.

Chloe still wore those cigarette jeans, but now with a turtleneck that covered her freckled collarbone. Lian had pulled her hair, so much darker than the rest of theirs but still so red, into a bun that was already falling out. She rested her elbows on the table, one hand cupped loosely in the other. Peyton was tracing her finger along the circle of a water stain, her hair in a braid so much like Chloe's that Chloe must have done it.

Ivy leaned against a sideboard, hip against a drawer.

They all looked at Miel.

They'd all been waiting.

"You're not going to kill your roses anymore," Ivy said.

It wasn't until that moment that Miel noticed the vase at the table's center. She wondered how she'd missed it, the glass as dark blue as the Bonners' house.

The sleeve of Miel's sweater covered her newest rose, as pale yellow as a candle flame. But Lian and Chloe were looking at her wrist as though they could see through the fabric.

She pulled her eyes away from the vase, to the Bonner sisters' faces.

Miel looked at Ivy. "They don't do what you think they do," she said. Her roses, left under a pillow, would not make boys fall in love with the Bonner sisters. They would not give them back what they had before Chloe's body held another little life.

"You're not going to kill your roses anymore," Ivy said again, opening a sideboard drawer. Each word was as calm and sure as the first time. "When you grow one, you're going to bring it to us."

In Ivy's face, Miel saw a calm that fell between them like a sheet. The Bonner girls were losing their strange power, but Ivy thought these roses could get it back. They could make any boys they wanted fall in love with them. This town would understand that the Bonner girls could take whatever they wanted. And that fact would ring louder than any whispers about Chloe.

Miel looked around the downstairs, wondering where Mr. and Mrs. Bonner were. Either they weren't home, or they were upstairs, or the sisters didn't care. If they thought their daughters were, for once, having someone over, they might be keeping their distance, not wanting to disturb the strange, unknowable act of girls becoming friends.

"No," Miel said. "They're mine." The words sounded petty, but they were true. Her roses belonged to her. Her cutting them away and then drowning them was her offering to the mother who had feared them.

Chloe tilted her head. Her braid skimmed the side of her neck and traced the outer curve of her breast. Miel wondered if her breasts were heavy and full, and if so, how long it would take her body to realize there was no baby here, no one needing her milk.

But Lian spoke before Chloe did.

"It must make you sad," Lian said, in a way that wasn't warm enough to sound kind or sharp enough to sound mean. "What happened with your mother."

Miel's neck turned as perspiration-damp as the night she and Sam saw a lynx in the woods. Its pale fur had shone in the dark, its ruff banded in black. It had eyes the color of the dark yellow veins in canyon jasper. Two wisps of dark fur curved off the tips of its ears.

Don't run, Sam had told her. *You'll just be telling her you're less than she is.*

I am less than she is, Miel had said. The lynx's fur, gray tinged with red and gold, had looked like strands of light.

"You don't know anything about my mother," Miel said.

"I heard a story from a woman a few towns up the river," Chloe said. "One of my aunt's friends. This old lady who talked about a woman who tried to kill her children and then killed herself."

"That's not what happened," Miel said. None of that was the way it happened.

"I doubt that's what people would think if they knew," Chloe said.

Lower your head, Sam had told her the night they saw the lynx. *And your eyes.*

Miel had, tipping her chin down, still watching the lynx's face. She still remembered the feeling of perspiration dampening the small of her back.

Now back up, he'd said. *Slowly. You don't want to look like you're retreating.*

I am retreating, she'd said.

Miel met Chloe's gaze, shrugging and shaking her head to say, *I don't know what you're talking about.* The woman in the old lady's story could have been any woman, anyone else's mother.

"You look like her," Lian said, without malice, not baiting her. But Miel almost asked where they had gotten a picture of her mother, did they have it or was it pasted into that old woman's photo album.

She didn't ask. But stopping herself was enough of a flinch to tell them they were right.

One flinch, and they had her.

Miel not only had the petals they thought could root them back into being the Bonner sisters. She had committed the crime of witnessing one of them fail, seeing Ivy and that bored, polite boy.

Peyton was still tracing that water mark. She couldn't meet Miel's eye. Of course she couldn't, not after everything Sam had done for her.

Miel tried to make her feet move, but her shoes felt heavy as glass.

The night they saw the lynx, Sam had put his hand on her shoulder blade, and guided her out of the lynx's line of sight. The warmth of his palm had come through her shirt so quickly she thought the pattern of blush-colored flowers would turn dark as wet cranberries.

But she was not as calm, as steady with logic, as Sam.

"Isn't it worth it to you?" Chloe asked. "So everyone doesn't find out all the terrible things she did?"

Of course it was worth it to Miel. If people told those stories about her mother, her mother's spirit would feel it. She'd be haunted, weighted by all those lies. Her spirit would never find any rest. She was already weighted down having a daughter born with roses in her body, a curse that spurred those petaled children to turn on their mothers.

Now, because of Miel, because of the roses the Bonner girls wanted, her mother would be blamed, slandered. What worse could Miel bring on her mother's soul?

Without even meaning to, she had become everything a rose-cursed daughter was feared to be, a disgrace and burden to her own blood.

A breeze came in the screen door, ruffling Miel's skirt. The damp hem brushed the backs of her knees. Streamers of chilled air snaked up her sleeves, cooling the wound her roses grew from. They felt solid as ribbons, tethering her to this spot on the Bonners' floor.

The sideboard drawer slid shut, the wood rasping against a worn track. But Miel didn't see the scissors until Ivy was peeling back her sweater sleeve. Tarnish dulled the brass of the blades, the handle rubbed shiny by the oils of the Bonners' hands.

It didn't make sense.

They thought Miel could give them back whatever they had lost.

They didn't understand that the only way to do that would be for Chloe never to have gone away. Chloe was a tree ripped out of and then planted back into an orchard, her roots and the roots of every tree near her shocked by the turning over of earth.

But Miel couldn't move. She was letting them, because they were the Bonner girls, and all of them had their stares on her. Ivy's, her eyes a gray that made the red of her hair look hot as a live coal. Lian's, a green as deep as her hair was dark red. Chloe's and Peyton's, both their eyes a brown that in certain lights looked dark gray.

Because together they had so much shared gravity they pulled toward that navy blue house anything they wanted. Because they were four brilliant red lynxes, and she could not run.

Ivy snipped the stem.

The cut bit into Miel, like thorns waited under her skin. She cried out for just a second before biting back the sound.

The feeling came back into her body. Pain snapped away the ribbons of cool air tethering her to the floor. And she ran, holding her wrist against her chest. The stub of a cut stem dripped blood onto her sweater sleeve, like a broken branch of star jasmine letting off milk.

She threw the screen door open and let it slam shut.

Among the flecks of orange and white in the pumpkin fields were small glints of light, like the field was dark velvet dotted with white opal.

Her eyes adjusted, the vines and little points of light sharpening.

Glass. The pumpkins were turning to glass. Everything that whirled between the Bonner sisters had not stayed inside that house. It had not huddled inside the sisters' bedrooms. It would not be locked inside their closets or hidden on shelves under their sweaters.

It had slid out here, creeping over their family's fields, this land they would inherit. It was seeping into the pumpkins so that each one now held a little storm spinning it to glass. It made the pumpkins brittle and hard and unyielding as the bond between those four girls. Miel could almost feel it skimming her neck like fingers of cold air. If she stayed still, it would find its way into her. It would make her breakable.

It would turn her to glass.

Miel ran down the path to the road, keeping as far from those pumpkins as the spread of the land let her. Her sweater clung to her skin, and the scalloped neckline of the shirt she wore underneath bit into her like teeth.

The pain in her wrist shot through her body. But she ran, fast enough that she could pretend she didn't see the pumpkins at the fringes of the fields, hardening and turning clear, shining the faint gold of hot glass.

sea of vapors

☽

*S*am and his mother had just finished cleaning up from dinner when Aracely called.

"Can you come help me?" she said when Sam picked up.

His mother stood at the stove, firing the cast-iron pan, the way she dried it so it wouldn't rust.

Sam propped the phone against his shoulder and looked over at her, his silent way of asking, *Do you mind?* They'd held to the unspoken agreement that as long as he asked permission to go out when his mother was awake, she wouldn't comment on the times he snuck out to see Miel when she was asleep.

Did you finish your math? his mother mouthed.

He nodded.

His mother turned off the fire and nodded back.

"Sure," Sam told Aracely.

"Good," Aracely said. "Because I'm about three seconds from strangling your girlfriend."

She hung up, leaving Sam to pick apart what little she'd said. The clench in his throat when he wondered if Aracely knew. The breath out when he realized that if she did, she didn't seem to want to kill him. And the question of what had gotten her in a bad enough mood that she was ready to kill Miel.

His mother threw a jacket at him. He shrugged into the sleeves on his way out, and followed the moons he'd set out for Miel, a path of light between their houses.

Miel didn't cure lovesickness herself. She didn't have what she called el don, the gift Aracely had. But often Miel helped her, passing her matches and glass jars and the right kind of egg. She went out and picked lemons from the tree outside, the gold rinds rain-slicked. Aracely couldn't set these things out beforehand because she never quite knew what she needed until she met the lovesickness living inside a broken heart.

Sam walked up the front steps, and like always, the color of the outside made him think of a paint he'd once used. *Wisteria*, the tube had called it. It had sounded like a place, somewhere that was both beautiful and too small to show on a map. But when he asked his mother, she told him it was a flower, a vine that dripped blossoms like icicles.

Aracely met him at the door.

"Watch her," Aracely said, tilting her head inside.

Miel stood with her back against the wall, shoulders rounded. He would have wondered if Aracely had yelled at her, but in front of those who came for lovesickness cures, she never did.

Aracely's heels clicked against the floor, Sam and Miel following.

"What happened?" Sam said, keeping his voice low.

Miel shook her head. *Not now.*

Tonight, Aracely was curing a man. Sometimes Aracely called Sam over to hand her eggs and herbs and the right kind of lemon. Having a boy around made the men more comfortable. They were already skittish about having Aracely's hands on their chests. Having a girl passing blue eggs to Aracely unnerved them, like the fact that there were two of them made it more likely they were witches.

This man looked a little older than Aracely, maybe twenty-eight or thirty. Everything about him seemed so pale against the dark walls of this room, the color of a blue milk mushroom. The waves of his hair, a dark blond like dried corn, had been cut short. He wore pressed slacks, nice enough for church, and a gray sweater in a knit too heavy for the weather, like he was trying to protect his heart from the thing he was paying to have done to it.

Aracely asked for a Faverolles egg, and Miel, staring at the patch of indigo wall, reached for a Copper Maran egg. Sam slipped it from her palm, replacing it with the cream egg Aracely wanted. Aracely asked for a blood orange, and Miel reached for a lumia lemon. Sam stopped her.

So that was the problem. Miel wasn't paying attention.

"Sorry," Miel whispered.

"What's going on with you?" he asked. She'd taught him which kind of egg was which. She could usually help Aracely half-asleep. The only thing Sam was good for was reassuring the men.

Aracely cracked the egg into a jar of water. She studied how the yolk spread, in needles like comet trails, or thick full light like a cord of dawn outlining the hills, so she would know how the lovesickness was holding on to him.

She swept herbs and a new egg over the man's body, put her hands on his shoulders. She pressed down on his upper rib cage, feeling through his skin. Her hands drew the lovesickness out.

Lovesickness resisted leaving, Aracely had told him, always. Whenever Sam watched Aracely, he saw the strain in her face when she drew it out, like pulling a full, heavy bucket up from a well.

But this man was no different from any other visitor on Aracely's table. His heart was swollen and sore with unwanted love. It fluttered inside his rib cage like wings. When Aracely took it out, it might flit around the room, running into a cabinet, bothering the apricots in the fruit bowl. But then Miel would fling the window open, and she and Aracely would chase it out the window like a bird that had wandered in.

Except tonight Aracely opened her hands, and Miel forgot to open the window. She stood against the wall, watching the floor.

Sam jumped toward the window, pulling the sash up from the sill. He tensed, only relaxing when he didn't hear the unseen lovesickness skimming the walls or knocking against the glass jars.

Aracely caught Sam's eye, and then nodded between Miel and the door, a look of *get her out of here*.

Miel caught that look, and turned to the door before Sam did.

She left the indigo room and then the house, stopping at the front steps.

Sam caught up with her.

"I don't know," she said before he could ask. "I'm just off today." She shut her eyes, and shook her head again.

He wanted to touch her. It should have been easy now. But since that night in his bed, he hesitated putting his hands near her, like his fingers and her skin carried the static of the driest days. Once they'd been like glass, and the little shocks, his forearm grazing her breast or her hand accidentally finding the thigh of his jeans, passed through them. But touching each other that night had turned them to copper. Their bodies would conduct the heat of every little moment. When his arm touched her back. When they were in his mother's kitchen making sohan, and they realized that the flame under the sugar and honey was up too high, both reaching at the same time to turn it down.

But now she was pulling away, and his own questions felt like threads of spider silk catching on his skin. What version of him did she want? Sam, or Samir, or some boy named Moon that this town had made up?

Did she want him because he hadn't grown out of this, or because she assumed he would? How long could he want her, as Sam, before he grew up and became someone else?

"Miel," he said. "What's wrong?"

"I'm fine," she said. "I'm fine." She kissed him, but it was as stiff and uneasy as the first time she'd done it, when they were children and she set her lips against his for no longer than it took to blink.

He could taste the clover and sugar on her lips, like sage honey. It made him think of her licking it off a knife when Aracely wasn't looking.

She went inside, and he heard the soft creak of the stairs and then saw her bedroom lamp turn on. Light filled the window, and she felt as far and unreachable as the moon.

bay of trust

)

*A*racely had tried to make Miel immune. Often, she brought home blue-rinded Jarrahdale pumpkins and deep orange Rouge Vif d'Etampes, and Miel would hide in the hallway closet. Aracely would narrate her progress from the kitchen. *I'm splitting it open, Miel. Okay, now I'm hollowing it out. I'm putting it in the pot now.* But Miel stayed in the closet, worried that new vines might sprout from the pumpkin's severed stem.

That was probably another thing Aracely had almost asked ten times, opening her mouth and then hesitating. Why, to Miel, a pumpkin couldn't just be a pumpkin. A question Aracely knew better than to say out loud. That hesitation always told Miel that the words on Aracely's tongue had more weight than *Are we out of blue eggs?* or *Have you seen my yellow sweater?* Miel wondered if a look crossed her face that showed Aracely the thread of fear in her. *Please. Please don't ask questions. Please don't wreck this, this life I have with you, by making me tell you.*

Now, standing at the edge of the Bonners' farm, Miel wrapped her arms around herself, fingers digging in. Light from the Bonners' house poured onto the fields, warming the soft gray color of the Lumina pumpkins. The sight of each rind covered Miel in the feeling that it could crush her, that it could put out vines and sink them into her. It would draw the life out of her and grow bigger, and she would become small enough for it to swallow.

She was stupid to come here, and she knew it. It was after midnight, hours too late to pretend she'd stopped by to find Sam, or even to lie that she'd come to see Lian or Peyton.

But she had to see the pumpkins.

It hadn't been the fever of Ivy cutting away her rose. More of the pumpkins had become glass. Constellations of them glinted, each one heavy and shining. The living flesh of a few pumpkins had turned, like flowers freezing into ice.

The little storm held between the Bonner sisters had spilled out of their family's house. They were shifting to try to give Chloe back the space she'd held, but they couldn't settle into where they'd been before she left. They still held that shared power of being Bonner girls. It had kept its sharpness. But it was turning into something halting and jagged. And now the fields were showing it.

The night air covered Miel. The cold threaded through her, and in the hollow of the wind she heard the sad murmur of her mother's voice. To everyone else, it would sound like the warning of a storm. But if Miel listened, if she shut her eyes and found that humming under the wind, she heard her mother, caught between this life and leaving it.

She could never hear her father. She couldn't even remember if he'd died or if he'd left them. But how could he have left them? Miel held on to the thought of him wrapping a bandage around her wrist. Her saying *It's hurting me* when he fastened it too tight, and his calm voice saying it needed to be tight, to heal.

His mild dismay when he checked on the wound and found it growing new leaves. His assurances that *don't worry, mija, we'll get it next time*, as though he could will her rose to vanish.

Those memories—even if they were laced with the feeling that they were not real, that they belonged to some other girl and Miel had stolen them—were her certainty that her father did not leave them.

That left the awful possibility that they'd lost him. It left Miel to guess how, to wonder if it was her fault.

With each wink of glass the moon found, her mother's song sounded a little sharper, a little more like weak sobbing.

Mr. and Mrs. Bonner would notice. And if they asked, their daughters would blame Miel. Chloe and Ivy would tell their mother and father that Miel was not only a girl once made of water, but that she'd had a mother who tried to kill her. The girls half this town thought were witches would call Miel a witch, a wicked girl the river had kept and then given back, and who was now turning their fields to glass.

The lies in the Bonner girls' hands were a thousand pairs of scissors, brass and tarnished. If they spread that story, her mother's soul would never be free of it. It would follow her, pin its weight to her and drag her down. Her mother already stayed too close, watching Miel and looking for the brother Miel would never see again.

She had to do what Ivy said. She had to wait for her next rose to grow and open, and then she had to let the Bonner sisters have it.

The question of why they wanted them pinched at her. It couldn't have been as simple as making boys fall in love with them. They already knew how to do that. Even Chloe, months gone, with the rumors trailing through her hair like ribbons, hadn't lost the shimmer that lived on their skin.

That was the worst thing, the not knowing. If them wanting the roses was about any boy in particular, or all of them. If it meant Ivy was set on the boy who'd been so disinterested at the river, or if one of her sisters had decided on a boy from another town who had never heard of the Bonner girls, and would be unprepared for the force of them.

Or Sam. That possibility whispered to Miel too. He worked at their family's farm. No other boy had ever gotten that close to the Bonner girls without wanting them.

Miel put her palm to her wrist, the muscle still sore. And the words she hadn't been able to find when Ivy opened those scissors filled her mouth.

No, she whispered over those fields. *No, you can't have this part of me.*

If they tried to take Sam, she'd do anything she could to stop them, but that choice was his. This one was hers.

I am not your garden, she said, the words no louder than the thread of her mother's voice the wind carried.

I am not one of your father's pumpkin vines.

You do not own what I grow.

The wind, and the crackling sounds of leaves and vines, answered her.

Those glints of glass looked a little duller. Instead of their shine, she saw the cream gray of the Estrella pumpkins or the deep blue-green of Autumn Wings.

The wind, and that thread of her mother's voice, quieted.

It was the first time the sight of pumpkins, fresh and alive, had warmed her. She stood facing those fields instead of cringing away. And this was as much of a sign as her mother had ever given her. Between them, pumpkins were a language as sharp as it was unknowable to anyone else. If she heard the distant rush of her mother's voice, it was her blessing.

Miel wouldn't do it. The next time she had a full rose on her wrist, she was staying far from the Bonner girls.

A tired feeling swept over her, equal parts exhaustion and relief.

She wanted to sink into it, fall onto her bed with her clothes still on. No matter how the Bonner sisters thought they could threaten her, she wouldn't give in to it. The decision had left her worn out, ready to slip beneath the glow of Sam's moons.

She went home to the violet house, and found the light on in the kitchen.

Aracely was standing in front of the wall calendar, the belt on her robe tied in a halfhearted bow.

Aracely looked over at Miel, eyeing her sweater, her jeans, her lack of a nightgown. "Where were you doing out?"

"What are you doing up?" Miel asked.

"Trying to remember the last time Emma came in." Aracely studied the calendar. "I think we're about due."

Emma Owens, the wispy blond woman who ran the school office, managed to get her heart broken at least once every couple of months. She fell in love with men who didn't call, or men who did call and who she scared off with her gratitude and hurry. In her early thirties, hell-bent on getting married before thirty-five, she ended up sobbing on Aracely's table at least once a season.

Every time she set her hands on her rib cage, Aracely told Ms. Owens to slow down, that the right heart would find hers, but only when both hearts were ready. But every time Aracely cured her, rid her of wanting whatever regional produce buyer or accountant did not want her back, she was barely off the table by the time she had another date with another man who would drift between interested and indifferent. Even in her prim pearl-buttoned cardigans, she was pretty and white-blond-haired enough that she was rarely alone on a Friday night.

Miel stood next to Aracely. "Don't you worry about how often she comes in?"

"First rule of business, never argue with a repeat customer," Aracely said. "Besides, I know what I'm doing."

"One day you're gonna pull her whole heart right out of her."

"Oh, I'd love to explain that," Aracely said.

Miel extended a hand in front of her, like she was setting a headline. "'Curandera accidentally kills local woman.'"

"Screw 'accidentally,'" Aracely said. "They'd never believe it."

"A correction to Monday's front page," Miel said. "'Bruja did it on purpose.'"

Aracely clicked her tongue and shook her head, like the women gossiping at the market. "'Tore that poor woman's heart straight out of her body.'"

Miel looked at Aracely. "You know my ancestors could do that in under fifteen seconds, right?"

Aracely held her hands out in front of her. "Not with this manicure."

Miel felt the air settling between them, Aracely letting fall her irritation over needing to call Sam.

"I'm sorry," Miel said. "About before. It won't happen again."

Aracely nodded, as much at the calendar as at Miel. "I know."

lake of death

)

Aracely washed out a blue glass jar, the inside milky from when she'd used it during a lovesickness cure. The mix of water and egg always resisted coming clean.

Miel was at the yellow kitchen table, making a stack of books she needed and another of books she didn't.

She felt Aracely watching her even as she scrubbed the glass.

"You're gonna go study?" Aracely asked, in a voice she must have meant to be joking, but it made Miel blush more than laugh.

Aracely had caught on to what she was doing when she put her books into her bag each afternoon, the class assignments she'd read while she waited for Sam.

"You just make sure you let him get his work done," Aracely said. "He's got his hands full finding enough pumpkins to cut."

"What are you talking about?" Miel asked.

"The glass." Aracely set the jar on the drying rack. "It's spreading.

Now when he's cutting fruit off the vine, he has to make sure he's not breaking anything."

Miel could imagine him like that, stepping through the fields, feeling for rough, living stems instead of glass. He would look like a cat, crossing a crowded shelf without knocking anything over.

But the thought of those glints in the fields still felt like a chill along Miel's ribs. Of course Mr. Bonner would have his farmhands continue as though nothing had changed. Of course he would ignore all that glass, pretending it wasn't there. It was the way he treated the force that was his daughters, as though they were still young girls settling ribbon headbands into one another's hair.

"What?" Aracely asked, her eyes going over Miel's face. "You know something about it?"

"No," Miel said, a little too fast. But whatever was happening between the Bonner sisters, however their land felt it and reflected it back, it was neither Miel's business to question nor her responsibility to explain.

Sam was the one thing that could get Miel close to the Bonners' farm. But she didn't let the sisters see her. Especially not now, a week later, when she'd grown and drowned a white rose with petals tipped in faint green. Last night the petals had spread wide, showing her the breath of yellow at the center, so she'd cut the stem and let the river take it.

In moments of lying to herself, she told herself it was just Sam, just that she wanted to see him and touch where the sweat off the back of his neck had left his hair a little damp. She wanted to kiss him when his mouth was still wet from having just taken a swallow of water.

And that was true. But in moments of letting the rest of the truth edge into her, she knew she wanted the Bonner sisters to see her. Wanted them to catch her pulling Sam into the woods, kissing him before they even reached the trees' shadows. She wanted them to see her bare wrist and know that just because they were the Bonner girls, just because they'd gotten Hunter Cross and Jerome Carter and every other boy they wanted, didn't mean she'd turn over to them the things her body grew.

If they thought they needed her roses, they had lost something. That left Miel less afraid of them knowing she wanted Sam, and more intent on them knowing he did not belong to them. He belonged to himself, and to his mother, and maybe even to Miel, but not to them. He wasn't theirs any more than Miel's roses were.

Today she caught Sam at the edge of the pumpkin fields, pulled him under a sycamore big enough to hide them both. For a few minutes, before he went back to work, and she left to finish her reading or pick up eggs from the Carlsons' farm, this canopy of leaves, orange and gold at the edges but still green at its heart, was their whole world.

She backed him against the bark, kissing him hard enough that it stung. Her hand brushed his chest, and without her realizing she spread it flat, fingers fanned out against his shirt.

She only noticed when he shuddered, his shoulders pressing back harder against the tree.

"Sorry," she said, her mouth still near his. "Sorry."

They both stayed still, taking in a long breath of air that was wet and earthy with fall but sharp from the smoke of farmers burning leaves.

Miel told her palm to move. She tried to send the impulse to her fingers to pull away from him. She knew so much of his body, but this was a place she hadn't touched. His chest had been against her when they were in his bed, but she hadn't mapped it with her hands.

Even with the undershirt that pressed it down and, through a shirt, made his chest flat as any other boy's, she never put her hands here. Not even poking a finger just under his collarbone when she teased him or flirted with him. It was a part of his body he didn't like being reminded of, and she understood, now, that her hands were the worst kind of reminder.

She checked his watch for him, always checked his watch for him, because she knew he didn't like telling her he had to get back.

"You're late," she said.

He kissed her again, hard, and it felt like him telling her that they could forget this. He would forgive her. Not even forgive her. He would let it go, treat it like the accident it was. Like him holding her in a way that pressed the edge of his belt buckle into her, or her, without meaning to when she put her hand to the side of his neck, scratching him.

When he left, she leaned against the tree, hands flat on the bark behind the small of her back, and watched him. To her he had always been Sam, the boy who made the moon for her, the boy whose silhouette she'd found a hundred times on that wooden ladder, light filling his hands. That didn't change when she saw him, through the bedroom door he thought he'd closed but with a latch that sometimes sighed open, changing his clothes or getting dressed after taking a shower. It was only then that she saw that part of him he bound down with that undershirt, or his hips, a little wider in a way that didn't show through jeans but she could see when he had on just his boxers.

None of it had been a surprise. She knew what he was, the tension in the fact that, to anyone who didn't understand, there was contradiction between how he lived and what he had under his clothes. How he had to wear pants loose enough that no one noticed what he did or did not have.

His face was softer than the other boys in their class, but his work on the Bonners' farm had added enough muscle to his back and shoulders that he looked a little broader than before. Boys at school had almost stopped calling him a girl, a thing they meant as something else, a thing they said without knowing what they were saying.

From what little Miel knew, from what little his mother had been willing to say, this was something Sam thought he would grow out of.

He didn't seem to realize he was growing into it.

Miel walked alongside the road, the points of wet, fallen leaves brushing her ankles.

A swath of copper swept out of the woods, like a whole branch of leaves breaking loose.

Ivy Bonner stood, watching her.

"I want to show you something," she said. No greeting, no introduction. Not even a glare for Miel's bare wrist.

Miel could have kept walking. But ignoring her would have felt like provocation. Keeping quiet, not telling her no, had cost her that candle-yellow rose.

"What?" Miel asked.

"If I could tell you about it I wouldn't need to show you." Ivy said it like it was a secret shared with a child, not with the allure, the tilt of her neck, that the Bonner sisters liked showing both boys and other girls.

Miel looked over her shoulder at the road. But running again felt like both an admission that she was afraid and a kind of escalation.

"Will you relax?" Ivy said. "I'm not mad."

"You're not?" Miel asked, hating the deference in her own voice.

"I don't get mad," Ivy said. "Nobody should. What does that do?"

She sounded like Sam's mother, and Miel wondered if she'd picked it up from her. Even the Bonner girls must have appreciated the glamour of Yasmin's pressed white shirts, her thick eyeliner and jewelry made of oversized quartz and jasper. She'd tutored the Bonner girls a few times, not every week the way she did with the children of so many families, but when Mrs. Bonner had a bad cold, and they fell behind on their lesson plans.

"You're mad though," Ivy said.

"No, I'm not," Miel said.

"Yes, you are. You feel like I took something from you without giving you anything."

The thought of the tarnished scissors in Ivy's hands made Miel clutch her forearm.

It wasn't about Ivy not giving her anything. It wasn't about her and her sisters keeping their stares on her, the numbing spell of those eight eyes, so she didn't realize what they were taking until the snap of those brass blades.

"That's why I want to show you something no one else gets to see," Ivy said. "Something I haven't shown anyone."

A flickering in Miel's rib cage told her to run. But another current inside her pushed her toward following Ivy. Both because she was a little curious, and because when a Bonner girl offered a secret, it seemed foolish and antagonistic to refuse it. Once Lian Bonner had a birthday party, one of the few the Bonner girls had invited anyone but family to. Lian heard Elise Shanholt calling the girls creepy, saying she wouldn't come within a mile of that house, wouldn't go to that party even if Nate Stuart's hot older brother wanted her to be his date to it.

So Ivy and Peyton had stolen her cat, a beautiful orange tabby as big as a raccoon. They petted it, gave it cream they skimmed themselves, laughed when a dose of catnip made it bat at its own tail.

It didn't take long before Elise discovered who'd taken it. But when she came to get it, it wailed and clawed and wouldn't go with her. It ran from her, circling Ivy's legs and then jumping onto Lian's lap. Elise's parents said they'd get her another cat, told her to look, weren't the girls taking good care of it, and it wasn't their fault if it had taken to them.

Miel remembered Elise crying in the halls for a week over that. Even her parents had taken the Bonner girls' side. And that cat roamed the Bonners' farm until it died last spring, always running back to the girls who'd stolen it.

For Miel to refuse Ivy's gift, to turn her back now, would be a declaration of war. The girl from the violet house against the sisters who lived in the navy one.

So she went with Ivy.

The deeper they walked into those gold and orange woods, the more she flitted between fear and excitement. That was the thrill of the Bonner sisters, she guessed, to the boys who loved them. That they never knew in which parts to be elated and terrified. Their time being loved by a Bonner girl might be short and sudden as a firework, or long and spun out, and they never knew which. The letdown would be either soft or brutal, and they never knew which.

Only a few columns of light pierced the trees. But this time of year the trees were their own light, amber and coral and butter-colored. Ivy stopped in a grove that was almost all yellow, the flat gold of cottonwood and birch and tulip poplar.

A large box, long and wide as a florist's case or a coffin, sat on the ground, its sides and lid and even its floor made of stained glass. It had been laid down, on the base where a body would rest flat, as though at any moment the whole box might sink into the ground and become a grave. Whorls of deep red and violet crossed the panels. Sprays of milky stars floated over a field of dark blue and green. Even the long cracks slicing the planets and constellations didn't make it less beautiful.

"So it's true," Miel said.

"Half-true," Ivy said. "It doesn't make us pretty if that's what you're wondering."

Miel wondered how long it'd been here. Where the Bonner girls, whichever generation of them, had gotten the stained glass, Miel would never know. Maybe they had bought it, bartered for it, or stolen it. Not that the Bonner women ever needed to steal any-thing themselves. From what Miel had heard, sets of beautiful sisters glittered through this family like flecks of mica in sand. It made Mr. Bonner as terrified of his daughters as he'd been of his sisters and aunts, and Mrs. Bonner baffled by her husband's family, all those flame-haired women.

All they would have needed to do was lower the soft screen of their red-gold eyelashes to get men to tear the bright glass panels from the windows of their own church. With flashes of their cream-white shoulders, they could have gotten those same men to hand over the stained glass like boxes of violet candy. Miel imagined them flirting with metalsmiths, who would have charged them nothing to join the loose panels into this box and trim the corners and edges in rose brass.

"It got covered over for a few years," Ivy said. "Vines and leaves practically buried the thing." She made a half-circle around the stained glass, and Miel felt the unease of thinking that somehow, if there were smudges or fingerprints, Ivy would hold her responsible. "My parents didn't want us to know about it. They pretended the whole thing was a rumor. But we found it."

When Ivy said something she hadn't shown anyone, she'd meant anyone except her sisters. It hadn't so much been a lie—the Bonner girls were as linked as cells in a single organism, breathing together—as the fact of Ivy keeping no secrets from her sisters was implied.

"Well, Chloe and I found it," Ivy said. "But we all cleaned it up."

"Why?" Miel asked.

Ivy stopped, her face scrunching into a smile like Miel was slow. "Because it's ours," she said. "Everyone should take care of what's theirs."

Miel caught the movement of two shadows. She couldn't make

out their shapes yet. She just sensed them passing under the trees, like the minute before she and Sam had seen the lynx.

"I'm surprised you don't know already," Ivy said.

Miel turned back to Ivy. "Know what?"

"That things go easier when you just give people what they want."

Miel felt that pair of shadows drawing closer. The second she looked toward the trees again, Ivy grabbed her. Miel tried to wrench away from her hold. But Ivy's fingers were hot on her wrists. When she grabbed the place Miel had just trimmed a rose from, pain spun through her arm.

Miel tried to twist away from her, but then everything was orange and red, not just Ivy, but Lian's loose auburn hair and the muted orange of Peyton's curls. And when their hands all fell on her, she knew it was true, that they were one animal in many bodies. When one set of fingers lost its grip, another tightened. When Miel threw her weight against one of them, another pulled her back so the force dissipated and did not land.

Ivy pushed the lid of the stained glass coffin open, and they forced Miel in. Miel's knees hit first, the impact reverberating up to her wrist. She collapsed on her side, and all those hands shoved her limbs within its walls so Ivy could throw the lid shut.

Miel turned, holding her hands up to stop it from closing, but the weight drove her down, and the sound of a latch clicking echoed through the glass.

She pushed up on the lid. It did not move. She shoved her weight against the panel. It stayed in place, sealed shut.

That latch would not open from the inside.

She banged on the lid.

The walls barely gave her enough room to twist her body. She tried to throw her shoulder at the side, and then the lid. She tried to shove her weight against the panels, aiming for the places where long cracks cut through the patterns. But the cracks, even the long ones, were shallow, and didn't give, and she was trapped like a moth in a killing jar. Only the cold wisp of a few holes in the glass let her breathe.

Movement outside the glass made her turn her head.

The bright fall trees and the color of the stained glass blurred her view. But she thought she made out Ivy's copper hair vanishing. Peyton and Lian stayed, the orange and auburn of their hair still. They left their pale arms loose by their sides, standing guard.

Miel tried to scream, but there was so little air in here that the heat and the walls stole the sound from her throat. She tried to grab on to something that would let her breathe. The smell of Sam's skin and hair.

The way Aracely had just painted her nails with plum polish and tipped them in silver, or how she put on her alexandrite bracelet, sparkling like the soft purple of hydrangeas.

The roof tiles on Sam's house, varied like kernels on an ear of glass-gem corn. Slate blue and deep yellow. Dull rose and dusk violet. She thought of the rows of flat stones, set in the grass, that led to the door of Sam's house.

But she could only smell the salt on her own damp skin. Thinking of Aracely's nails or those roof tiles made her think of the colors of all this stained glass. She was losing her breath to it. It was taking her under.

southern sea

)

That afternoon, Sam ran into Lian on the brick path that led to the Bonners' door.

"So what do you think?" he asked.

"I think you should go fuck yourself," she said, and turned around fast enough that her hair fanned like a wing.

Go fuck yourself. Sometimes varied as *fuck off.* Always the same response, as classic and timeless as the moss-colored eye shadow the Bonner sisters all seemed to share.

He shrugged. "Just checking," he said.

Sam had the distinction of being the only person in this town Lian Bonner was rude to. But he took it as a compliment, and every few months he offered.

When the Bonner sisters went to the same school as Sam and Miel, everyone thought Lian was as dull as the patina on her copper bracelets. They said she passed her classes only because her sisters did her homework, and she was so compliant and docile the school administrators couldn't bring themselves to fail her. Teachers never called on her, or asked her to read out loud, or write on the board. Sometimes, if people at school were feeling brave and sure that none of the Bonner sisters could hear, they'd laugh and say that the reason Lian's hair was the darkest red of the four of them was because every one of her sisters was so much brighter than she was.

But he knew better. Even with the jokes that the Bonner sisters were now homeschooled because the only teacher who'd pass Lian was her mother, Sam knew better.

He also knew better than to push it. So when Lian told him to fuck off, he did.

That was the second Bonner sister he'd pissed off today. That had to be some kind of record. But the whole Bonner family was on edge, made nervous by the glass spreading through their fields, and the whispers about their brittle harvest. That afternoon, Mr. Bonner, a man as mild as the loaves of bread in plastic sleeves at the grocery store, had yelled at Sam for the first time since he'd started work at the farm. It had startled Sam, but he wrote it off as a result of how, each morning, the Bonners woke and found that more pumpkins had turned hard and shining, dew beading the glass.

Earlier, at school, he'd seen the Bonner sisters hanging around Ms. Owens' desk, acting like they were still enrolled. Ms. Owens, the young and pretty but bony and very pale woman who ran the school administration office, had near-permanent mascara stains around her eyes. She always seemed to be crying into a frill-edged handkerchief, but he knew from experience that asking her what was wrong just earned him her sharp insistence that it was allergies, and he should mind his own business.

Today the Bonner sisters, all of them, even though Chloe had graduated and the rest were now homeschooled, had crushed around Ms. Owens' desk. Not even in front of it, but behind it, with Ms. Owens, sharing empty desk chairs and whispering to her as she nodded. Her thin ponytail bobbed enough to reflect the fluorescent lights. What were they doing with that poor woman?

When the four of them left, Sam had caught Peyton in the hallway.

"Isn't she a little old for you?" Sam asked.

For a second Peyton looked terrified, the way she always did at any mention of the fact that she liked girls and not boys. Her eyes spread so big he could see a thread of white around each iris.

But then she glared at him and caught up with her sisters.

Sam should've known better than to cross anyone he didn't have to. In this town, he was too dark to blend in among the fair-haired boys crowding the classrooms.

A few of the blond ones, their skin so pink their necks looked red even in winter, told him to go back home, and it had taken him a week of first grade to realize they didn't mean the bright-tiled house where he lived with his mother.

The sons of the farmworkers assumed he thought he was better than they were, and he didn't know how to correct them without proving their point. Being friends with Miel didn't change anything to them. Their blood traced them back to the same parts of the world, but their grandmothers had taught them to stay away from any girl whose body grew something more than hair and skin, unless she was a saint.

After his shift, Sam walked home, the air cooling down and the sky turning from the blue-gray of Jarrahdale pumpkins to a deep, clear blue that made the clouds look sponge-painted.

On the way to his house, he always passed Miel's. That house had become almost as much of a home to him as his own.

Miel hadn't turned her bedroom lamp on. But light filled the kitchen window. As he passed the house, he found not Miel's dark hair, full and messy, but Aracely's, blond and brushed.

Aracely stood at the kitchen sink. She lifted her wet hands to her head and twirled her hair into a bun, pinning it in place by spearing it with the handle of a spoon.

Maybe sleeping with Miel had made Sam's world a little sharper. He'd already felt it, how the rinds of pumpkins felt cooler against his hands. How Miel's hair smelled like the rain-slicked lemons Aracely sent her outside for.

Maybe nothing would go dull and unnoticed now, and maybe that was why the sight of Aracely felt like a hand's worth of finger-nails digging into his upper arm. Her features struck him in a way they never had, each on its own.

Her nose was longer and narrower than Miel's, thinner at the bridge, but they had the same slope. Both Miel and Aracely had the same smooth line to their top lips. No bow. Their eyes were different shades of honey. Aracely's were the near-black of buckwheat and Miel's were the gold of orange blossom or eucalyptus. But they were degrees of the same color.

These things would never have been enough to make a stranger ask if Miel and Aracely were related. But to Sam, now, they stood out, sharp as winter stars.

lake of fear

)

*M*iel had a few memories that were only stray threads, frayed from her going over them so many times. Now, locked in these walls of stained glass, they unfurled and spread out, made brave by how little space they had to fill. The air inside these walls, hot with Miel's breath, gave them life and blood.

She shut her eyes against the deep colors of the stained glass, but when she shut her eyes, that night came back to her.

On the advice of an old woman from her church, Miel's mother had gone out into the pumpkin fields and hollowed out the biggest pumpkin she could find. A cream white one as big as the space under a chair. She had left the stem attached to the vine, the carved top clinging to it so that when she put it back on, the pumpkin would still be tied to the earth. When the shell was cleared of its seeds and string, the inside scraped so clean it was damp instead of wet, she forced Miel inside.

Miel remembered screaming, begging her mother not to make

her. When her mother had shut her inside, Miel beat her hands against the shell, trying to break it. She had cried and called for her mother. She had heard Leandro begging their mother to let her out. He even tried to unpin the lid before their mother slapped his hand, telling him to stop, didn't he want his sister cured.

She didn't remember calling for her father. He must have already been gone from them.

The señoras had thought this would work, putting Miel inside the pumpkin, pinning the lid back on and leaving her there over-night. She thought that tying Miel this closely to the earth would make the earth take back her rose. It would claim it. Her rose would wither and fall off her wrist, and become part of the soil.

Miel remembered tiring herself out, being so cold and thirsty she fell asleep. And in the morning, the slices of gray light when her mother opened the top. Her mother's sadness, her disappoint-ment, when she saw the crushed rose still on Miel's wrist.

Miel remembered overhearing the priest's advice to her mother, the judgment in his voice. The fear that ran through Miel's body when she realized what would come next.

A rush of cold air spun through the stained glass coffin. It wrapped around Miel's neck and slipped between her parted lips, and she took a breath like she'd come up from underwater.

She opened her eyes.

Peyton was leaning over her, holding the rose brass edge of the stained glass coffin's lid.

Miel sat up, startled to find neither stained glass nor the shell of a pumpkin stopping her. She put her hands against her chest, the new air stinging her.

She looked around. She found only the clean yellow of the thin hornbeam leaves and fanned gingko leaves, not the copper of Ivy's hair or the almost-maroon of Lian's.

Peyton stood over her, her curling-iron curls almost touching Miel.

"She wasn't gonna let you out yet," Peyton said. "We had to ask."

Miel scrambled out of the stained glass coffin, getting her breath back but too unsteady to stand. Still on her hands and knees, she looked up at Peyton. "Do you want me to say thank you?" she asked.

Peyton's wince was just enough to let Miel see it. She wondered if her guilt was because Miel was Sam's best friend, and Sam had helped Peyton so much. Peyton walked the road back to her parents' farm every Thursday night with marks on her neck that were just as often lipstick as hickeys. Miel knew because Sam had been covering for her since Chloe left, saying he was helping her with her math homework, which everyone but Mr. and Mrs. Bonner knew was a joke. Sam spent an hour writing English papers that took Miel a week, but if the two of them didn't study for math tests together, he didn't pass.

Thank God, Miel had often thought, Peyton was one Bonner sister she didn't have to worry about. A couple of years younger than both Miel and Sam, and not interested in anyone who wasn't at least as pretty as she was. That meant Jenna Shelby or sometimes, when she and Jenna weren't speaking, Liberty Hazelton.

But now Peyton scared her worse than Ivy. She had a look that was both guilty and passive, as though she could apologize for her sisters and in the same breath run to catch up with their shadows.

"It's hard to breathe in there, isn't it?" Peyton asked, crossing her arms so she cupped an elbow in each hand. "There's the little holes to let you breathe but it's still hard."

The air in Miel's throat turned hot and sour as the tea Aracely made her drink when she had a fever. Ivy said it was all rumor that the stained glass coffin made them beautiful. But maybe those walls of bright glass made them the Bonner sisters. Maybe they'd put

Peyton in there when they realized she was leaving her lip gloss on other girls' sweaters. Maybe they'd let her out when they realized she would always put them before anyone else, boy or girl, and that the girls she liked were as expendable to her as the boys.

Miel grabbed the edge of the stained grass, pulling herself up.

"They lock you in there?" she asked. "They can't do that. You should tell your parents."

"We all do it," Peyton said. "It's just about who needs it."

Peyton's look was calm but not cold, unafraid without being defiant.

She didn't fear her sisters, even if they'd locked her in the stained glass coffin. Even if they had taught her to do the same to them.

"Do what we want," Peyton said. "Do what we want or we always make you."

Her tone, like she was both herself and one cell in that body that was the Bonner sisters, made Miel feel pressed back inside those glass walls.

"Is that a threat?" Miel asked.

"No. It's advice."

Peyton left, curls spinning like streamers, and Miel did not follow her. She looked for the way out of the woods, running so the trees turned to a blur of scarlet and rust and yellow. When she found a place where the trees thinned into open air, she took a full breath, a breath clipped when she heard the sound of glass cracking under her feet. Shards scratched her ankles.

She looked around, her stilled breath prickling the back of her throat. She was at a different corner of the Bonners' farm. And her hurried steps had smashed a few of the glass pumpkins. The bigger ones had cracked open, leaning on their sides. The smaller ones had shattered into pieces that ringed where she stood.

Miel's steps, breaking the glass of a few pumpkins, had released into the air everything they'd held, the little storm the Bonner girls had not been able to hide in their drawers. Now she could almost smell the eye shadow and blush palettes they passed back and forth, the shirts they borrowed from one another so often they forgot whose they were first. The scent landed bitter on her tongue, like wildfire smoke turning the sun red and the air to ash.

A few pumpkins shone like they were wet. Their colors were so deep that at first she thought they were the knobby, almost-black rinds of the kind sold in the grocery store as Marina di Chioggia or Musquée de Provence.

But they weren't all deep green. Some were dark red, like the wide planet on the lid of the stained glass coffin. Others were violet and blue as the sky, or pure white as the star sprays.

And they were all glass, smooth and shining and cold.

No matter what Miel whispered or screamed, they were all glass.

lake of solitude

☾

She could not move. In the woods, that stained glass coffin waited. And here, all these pumpkins, both made of jewel-colored glass and made of the same kind of flesh that held her years ago, pinned her in, keeping her from running. She could not cross these rows of glass.

Miel sank to the ground, settling onto a small patch of ground not flecked with broken glass. She pulled her knees in, clutching her ankles, trying to take up little enough space that she would not touch the vines or the pumpkins or the shards her own steps had made. But a few pieces of broken glass crushed under her feet, her heels grinding them down against the hard earth.

The world was made of everything that wanted to take her in, and make her disappear.

It was all noise. Her mother screaming. Her brother calling out for her. But the air was still and cold, no wind, and there was no trace of her mother's whispering.

She set her fingers to her temples, pressing hard, hoping the spaces inside her would go silent.

"Miel?" She heard Sam's voice, cutting through all those echoes.

His steps were so quiet she hadn't even heard glass ground down under his shoes.

She looked up.

He was holding one of his moons, the features of *palus somni* and *sinus iridum* painted on an old glass globe. Over his shoulder was the thin wire that would go unseen once he cut it and hung the moon. She wondered where he'd set the wooden ladder. He hung his moons anywhere he got away with it, and this town let him get away with it almost everywhere. The light of these moons, they said, so much closer and steadier than the one in the sky, kept away their children's nightmares. When children were sick, they called him, and he hooked moons onto boughs outside their weathered houses.

Sam crouched near her, tucking the moon under one arm, and now his weight crushed the glass under his feet. But he didn't startle, or pull back. "What happened?"

She looked past him, shaking her head at the pumpkin fields and the trails of broken glass.

He gave them a quick look and then looked back at her, not taking them in. He must have thought this was her fear of everything those vines grew.

But the sheen of glass must have pulled him back. He looked again, his eyes settling. His stare moved over the cluster of glass pumpkins, the deep red and violet, and dark blue and green. He was reconsidering these things he'd had to work around while cutting fruit off the vines.

He looked at her again.

"You didn't do that," he said. "That's not your fault. You know you didn't do that, right?"

Sam was so stupid. He was stupid and kind and always had a

guard up against Miel being blamed for things. He knew that the only people in this town called witches more often than the Bonner girls were her and Aracely. When anyone came to the violet house blaming them for too much rain or not enough, or because a bad cough was spinning through the grade school, his mother was the first one to tell them to go back to their homes. And Sam was the first one to say that if they didn't, he'd tear down every moon in this town.

Both Miel and Aracely knew he'd never do it. He'd never take down anything that was letting this town's children sleep. But he was a dark-skinned boy, a kind of dark they could not place, so when he threatened them, they believed him.

Sam and his mother were right to defend Aracely. But they should have let the town do whatever they wanted with Miel.

It was her fault Leandro was dead. It was her fault her mother was dead.

Sam reached his hand out to her, slow as the sway of the trees.

"Let's go home, okay?" he said.

He touched her sleeve, and she pulled her arm away, her skin shrieking with everything she couldn't say.

Please don't touch me.

Please don't leave me.

Please don't let me be this anymore. Afraid of everything, and angry at everyone, and so awful at holding all of it within her own skin that it burst from her wrist as thorns and petals.

She was poison. And the last boy who had hair as black as wet ironbark and who tried to save her ended up dead.

The motion had felt small to her, pulling back her arm. But Sam looked startled, worried, the border between his dark eyes and the white looking clear and sharp.

He set the moon down so close to her that her skin turned a little blue.

"I'm gonna leave this with you, okay?" he said.

The moon, big as Aracely's bedroom mirror, cast a faint glow on his skin like the reflection off snow at dusk. He had painted the craters and lunar seas, *mare insularum* and *lacus hiernalis*, the sea of islands and the lake of winter, in pale and dark silver. The glow looked like moonlight filtering through shallow water.

He'd already lit this one, the candle cupped and burning inside.

"And I'm coming back," he said.

sea of serenity

☽

He found Aracely sitting at the yellow kitchen table, rubbing polish off her fingernails.

"Where's Miel?" she asked when she saw him. "I thought you two were making out in the woods somewhere."

"Not exactly," he said.

He looked down at the pattern of tiles on the kitchen floor. He'd never noticed how close the brown of the worn ceramic was to the shade of Miel's skin in winter. In summer, her skin turned darker, cutting the sharp outlines of the foil stars he set against her skin. But after months of gray skies, this was the color she was, and he'd never noticed it before.

It made him feel odd about standing on it, like she'd feel his weight even from where she sat at the edge of the Bonners' fields.

"Words, Sam," Aracely said. "Use some."

She'd been saying this since he was in middle school, when he'd gone quiet so no one would notice his voice wasn't lowering like other boys'. They'd written it off as evidence that he was waiting out his own voice change, self-conscious of it hitching if he talked. Alone, in his room, Sam had practiced driving his pitch lower, so that when other boys, frightened into silence by unexpected cracks and breaks in their words, emerged with dropped voices, so would he.

But Aracely had little patience for his silence, then and now.

He looked up. "I need your help."

That was all it took. She didn't panic or ask him questions. Aracely had a calm that rivaled his mother's. When his mother didn't know how to talk to him when he started bleeding between his legs, Aracely spoke to him once on his own, and then herded him and Miel into the wisteria-colored house's living room for the kind of talk their school used to give in health class, before they cut health class altogether. Aracely had been the only one who didn't squirm through the whole thing. Sam and Miel had sat, cringing, at opposite ends of the sofa, his hand in his hair, fingers digging into the roots, while she buried her face in a throw pillow.

Aracely threw out the remover-soaked cotton balls, and went with him.

Miel shuddered when Aracely touched her, the way she had when he tried the same thing. But Aracely spoke to her in a voice so soft Sam couldn't make out the words. She talked her down in a way Sam didn't know how to, like her words were a rhythm she was helping Miel follow. Her voice was a frequency she was getting Miel to tune in to, until Miel was nodding, and letting Aracely take her hands. Aracely helped her stand, guided her through the constellations of broken glass.

There was something about it so different from what he would have done, different even from the way his mother talked to Miel.

There was something not quite sisterly, and not quite maternal. Not just the familiarity that had grown between a woman and the girl who'd lived with her for ten years.

Tonight Sam would paint another moon for Miel, one warmer than the bluish one he'd carried into the woods. He'd make one big enough to fill his arms, the light both full and crescent. He'd paint its face the blush of a flower moon, its edge darkened almost to red, like a strawberry moon. He'd paint its *mare serenitatis* and *mare tranquillitatis*, the wide seas of serenity and tranquility crossing the crisp white of a snow moon.

All the colors would look like the rose moons he and Miel had found in the sky that summer. He'd hang it in the beech tree outside her window, and under its light she'd sleep. He wanted to give her every light that had ever hung in the night sky. He wanted to give her back what she thought she'd lost years ago.

Sam could stay with her. He could tell her what his grandmother had told him about the crocus fields, how they sometimes smelled like hay, and sometimes like leaves, and sometimes like the spice they held. He could tell her his favorite story his grandmother had told him. A prince and a fairy who fell in love, and could sometimes be seen over the water of Saif-ul-Malook on nights lit by the full moon.

But it took Aracely to get Miel home, to get her in bed, to get her to sleep. Aracely stood in the doorway of Miel's room, watching her breathe, lips parted.

There was something proprietary in that look. Something possessive, both defensive and proud.

Sam had disregarded that moment of thinking he'd seen a resemblance between Aracely and Miel. He'd let it fall like a stone he picked up, turned over, and then decided not to keep. But now he looked for it again, like brushing his fingers through a carpet of leaves, finding it a second time.

He couldn't ask Aracely, not now, with Miel settling into the space between those glass pumpkins and her own dreams. But he wouldn't forget. This time he wasn't letting it go.

lake of forgetfulness

☽

Ms. Owens' voice came up through the floorboards, her nervous laugh and her chatter to Aracely.

Miel opened her bedroom door. She heard Aracely answering back in her slow, calming voice, her *aren't-men-awful* voice. Ms. Owens' voice was unsteady, and Miel wondered what actuary, what mattress-franchise millionaire, had broken her heart this time.

And why Aracely hadn't called Miel down to help her.

Aracely stood at the stove, boiling water for lavender and ginger tea. After the second time, Aracely always gave it to Ms. Owens, to relax her, to make sure the inside of her wasn't becoming too stiff and brittle from so many lovesickness cures.

Miel leaned against the counter, her elbows on the tile. "Where is she?" Miel whispered.

"Just fixing her face," Aracely said, giving Miel a pained look. "It's a bad one this time. Mascara everywhere."

"Why didn't you call me?" Miel asked.

Aracely leaned in. "I think that's the same thing she wants to ask the guy."

Miel elbowed her, and Aracely pressed her lips together. Only Aracely could make those kinds of jokes without sounding cruel.

"I meant why didn't you tell me to come down," Miel said, her voice still low. "I always help you."

Aracely's eyelids pinched. "You had a long night last night. I thought you might be tired."

Miel felt the unease of slipping from a place she'd claimed as hers. She always handed Aracely the eggs and the oranges. Aracely always signaled to Miel to open the window at just the right time to let the lovesickness out. They both carefully shooed the lovesickness out the window, watching so it wouldn't fly back, or end up stuck in a bowl of fruit or a vase of flowers, the ceramic trembling like a wasp's wings. Or worse, rush back into the body it came out of. To visitors, curing lovesickness seemed all instinct and flourish. But Aracely treated it as a craft that took as much patience and method as cutting raw opal.

And Miel had been part of that for almost as long as she'd lived with Aracely.

"I'm fine." Miel stood up straight. "I can do this."

The kettle sang, and Aracely took it off the burner. "Are you sure?"

"It was just bad dreams," Miel said. "That's all."

"That's not what I hear."

The gossip had already bubbled through the town about the newest glass pumpkins in the Bonners' fields, deep and bright as topaz and bloodstone.

"Are they saying I did it?" Miel asked.

"No." Aracely poured the hot water. "Why would they?"

Miel felt the tension in her fingers pulling back toward her heart.

No one but the Bonner sisters knew they had brought the stained glass coffin back from its distant place in their family's stories. No one but the Bonner sisters knew they had locked Miel inside it.

No one but Miel saw those jewel-glass pumpkins as the threat they were.

Miel handed Aracely the hard cone of piloncillo she always grated into Ms. Owens' tea.

"I can do this," she said.

Aracely took the piloncillo. "Are you sure?"

"I always help you," Miel said.

"I've cured her more times than I can count. I know her heart better than mine. If there's one you had to miss, this isn't a bad one."

"But it's important," Miel said. "You're always saying keep the repeat customers happy."

Aracely eyed the door Ms. Owens was behind. The sound of the sink running came through.

"Fine," Aracely said. "But take it slow. You don't have to get me what I ask for so fast you throw it at me. I can wait. So can Emma. If it takes an hour, so what? I don't want you handing me a pink egg when I want a green one."

"Deal," Miel said.

So they spread a sheet over the table in the indigo room, and Ms. Owens came in, clutching a pocket square that must have belonged to whatever man she had last fallen in love with. It looked like it cost more than any dress Miel owned. The candles turned the silk the color of Aracely's Spanish rice.

Aracely tried to take the pocket square.

Ms. Owens held on.

Aracely ran her fine-boned fingers through a lock of Ms. Owens' hair. "Let go," she whispered, her voice warm with the assurance that everything was good and right, that it was the golden hour of afternoon and not night, that there was no fear in the world.

Ms. Owens shut her eyes, and opened her hands, and Aracely took the pocket square.

Miel folded her elbows, hands gripping her upper arms. All the heat in her body pulled to her wrist. She could almost feel the weight of Ms. Owens' heart, how she wore her disappointment like wet clothes.

"Lie down," Aracely said.

Ms. Owens did. The almost-white blond of her curls fanned out from her head. Flakes of mascara clung to her cheeks like ash, and tears trembled at her lash line.

Aracely tore a scrap from the pocket square. Ms. Owens winced as though she felt it. Aracely burned the cloth in a glass jar and said the prayer of Santa Rita de Cascia. The edges of the satin blackened and curled in on themselves.

Miel handed Aracely a purple onion, the green stalk still on. Aracely always knew which color egg, which orange, which herb. She swept the onion over Ms. Owens as she said the prayer again, her whisper softening the air in the room.

Ms. Owens kept her eyes shut tight enough to wring tears into her hairline.

Miel stood, waiting for Aracely to tell her what to do. She waited long enough that she thought she saw ribbons of faint light shining along the floor. They snaked and twirled, skimming the baseboards. They wrapped around the legs of the wooden table.

At first they looked like tiny streams, bands of water no thicker than her wrist. Then they looked solid, their glint a hard edge.

Like glass. Like vines of glass, not just deep green but dark blue and red and violet. They spun up the indigo walls. They reached out toward Miel, trying to wrap her forearms. She felt them without them touching her, a cord of pain from each elbow to each wrist.

They pricked her like thorns and leaves growing under her skin, and she felt the ache of a glass vine caging her forearm. They would crack, and the jagged pieces would cut into her wrists. Her blood would tint the glass. It would splinter and cut deeper into her.

A bump against the window, like a bird hitting the pane, cut through the room. A sharp scream followed it. It streamed into the air, skittering along the walls.

"Dammit, Miel," Aracely said, her hands on Ms. Owens' shoulders. "Did you hear me? Open the window!"

Ms. Owens sat up, clutching for the pocket square she no longer had. She looked down, startled to find her hands empty.

Miel hadn't even heard Aracely ask the first time. But she could see the startled look in Ms. Owens' face, the way her eyes looked almost white.

Aracely had taken out her lovesickness.

And because Miel hadn't opened the window fast enough, it had struck the glass, and then rushed back into Ms. Owens.

Miel leapt toward the window, pushing up the sash as wide as it went.

"It's okay," Aracely said to the trembling woman on the table. "It's okay."

But Ms. Owens' breathing fluttered, and she broke into screaming again.

But Aracely kept her hands on Ms. Owens.

"Lie back down," she said.

However assuring Aracely's voice sounded, Miel caught the straight line of her back, like a current had gone through her.

Ms. Owens lay down again. But she shivered. She clutched at the air.

Aracely hovered her hands over Ms. Owens, ready to set her palms against her collarbone.

But Miel could see the lovesickness, even more restless now that it had left and rushed back, kicking around inside Ms. Owens.

Ms. Owens sat up, and her hair spilled down her back. "No," she said. The tightening of her face pinched two more mascara-darkened tears from the corners of her eyes. "I can't."

She ran out of the indigo room, the waves of her hair sweeping her shoulders.

These were not words Aracely drew from those who got up from her table. Each time Aracely gave a cure, the visitors always said they were tired. *It's so strange, I'm so tired. I've never been this tired.* Aracely's lovesickness cure often made people sleep for days. They felt fine at first, awake and alive, and then they sank into relief and exhaustion. Once the lovesickness cure had made a man fall asleep to the rust-colored leaves of late November and wake to the first snow silvering his window.

But Ms. Owens was running out of the violet house, startled and awake.

The door slammed. Ms. Owens' steps scattered the gravel outside.

The torn pocket square had fallen to the floor.

Miel bent to pick it up.

Aracely's steps clicked on the wooden floor, and Miel looked up. Aracely was rushing toward the front door.

Miel followed her outside, the air cool and green with the smell of grass and light rain.

But Ms. Owens had already started her car. In the distance, the taillights were growing smaller.

"Just let her go," Miel said. "She'll come back."

Aracely turned to her, so close Miel could smell the amber of her perfume. "You told me you were ready. You told me you could do this."

"I thought I was," Miel said. "I just wasn't paying attention for one second. I'm sorry."

"Do you realize what you've done?" Aracely looked stricken, possessed, like she'd witnessed sons and daughters scratching out the names on their family's headstones.

"I'm sorry," Miel said.

"Great," Aracely said. "You're sorry. Well, that solves everything, doesn't it?"

Miel felt the aftertaste of her own apology turning, growing sharp on her tongue. "Look, if you're so mad at me, why don't you call Sam?" she asked. "He's better at helping you anyway, right?"

"Sam." Aracely's laugh was a sharp inhale, almost a gasp. "You wanna talk about Sam? How do you think he and his mother have kept that secret this whole time?"

"What are you talking about?" Miel asked.

Aracely grabbed a handful of Miel's sweater and tugged her close, more like she didn't want anyone to hear than to shake Miel.

"Emma Owens is the only one who's seen his real paperwork," Aracely said, her teeth half-clenched. "She's the reason he's registered as Samir and not Samira."

The grass under Miel felt soft, like it would turn to water and pull them both under.

"What?" she asked.

"Did you think we got lucky this whole time?" Aracely asked. "That the school just took his mother's word about his name and his date of birth? Sam's mother got away with saying she didn't have the papers for grade school or middle school, but they wouldn't let it go for high school. They wouldn't register him without official documents. So I called in a favor, to the one woman who's on that table more than anyone else. She owed me. She's the only one who knows his birth name. And she's kept quiet because of everything I've done for her, but now . . ." Aracely's words trailed off, and she looked down the road Ms. Owens had left by.

Now Aracely had failed. So many flawless cures, as much mercy as medicine, and now she had failed. It hadn't just been Aracely's good name resting on her giving a remedio so skilled it felt like a soft, shimmering dream.

It had been the secret name Sam didn't want anyone knowing. And it was Miel's fault.

Dread billowed through her.

Aracely went back inside.

"Can you fix this?" Miel asked, going after her.

Aracely slid into her coat and lifted her hair out from under the green velvet of the collar. "I don't know." She grabbed her car keys. "But you better hope so."

marsh of sleep

☽

Pain sparked through Miel's wrist, startling her awake. She shuddered at the feeling that there were words she'd just heard, but that she'd been too asleep to hear them, and their echo had become too weak for her to catch now.

She scrambled from where she was curled on the sofa, waiting for Aracely to come home, and she sat up.

"Aracely?" she called toward the door.

She was still breaking through the feeling of being half-asleep. But through the blur she saw the deep red of Ivy's hair.

Ivy was standing over Miel, staring at her wrist. Her eyes looked gray as the pumpkin Peyton had held that night by the water tower. Her expression hovered between satisfied and relieved, like she'd just checked a door or a stove and found that yes, it was locked, yes, the blue gas flame had been turned off.

Without meaning to, Miel followed Ivy's stare. She looked down at her own wrist. Two new leaves lay bright green against her skin.

They were young and soft, not yet showing the hard stem of the coming rose.

To Ivy and the rest of the Bonner sisters, those two leaves were evidence that a new rose was growing, that Miel hadn't destroyed another one of the blooms they'd decided was theirs.

Miel looked up, but the copper sweep of Ivy's hair and the gray of her eyes was gone.

She shook off the feeling of sleep, and ran to the back door.

It was a little open, a few inches left between the door and the frame.

The smell of the grass outside, clean and a little sour, filled the hall and the kitchen. But cutting through it was a scent that did not belong in this house. Not the tart fruit smell of the soap she and Aracely used. Not the heavy amber of the glass bottle that sat on Aracely's dresser.

It was a smell like almonds and Easter lilies, the kind of perfume Mrs. Bonner might have bought her daughters, and that the four of them would have passed between them. It held the undertone of Ivy's camellia-scented soap.

Miel left the door open, letting in more of the night air so the perfume would fade. She stood there, waiting for it to become so faint she could tell herself that Aracely, rushing out to Emma Owens' house, had just forgotten to close the door.

serpent sea

)

It took more nerve than Sam had expected. He'd been so sure, looking between Aracely and Miel. But in the morning, that certainty had vanished, the sun and its white-gray light washing it out. Then, at night, it came back, deepening with the sky. By the time he got home from the Bonners' farm, it was spinning inside him, its weight wearing him down.

Later that night, after his mother had gone to sleep, he stepped out into the cold air, filled with the dull spice of falling leaves. He followed the trail of moons toward the wisteria-colored house.

Most nights, he stood outside where Miel could see him, the moon in his hands calling her out into the dark. But tonight he stood in the house's shadow, hands in his pockets, waiting for Miel's light to go off.

Her window went dark, and he knew she was asleep. His fingers brushed the metal in his pocket. His mother and Aracely both kept spare copies of each other's house keys in their kitchen drawers. He'd taken theirs with him in case Aracely was locking her doors earlier now that it was getting dark faster. But she hadn't.

He paused in the doorway. For the first time since he left his house, he felt the force of how strange, how invasive this was. It didn't matter how well he knew Miel. He was walking, without being asked, into a world ruled by women. Even at the threshold he could smell perfume and the sugary fruit scent of their soap.

The longer he stood there, the sharper that hesitation felt. He listened for the creak of floorboards above him. If Aracely had already gone upstairs to bed, he'd turn around, work himself up to this again another night.

The creak of wooden cabinets came from the indigo room. Aracely was awake, still down here.

Sam found her checking her store of eggs.

He wasn't sure if she'd heard him come in the back door. So he knocked on the doorframe, to let her know he was there.

Aracely jumped, clutching the basket of eggs.

"You scared me," she said. "What are you doing here?"

She had on her coat, the heavy velvet one Miel had found her at a secondhand store last Christmas.

"You going somewhere?" he asked.

"Just got back," she said, looking down at her coat like she'd forgotten she had it on. "I had to make a house call. What's going on?"

He could map her features against Miel's. Their shoulder blades, Miel's as pronounced as Aracely's even though Aracely was thinner. The slope of their eyebrows. Even the shape of their ears, how the right lobe was a little different from the left.

"Is everything okay?" she asked, slipping out of her coat.

Sam leaned against the doorframe. He hoped it would make him look patient, unhurried, that Aracely wouldn't be able to tell he was using the frame to keep himself steady.

"Who is she to you?" he asked.

Aracely set down the eggs and smoothed a new sheet onto the wooden table. "What are you talking about?"

"Miel," he said. "Who is she to you? You're not old enough to be her mother, so what is it?"

"I take care of her." Aracely tugged on the sheet so the edges wouldn't drag on the floor. "Why does it need a name?"

"No, I mean, who are you to her?" he asked.

Her eyes drifted to the walls, that same indigo as the mushrooms his mother found at the markets when she was a child. The caps pale lavender, the gills deep blue-violet, stems bleeding that same color.

"I can't do this right now," she said. "Can we talk tomorrow?"

"Are you her sister?" he asked. "Cousin? Aunt? I don't know."

Aracely looked up. "I'm nothing, Sam. I'm a woman who had a room free."

Sam put his hands in his pockets. "I don't buy it."

"You don't have to."

She could not talk him out of this. He would not forget that he'd realized Miel and Aracely both wore out their shoes the same way, the right sole thinning before the left, the wear heavier on the outside edge than the inside. These were things that did not come from living with each other. These were traits and tendencies each had been born with, and there were too many of them.

"You don't owe me the truth," he said. "But you owe it to her."

Aracely turned around. "If you think the truth is so great, how about you start?" She scanned his shirt and his jeans. Under her stare, his binder felt a little tighter, his jeans not quite loose enough to hide what he didn't have. "This thing you're doing . . ."

"It's not a thing," he said.

Maybe *bacha posh* were words that did not belong to him. They were only his through the stories his grandmother had told him, of families across the border from Peshawar, mothers and fathers dressing their youngest daughters as sons.

But they were so much more his than they were Aracely's. His grandmother's father had welcomed into his home men whose youngest daughters lived as boys until it was time for them to be wives. He had done business with these men. To mark their arrival, Sam's grandmother and great-grandmother had shelled almonds and pistachios for sohan, their whole house sweet with the smell of cardamom.

Miel understood this. That day she'd seen enough of him naked to wonder, when she'd waited for him on the back steps, she'd been quiet enough to let him explain bacha posh. He remembered grasping at the words that would distill it down, words he could get out fast enough to keep her there, to stop her from running back to the violet house and telling him she never wanted to see another of his moons outside her window.

Where my grandmother comes from, sometimes parents who have girls but no boys dress one of their daughters like a son. Then it's like they have a son. She can do things boys can do and girls can't. And she can be a brother to her sisters. Does that make sense?

Miel hadn't been looking at him as he spoke. She'd been looking down, at their legs next to each other, his in jeans, her knees showing at the edge of her skirt.

But she'd nodded, and she'd stayed.

If Miel had been able to understand when she and Sam were both children, Aracely, a grown woman, had no excuse now.

Sam looked back at Aracely. "You don't get to pick apart bacha posh," he said. "You don't know anything about it."

"I know enough," Aracely said. "I asked your mother because I'd never heard of it before."

"That's right," he said. "You'd never heard of it. So don't pretend you know anything."

"I know that these girls live with the freedom of being boys for years and then they're expected to become wives. They're expected to forget everything they knew about being anything other than what they're supposed to be."

The words turned the back of his neck hot. They left him tense with the feeling that Aracely was lecturing not only him but the grandmother who had told him about Pakistan, and about bacha posh, and who was no longer alive to speak for herself.

These girls. What they're supposed to be. All of it felt like Aracely's judgment of a world she did not know, and a world that had given him a quarter of his blood.

"You want to play whose culture is more backwards?" Sam asked. "Because I can do that. Women like you, with your cures and your prayers and your different-color eggs, you know what they say about you? Those old women—what do you call them, the señoras?— they're nice to you to your face. They send their sons and their daughters to you. And then they call you a witch behind your back. A bruja. Even *I* know that word."

Aracely's eyes were still as open as they'd been before, neither closing with a flinch nor spreading wider.

"And these are your own people," Sam said. A cruelty, a kind of rubbing it in, had slipped into his tone before. Now he let it wrap every word. "They want you for what you can do for them when no one's looking, and then in church they curse you. That's your culture. I pick mine any day."

Aracely watched him, her face unchanged.

"And where do you get off acting like it's any different here than where my family came from?" Sam asked. "You think girls can do whatever they want here? You think Miel can? How do think girls here would do if they got to be boys growing up and then had to be girls again?"

"But that's what you're counting on, right?" Aracely asked. "That one day you'll wake up and wanna put on a dress?"

"Fuck you," Sam said. It had never been about a dress. It had been about the clothes his grandmother would have wanted to see him in for family photos. Not a boy's kurta, but the sunrise colors and scrolled patterns of a girl's salwar kameez. A dupatta draped over hair longer than he ever wanted to grow it.

He looked for any cringe in Aracely's face. Some sign that she knew she'd gone too far.

Instead there was just the trace of a smile, curving one side of her mouth.

She'd baited him. She'd wanted him angry.

"So you've got that in you," Aracely said. "Good. You're gonna need it."

Sam gritted his teeth, hard enough to feel it in the back of his jaw. "For what?"

"To be this." She took in his clothes again, and again he felt like they were pinching him. "To live like this."

"I'm not living like anything," he said. "I do this for my mother. This country's no different than anywhere else. It's better for a woman if there's a man in her house, even if that man's her son."

"Stop pretending this is for anybody but you."

Sam turned around.

Aracely didn't know anything about him, or his family. Once his grandmother was gone, it had just been him and his mother. His mother had no sons, only him, born a daughter, and Sam had wanted, as badly as he wanted his grandmother back, not only to be a boy but to be a son to his mother. Years ago, when he'd first thought of living as a bacha posh, he'd felt the same shiver of triumph every time he was, in jeans and hair shorter than most girls, mistaken for a boy. He'd thought of having that all the time. How he could have something he wanted and at the same time do something for his mother.

He would be the man in their house, taking care of her. If he became a son to her, he'd thought, she wouldn't cast a nervous glance toward the windows when she locked the door at night. If he was a son, she would have let him paint over the letters sprayed onto the side of their house, instead of her doing it herself, having to look at it. She hadn't let him near that wall until she could get it covered over, and it wasn't until he was thirteen that he got her to tell him what slur those letters had spelled.

"Sam," Aracely said.

He left the indigo room and went for the front door.

"Sam," Aracely said, a whispered yell. He could tell she wanted to raise her voice but didn't want to wake Miel. "Get back here."

He looked over his shoulder.

Aracely still had a basket of eggs in her hands. She'd forgotten to put it down.

"Miel may think you know everything," he said. "But you don't know anything about me."

"I know more than you do."

"Oh really?" He turned around. "How?"

"Because I used to be where you are."

The lie of her words made him lonelier than if she'd said nothing. The fiction that anyone in this town had ever been where he was, caught between feeling bound by the clothes he wore and being so desperate to keep them he wanted to hold on to them with his teeth, made the slide toward resenting her quiet and fast.

"No, you don't," he said, and it wasn't until he heard the tremble in his own voice that he noticed the prickling damp at the edges of his eyelashes. How much tears irritated his eyes when he tried to stay still, how they refused to be forgotten until he blinked and let them go. "How could you?"

"Because you were right," Aracely said. "I am Miel's family. And not just because that's what we've become to each other. I always have been."

This was the thing he'd wanted to know so badly a few minutes ago. But now, how much he didn't want to talk cast a heavy shadow over how much he cared.

"What does that have to do with anything?" he asked.

Aracely crossed her arms, and her thin elbows turned pointed and sharp. "Because Miel remembers me as her brother."

sea of waves

)

At first, Sam could not understand why Aracely was telling him the truth. He felt the caution of wondering
whether it was a trick, another lie. He didn't understand why she
didn't say those words—*Miel remembers me as her brother*—and then order
him out of the wisteria-colored house. But then he noticed in her
face a tension that was half-hesitation and half-relief, a look that he
knew because he'd worn it himself.

He knew it from that day Miel had caught him changing, seen
him naked enough to know there was distance between his body
and what he let everyone believe it was. He knew it from that moment of sitting down next to Miel on the back steps of his house,
and telling her everything.

That was the truth of holding so much back, and then giving up
a little of it. The rest came.

Now that he knew Aracely was like him, he understood, and she
knew that both he and she were creek beds, quiet when they were

full and quiet when they were dry. But when they were half-full, wearing a coat of shallow water, the current bumped over the rocks and valleys in the creek beds, wearing down the earth. Giving someone else a little of who they were hurt more than giving up none or all of it.

Now that Aracely had told him this one thing—*Miel remembers me as her brother*—the rest came, as long as he was quiet.

So this time, Aracely did not lie. She did not tell him that she was just a woman who took in the girl from the water tower.

She spoke, and Sam learned all these truths he had never guessed. How Aracely once lived as a boy named Leandro, a boy who was years older than his younger sister but still small.

That Leandro loved his sister, that he almost died trying to save her from a river that wanted to take her.

That his mother had died trying to save them both.

But the water took Leandro, folded him into its current, brought him back as the girl he'd always wished he could grow into.

Not a girl. A woman, finished and grown.

That a summer covered in amber butterflies turned her hair to gold and welcomed her back into the world as someone else. How she did not know if this was the water's gift for trying to save her sister, or if it was only the water seeing her for what she was, and showing it to everyone else. But how she felt, as the water brought her back toward the light, was the certainty that she was not small anymore.

The water had felt her sorrow, her broken heart because she had failed to save her sister. That sorrow had aged her heart, made her grown instead of a child. So the water made the outside of her show the truth in all ways, not just by making her a woman, but by making her old enough to match her bitter heart.

That woman gave herself a name, and looked for her lost sister, and found her only when she was sure she had lost her forever.

Miel didn't know. Sam knew that. Not because she would've told him. She had so many secrets, so many fears and places she did not let him bring light into, that he couldn't count on it.

He knew from the way Aracely was touching the eggs, pretending to arrange them, but doing nothing with them. Her hands patted the nest of shredded paper.

Aracely took a few strands of the paper between her fingers, crushing them.

The moment of realizing, again, that Aracely had not lied, that she knew the narrow, rocky ground of being one thing and wanting to be something else, crept down each knob of his spine. It wrapped around his rib cage, harder and tighter than the bandage he'd used before Aracely had bought him these undershirts that pushed his chest flat.

He didn't want to think of that though, to open the door to her asking him questions because she thought they were the same. So he tried to imagine Aracely with dark hair, how much more she and Miel would have looked alike.

"You're family to her," he asked. "Why didn't you tell her?"

"Because there are things she doesn't remember, and never should." Aracely had set down the eggs, but now she turned a jar in her hands, the blue glass filled with water, ready for the gold of an egg yolk. "And if she remembers me, like I was, if she sees me and knows who I am, she might remember the rest."

Sam tried not to guess at all the things that could have happened to Miel. She might have slipped and fallen into the river. She might have once loved water, and swam with the current, realizing too late that it did not love her the way she loved it. Or she might have been small enough to see the moon on the surface, and think she could wade in and catch it.

So he would not think of these things, he looked at Aracely. Even with all the little ways she and Miel were the same, there were so many other ways Aracely was different, traces of who she might have grown to be if the water had not intervened. Her height. How she had bigger hands, but no one noticed because most of their spread was thin, wispy fingers.

"Is this what you wanted?" he asked.

Aracely looked at him. "Always. But my mother always told me how handsome I was, how happy she was to have a son. So there was no space for any of it."

It was the first crack Sam had seen in Aracely, sadness rather than annoyance or worry. She looked at her own fingers, the polished, rounded nails, her palms paler than the backs of her hands. Tears sat in the outer corners of her eyes.

She had the self-control he didn't, the gift of ignoring what prickled and stung and wanted to be blinked away.

"How did Miel end up in the water?" he asked.

Now Aracely smiled, and the shift in her expression forced one tear onto her temple. "That I'm not telling you."

"Because you don't want anyone to know?" he asked.

"Because I'm never saying it out loud."

Aracely pressed her fingers to the corner of her eye.

"The day she showed up," Sam said. "The day they emptied the water tower. Why didn't you come forward? Why didn't you do something? Why'd you wait until I did?"

The sadness on Aracely's face turned pure and pained, no bitterness or anger.

"I was going to," she said. "But then I hesitated. She had no idea who I was. This woman she'd never met before? If I would've come near her, I just would've scared her. You saw how she was looking at everyone."

Aracely folded one hand into the other, pressing both against her sternum.

"But you were little," she said. "Almost as little as she was. You didn't threaten her. I hesitated, and you did something before I did."

Aracely had a right to Miel, a claim on her as her sister. And Sam had acted before Aracely could. He had never once regretted coming close to Miel when no one else had. He'd always counted it as one of the few good things he'd done, pure and certain.

But now the sudden guilt rounded his shoulders.

"I'm sorry," he said.

"I'm not," Aracely said. "You made her feel safe. Enough that when I came to get her, she was ready."

"When are you gonna tell her?" he asked.

Now her smile was amused, almost cruel but not quite. "When are you gonna tell your mother you're not putting on a dress anytime soon?"

His throat tightened, and he felt them both settle into their stalemate.

With her words, everything he'd tried to pull out from her story rushed at him, like a paper moon he could not push underwater. It might vanish into a dark river for a second, but then it would appear downstream, pale and bright and bobbing along the surface.

The fact that Aracely might understand what he could not say, it seeded in him a want, new and raw, like not knowing he was thirsty until water was in front of him. No one else, not his mother, not even Miel, could understand this wanting to live a life different from the one he was born into, so much that his own skin felt like ice cracking.

It shouldn't have mattered, not when Miel and the other girls in his class wore jeans more than they wore skirts. Not when they went out as late as they wanted. Not when they told their brothers what to do, and borrowed their fathers' books.

But there was everything else. The idea of being called Miss or Ms. or, worse, Mrs. The thought of being grouped in when someone called out *girls* or *ladies*. The endless, echoing use of *she* and *her*, *miss* and *ma'am*. Yes, they were words. They were all just words. But each of them was wrong, and they stuck to him. Each one was a golden fire ant, and they were biting his arms and his neck and his bound-flat chest, leaving him bleeding and burning.

He. Him. Mister. Sir. Even teachers admonishing him and his class-mates with *boys, settle down* or *gentlemen, please*. These were sounds as perfect and clean as winter rain, and they calmed each searing bite of those wrong words.

"Does my mother know?" Sam asked. "About you?"

Aracely's laugh was not the wild, reckless thing he sometimes heard coming from the wisteria-colored house. Now it was warm, almost pitying. "Of course she does. How do you think you ended up here?"

"What are you talking about?" Sam asked.

"I met your mother before you two moved here," Aracely said. "She came with a cousin who wanted a lovesickness cure, and we started talking about you. I told her if she ever wanted to move out here, I couldn't promise much, but I could promise I'd watch out for you." This time Aracely's laugh was lighter. She combed back a stray piece of her hair. "I never thought she'd take me up on it."

"But we moved because she lost her job," Sam said. "The school was making cuts, and they let her go."

In Aracely's smile, clench-lipped and sad, Sam saw the truth.

The school hadn't been making cuts.

She hadn't lost her job.

"She loves you," Aracely said. "She loves you as much as a daughter and a son and everything in the world put together."

His mother had gone from being a teacher to being something between a tutor and a nanny, for him.

"That's why we came here?" Sam asked. "Because of me? It's my fault?"

"Not your fault," Aracely said. "Not because of you. *For* you."

Sam put the heels of his hands to his forehead, his fingers in his hair.

"Your mother wanted to move," Aracely said. "When you wanted to live as a boy, she knew how hard it was gonna be to stay in the same place. A whole town calling you Samira? What was that gonna do to you? She couldn't decide what was worse, you trying to get them to understand a tradition they'd never heard of, or her trying to get them to call you Samir."

Sam kept his palms on his forehead, his fingers still caught in his hair. But he felt Aracely watching him, her stare landing on the backs of his wrists.

"She wanted you to have the life you wanted," Aracely said. "So figure out what kind of life you want."

bay of roughness

☽

The phone rang, and Miel answered, barely getting a full breath out before Ivy's voice came through the line.

"Come over," Ivy said.

Miel let out a laugh so small that on the other end of the line, it must have sounded like static. "Forget it."

"Come over," Ivy said, "or I'm telling my father to fire her."

For the way Ivy said it, Miel felt something close to admiration. No taunting, none of the singsong of grade school playgrounds, none of the I-know-something-you-don't-know. Ivy's tone came clear and without pleasure. She wanted what she wanted. The rest was all transaction.

But that didn't mean Miel knew what Ivy was talking about. Aracely? Aracely didn't work for anyone. No one could fire her. They could only decide whether to trust her with their broken hearts. Sam's mother? The Bonners may have owned the biggest pumpkin farm for miles, but even they, with their acres of dark soil and their bright-haired daughters, couldn't cost her the work a half-dozen families in town gave her.

"Who?" Miel asked.

"Samira," Ivy said.

The three syllables cut into Miel.

Samira. The name sounded less like a thing that had once belonged to Sam than the name of some specter, a spirit that might come and take him if Miel did not keep it away. It was a name of a girl who had not died because she had never quite lived. She had never truly existed. She was a life that did not belong to Sam but that he'd tried too hard to belong to.

"Who?" Miel asked, but she heard the wavering in how she said it now. Not the true confusion of the first time she'd asked, but a false start to the word, a breath hitching before she got it out.

"Sam," Ivy said. "Samir. Whatever you want to call her. Come over, or I'm telling my father to fire her."

Ivy hung up.

A new rose stem twisted inside Miel's arm. The opening it would grow through looked as smooth and round as a cigarette burn in a blanket.

When they were ten, Miel had let Sam touch it, let him set his thumb against the little knot of scar tissue. He'd touched her so lightly, so afraid of hurting her, she'd taken his hand and pressed it against her skin, making him feel it.

Now these roses, these roses she hated more than she feared pumpkins or the deepest parts of the river, were what the Bonner girls wanted so much they'd rip apart the life Sam had built. They wanted them enough to drag back a girl Sam thought he had shed years ago. He was a comet burning through the night sky, and Samira was the trail of dust and ice streaking after him.

And the Bonner girls would make everyone tilt their faces and see them both. Sam, the boy he was. Samira, the girl he wasn't. And the blur of scattered light that would make everyone think they were the same person.

Miel was still buttoning her sweater as she left the violet house. Of course she would come, and of course Ivy knew that.

She felt a flare of anger toward his mother, that beautiful, kohl-eyed woman who told her charges stories of brazen, fearless daughters. Yasmin saw her son for what he was, a boy who would never feel like himself inside the name Samira, or inside clothes that let people see and judge his body. But she was as intent on letting things take their own course as she was indifferent to religion. She accommodated both the boy at the core of him, and his brittle, tight-held hope that one day he would want to be a girl.

So you're just gonna wait? Miel had asked her when Sam couldn't hear. Yasmin had just said, *He'll get there.* Her shrug was more a gesture of levelheadedness than an indication that she didn't care. Miel knew that. It still frustrated her, how well she knew Sam and how comfortable she seemed waiting him out.

Miel let that little shred of resentment float away from her. It wasn't his mother's fault. She had given him as much space as she could and as much time as he needed.

Neither of which would mean anything if the Bonner sisters dragged out the name he'd been born with. By saying that name that once belonged to him but that he never quite belonged to, they could strip him naked.

Mr. Bonner was in his truck, the wheels grinding along the dirt path that cut through the farm. He leaned out the driver's-side window and nodded at Miel, like she was coming to see his daughters so they could share library books or polish one another's nails.

She nodded back, because that was what people did in this town.

She kept her eyes up, not letting them fall to the glass pumpkins.

Las gringas bonitas sat in the same arrangement as the last time Miel had been here, as though she had left and they had stayed the whole time. The Bonner sisters had gathered around that dining room table, Ivy's and Lian's gray and green eyes bookended by the redless brown of Chloe's and Peyton's.

That blue vase sat in the center of the table. Miel saw the first rose they'd cut. It had barely wilted, the edges of the petals darkened to copper.

They hadn't tried using it. They hadn't yet found out that the rumors about Miel's roses were nothing more than town lore.

Miel felt caught in a second of wondering why, but then the Bonner girls' four faces, their four shades of red hair, made her feel so dizzy she could almost see four roses. Like they had multiplied in the vase, growing roots and new leaves.

Then those echoed roses vanished, turning to faint washes of color.

The Bonner girls hadn't used that rose yet because they were collecting them. They wanted four of them. They had decided that until all of them could have one, none of them would.

It made Miel unsteady with wondering how many of her roses were at the bottom of the river, whole and alive.

"You don't care about your mother," Lian said.

Miel tensed, even though there was no malice in Lian's words. Only a bluntness, a carelessness evolved to make up for how long thinking took her.

Remembering that stopped Miel from rising to the insult.

"I guess you don't care what anyone thinks of her," Chloe said.

You have no idea what happened. She tried to say it, to cut Chloe off. Just because she wouldn't give up her roses, just because she wouldn't barter away the thing her mother considered so dangerous, didn't mean she didn't care about her mother's memory. It meant she wasn't willing to put into the Bonner girls' hands the petals her mother feared, and that her father was so sure could be willed away.

But those pumpkins outside, the jewel colors of the stained glass coffin, were a threat she could wish away no more than her father could cure her with bandages wrapped so tight her fingers prickled. And her voice felt like a thing outside her, like a breath she had let out and could not pull back.

"You don't care about everyone knowing she tried to kill her own children," Chloe said.

Chloe's voice was more knowing than Lian's, but it was still soft, unthreatening, like she'd just woken Miel from a nap. Her voice was afternoon gathered in the folds of sheer curtains. It was her white hand on patterned wallpaper.

It was a lit match produced from her palm like a magic trick, and the whole room going up like kindling.

Miel looked toward Peyton, who stayed quiet. But she was looking right at Miel, not tracing her fingers along water stains, or looking for anywhere else to settle her eyes.

"But you care about this." Ivy tapped a finger on the table.

Miel noticed, for the first time, that a piece of paper sat on the wood. A photocopy. But the edging, the familiar border and spacing of the lines, made Miel feel like the Bonners' wood floor was buckling under her.

A birth certificate. Sam's. Miel knew without looking. And that knowing came with the sharp drop of realizing Aracely had not settled everything with Ms. Owens. Maybe she thought she had. Maybe she thought she'd left Ms. Owens hopeful, calm, sure in her faith that when she grew lovesick again, Aracely would be ready for her.

But because of Miel, Aracely had botched Ms. Owens' lovesickness cure. Because of Miel, Ms. Owens, scattered, sobbing, and flighty Ms. Owens, would have been so open to the kind words of four girls who told her how useless men and boys were. Miel could imagine them leaning their elbows on the office counter as though they were enrolled, their hands rising and falling in soft gestures. They would have whispered to Ms. Owens as though she was part of their club, told her how men and boys were animals that were easy to control once you knew how they worked.

Maybe they had gone in looking for Miel's file, something they could use against her. She had refused them something they demanded. Of course they would want to wrench her up against the truth that if she defied them, they would tear into her life like teeth into muscle.

But with all of them talking and laughing in hushed tones, how easily Ms. Owens could have let slip that she'd been keeping secrets for Miel's best friend. And the Bonner sisters would have charmed those secrets out of her so slowly, so gently, Ms. Owens would have barely noticed she was giving them up. Confiding in the Bonner sisters would have felt like an act so quiet and harmless, she wouldn't have realized the weight of what she was doing. Showing them the birth certificate would have seemed not like a betrayal, but like chatter between girlfriends.

Miel tried to smooth the wondering out of her face.

She looked at Ivy. "How do you know I care?"

"You're here, aren't you?" Ivy said.

Miel held her throat tight, wound with the feeling that every small movement was one the Bonner sisters would notice. If she swallowed, they'd know they had her. If she breathed in a little too quickly, or out for a little too long, they'd know they had her.

"What I'm wondering is what you care about more," Ivy said. "Everyone knowing she's a girl, or everyone knowing you like girls."

The second half of that threat was so weak, Miel felt the sudden rise of a laugh. She took a breath in, stopping it.

To this whole town, she was odd and unnerving. To them, she was the motherless girl who came from the water tower and grew roses from her wrist, a girl whose skirt hem was always a little damp even on the driest days. Whatever they said about her liking girls or liking boys was a handful of water next to the whole river. It could not make her stranger, more unsettling to everyone else, than she already was.

But what took that stifled laugh, what folded it into something so small and dense it turned to anger, was going over the rest of what Ivy had said.

"He's not a girl," she said.

Ivy eyed the piece of paper. "That says different."

The grain of the photocopy pulled Miel into wondering what they'd noticed, what that birth certificate had made them look at a little more closely.

How he fulfilled his PE credit with farm shifts.

That he'd never taken off his shirt outside, even for swimming; even when he and Miel found places the river pooled, shielded by rocks, he didn't.

That Miel, a girl, was his best friend; so many boys were friends with girls, but not the way Sam was with her, not so close they became names like Honey and Moon.

How often boys at school had called Sam gay or a girl. Even with muscle filling him out, he didn't have the hard angles to his face or the wide spread to his hands to keep them from calling him feminine.

Those boys had no idea what they'd been saying.

Miel's eyes crept over to Peyton. But she had nothing for her but that stare, her eyes the same brown as Chloe's.

There was so much art to it, how little they had to say to lay down the threat.

As far as they could take it, they would take it. They'd proved that the second they'd locked her into those walls of stained glass.

Miel's wrist needled her, like peroxide in a cut. Like something biting her. They were all watching her wrist for the first sign of a new rosebud.

Lian looked at her wrist. "You have time to think about it," she said, and because it was Lian, it sounded like nothing more than an observation, neither a threat nor an assurance.

Miel felt the point of a thorn dragging under her skin, ready to break it as easily as wet paper. She held her throat tight, killing the gasp.

This time she did not run. She slid the paper off the table, folding it over until it was small and would not stay folded another time.

She was halfway down the brick path when Peyton appeared from her mother's herb garden, her hair bringing the smell of rosemary needles.

Miel startled. A minute ago Peyton had been next to her sisters, and now she was here, a cat that was in an attic window one second and on a porch the next.

"Miel," she said.

The give in Peyton's voice sounded almost like an apology, but there was too much of that Bonner pride, that shared sense of being one life in the body of four girls.

"How could you do this to him?" Miel asked, pressing the folded paper between her fingers. "He's done nothing but cover for you."

If Sam didn't lie for Peyton, girls would laugh behind cupped hands when they saw her in the streets. Undisguised glances would needle her and her family at church. Mothers would forbid their daughters from visiting the Bonner house, not realizing their daughters were never invited there anyway.

And God knew what words, or worse, the Shelbys and the Hazeltons would have for Peyton and her mother. They probably wouldn't come by the Bonner house either. They wouldn't bother with discretion. This town punctuated its quiet with enough fury to sustain the gossips for months. Last year a woman shoved her husband's mistress into a stand of tomatoes at the market, sending red and yellow heirlooms spilling down the aisles. Three Christmases ago the Sunday school teacher, in front of everyone, ordered the girl playing Mary in the pageant to relinquish her blue dress, because she'd been caught smoking one of her mother's cigarettes behind the church. If Mr. Bonner were another man, less timid, less afraid of his own daughters, he probably would have flashed his shotgun at the boy who'd gotten Chloe pregnant.

"We don't have to do anything to him," Peyton said.

"You can't do this." Miel leaned in close, checking that Mrs. Bonner wasn't in the kitchen window or on the landing upstairs. "You can't out him. He is so screwed up about this, and he'll figure it out, but he needs time, and he's not gonna get it if the four of you put this out there."

Peyton's soft shrug came with a slight shake of her head. If her mother was watching from the upstairs landing, she wouldn't have even seen it. "Just give them what they want."

"Don't you get it?" Miel's hand opened and closed, twitching with how much she wanted to grab a handful of Peyton's curled hair and pull on it to make her listen. "A town like this, you have no idea what they'll do. Don't pretend you're hiding from your parents."

The openness in Peyton's face disappeared, quick and smooth as water slipping from cupped hands. "You don't know anything about me," she said. "Or my parents. After Chloe, they want me to be thirty before I kiss anyone."

Miel's laugh came out small and cruel, but she didn't bite it back. Because of the way Peyton referred to her own sister—*After Chloe,* as though the oldest Bonner girl could be reduced to the single event of her having a baby. Because of the implication that Mrs. Bonner wouldn't sob into her casserole dishes if she knew what Peyton was doing with Jenna Shelby and Liberty Hazelton.

"So that's it?" Miel asked. "That's the only reason you wear concealer on your neck?" Each word came out sharp and clipped, like yelling pressed down to keep it quiet.

Peyton flinched, and then recovered, her shoulders straightening.

She knew. Peyton knew that if the truth about her and Jenna and Liberty crossed the barrier from classmates to parents—if it moved from rumors in the halls of a school she no longer attended and into the whispers that covered this town—she would feel the scorn even through the walls of the navy blue house.

After Chloe. After Chloe, the blooms of red on Peyton's neck would make the town feel justified in calling the Bonner girls *loose, immoral, sinful.* Words the Bonner sisters would laugh off as old-fashioned, pretending each one didn't cut.

"Yeah," Miel said. "That's what I thought. And now you want to force on him what you can't even take yourself."

God knew what words, or worse, this town would have for a boy who'd been born female. They would wrap their contempt and their cruelty in the lie that they wouldn't have cared, if only he'd told them.

It's just the dishonesty of it all, they'd whisper.

All that lying, it's the lying I hate.

How can you trust someone who pretends like that?

As though the truth of his body was any of their business, as though they had a right to consider how he lived an affront to them.

As though who he was had anything to do with them.

Miel could hear those voices. She hated everyone who would say those words even if they hadn't yet.

And that was if Sam was lucky. This town would scorn Peyton, but they would hate Sam. That was how it worked, judgment for girls, and hate for boys. Boys had been run out of this town for sleeping with other boys, ones meant to marry pretty, pale-eyed girls. The boys who'd called Sam gay or a girl would hate him for what they would call a lie, solid in their conviction that his life was an insult to them, a deception, a trick.

Judgment for girls, hate for boys. And because this town would not know what to do with Sam, he'd have to take both.

"This will destroy him," Miel said.

"Then give them what they want," Peyton said.

This town had never seen anyone like Sam. If they had, they hadn't known. And Miel's fear over this, their reaction to that which they did not know, made her fight to keep her breath quiet. Girls who'd once thought Sam was handsome might let it slip to their boyfriends, who would beat Sam up because they could not stand the thought of their own girlfriends liking anyone born female. Boys who hated that he'd matched them, hated that for so many years they had not known, would corner him when he went out to hang his moons. Fathers, holding shotguns the same as Mr. Bonner's, would threaten him to stay away from their daughters.

"If he gets hurt, it's on you. Because you should know better than any of them what this could do to him."

"No," Peyton said, again with that slight shake of her head, so slow her curls barely moved. "If he gets hurt, it's on you. Because all you had to do was give up something you throw away."

It wasn't just throwing them away. It was killing them, destroying the petals her father could not heal her of and her mother could not baptize out of her.

Now she was supposed to hand them over to girls who misunderstood their awful force. Her roses didn't have the strength the rumors said, the power to compel love from those who breathed in the scent.

But her mother had feared them so deeply she was willing to do anything the señoras and the priests told her to save Miel from them.

"What do you even want them for?" Miel asked. "Just in case someone has the nerve not to fall in love with you?"

That got a tight-eyed blink out of Peyton, a tension in her cheeks.

"The four of you," Miel said. "You're worse than anyone on Aracely's table. You want to fall in love more than you want to be in love, and you want someone falling in love with you more than you want them loving you."

"That's not true," Peyton said.

"Then what are you doing with Liberty?" Miel asked. "You don't like her the way you like Jenna and everyone knows it."

Peyton's eyes opened a little more, a wild look that was closer to anger than surprise.

It satisfied Miel more than she expected. It may have been as surface-level as the cracks on the stained glass coffin, but it still cut across the color and shimmer that was the Bonner girls.

"I hope the three of them are all you need," Miel said. "Because they're gonna be all you have left."

Her wrist felt heavy, like the muscle had grown dense as a river stone.

It felt heavier when she realized Peyton was watching it.

A few more leaves had grown from her wrist, peeking out from her sleeve. They sheltered a tiny rosebud, the near-blue of an amethyst, shining with blood and water.

lake of winter

❯

he green shoot was already thickening into a stem, and the heat turned to a slashing feeling. Miel felt the stem's base anchored in her forearm, reaching almost to the inside of her elbow, under a veil of skin and muscle.

After she'd left the Bonners' house, the round pearl of the bud had fattened to the size of a marble. Now it was as big as an unbloomed peony, one flinch from shuddering open.

Miel thought of Sam's palm on her shoulder blade, and pain burned bright through her forearm. It felt as alive as if it had fingers and breath. Each time the stem crawled a sliver further out of her wrist, she wanted to let a scream pour from her throat.

Its perfume, like the warm sugar of figs and pomegranates, felt damning, proof to the Bonner sisters of how much she wanted him. It gossiped to the women at the market. It confessed to the priests at church. It spoke of the olives and lemon groves Sam's father ran through as a child.

The thought of cutting it off her own wrist came to her, and stayed. It scratched at her, like noticing a trickle of blood on her lip and trying not to lick it away. It pulled her, this rose that had grown faster than any other before it.

But she couldn't cut it away and kill it.

The Bonner sisters wanted it, demanded it. And Peyton had seen the start of this one, a deeper violet than the house Miel lived in with Aracely.

Without putting on her shoes, Miel crept downstairs and outside, taking a full breath when the night air hit her forearm. The grass smelled clean and strong as citrus pith, and each blade looked a little gilded, taking in light from the house like a cloth soaking up oil.

"Miel." She heard Sam's voice. Not the question he'd made of her name when he found her staring at the stained glass pumpkins. He was calling her.

He'd been coming from his house. Even from this distance, in the dark, she could see the tints of the roof tiles. The day she had spilled out of the water tower, her eyes damp and sore, those different-colored tiles had made Sam's house seem like a place out of a fairy tale.

Now it seemed like a place that the cruel force of her roses might wreck if she came too close.

The moon he carried was not the kind he hung outside her window, the pale blue-lavender of a frost moon, or the soft green of a corn moon, the kind he made for nightmare-plagued children. This one he'd painted in white, and black, and where they met, a thin band of gray. He painted not on paper or fabric but on a rusted metal globe, discarded by an antique shop; she'd gone with him to get it and a half-dozen others they were junking.

He'd covered it in the blue-black of a new moon, and then added the sharp slice of a waning crescent.

"Where are you putting it?" she asked.

"I don't know yet," he said.

She wanted to ask if she could go with him, watch him climb that wooden ladder and set the moon in a high tree, this gash of light.

It scared her a little. She'd never seen him paint a moon like this, all white and black, no hint of color, *mare insularum* and *sinus honoris* in gray. It was so different from every moon he'd ever brought her, the violets and blues of lunar seas painted on paper, or the plains in a gold so faint they looked like cream.

But that stark beauty made her want to kiss him so badly that the lack of it made her lips feel cold. Her tongue was ice in her own mouth. Her breath was winter wind that stung every surface inside her.

He knew. She saw the shift in how he looked at her, the way his lips parted, a breath held between them. He set down the moon and kissed her, the taste of him like the black cardamom Aracely kept in a glass jar. The smoke and spice filled the air whenever she opened it. Like ginger made darker.

Sam tasted like the one night each year when the air turned from fall to winter, the sudden cold, the smell of damp bark.

Winged cardamom. That was what Aracely called it. For the way the pods, split open, looked like moths about to take flight. The taste fluttered on Miel's tongue like a meadow brown on an iris petal.

Even when her lips broke away from Sam's, he kept his hand on the back of her neck, his mouth still so close to hers she felt the rhythm of his breathing.

He pulled her against him, his arm holding her waist. This morning her rose had given off the scent of honey and apricot, but now its perfume had the weight and spice of copal incense. It filled the air between them.

Each time he kissed her, that faint cardamom taste of his mouth made her shut her eyes. But then it turned bitter on her tongue. The more she cared about him, the more the Bonner sisters saw she cared about him, the more they'd know he was how to get to her. The more they saw how she looked at him, touched his arm when she laughed, pulled him into the trees when he was on his breaks, the more they'd wield that birth certificate.

He was her best friend, and everyone knew it. But half this town must have assumed they were best friends by default. The boy who hung dozens of copies of the moon, and the girl from the water tower. The girl afraid of pumpkins, and the boy who knew how to keep snakes away with cinnamon and clove oil and pink agapanthus. They were each so strange that only someone as odd as the other could get so close.

But if she loved him, the Bonner girls would feel it. She already had to do what they wanted, offer her roses in exchange for their silence. But she couldn't let them near him. He couldn't know that the secret held between him and his mother and Aracely and Miel was also in the hands of these four sisters. It would turn him frightened and skittish. He'd hide from the questions he needed to stare down.

She put her hands on his shoulders and pushed him away. "I can't." She cradled her forearm against her sweater. "We never should have done this. Any of it."

"What?" he asked. "Why?"

She reached into the dark for a lie, her fingers grasping for anything solid. "We know each other too well. We've been friends too long to do this." Her voice was thinning and breaking. "We can't do this."

"What are you talking about?" he asked.

"I'm sorry," she said, the first word clipped by a hard swallow. "I care about you. But I can't be with you." She turned her back to him before the damp sting of salt hit her cheek. "Not like this."

Even walking away from him, she heard him catch his breath in the back of his throat.

"Miel," he said.

But she didn't answer, so he didn't go after her.

She tried to get far enough away that she wouldn't hear the soft brushing sound of him slipping his hands into his pockets. And she didn't look back until she knew he was gone.

This time, when the Bonner girls found her in the dark space between trees, she did not fight. And because she did not fight, they did not dig their fingers into her, or drag her to the stained glass coffin. They just set their hands on her, like they were all in church and they were blessing her. Ivy parted the blades of those brass scissors, and Miel gave herself over to the blazing reds and oranges of the Bonner girls, bright as tongues of flame.

bay of honor

)

She kept the door to her room closed. She almost never kept the door to her room closed. But lately she and Aracely barely spoke. Miel didn't know if Aracely was still mad at her, and she didn't know if she should ask.

Miel lay curled on her side, cheek against her comforter.

Aracely was civil, and that made it worse. She poured Miel coffee in the morning, offered without speaking, but didn't hold her lips tight or look away like she was angry. She just handed over the cup and then went back to frying nasturtium blossoms. It reminded Miel of how badly she'd ruined the lovesickness cure, and how she'd thinned out Ms. Owens' loyalty so badly that she was open to the whispers and charms of four fire-haired girls.

Now it was all on Miel to save Sam, to make sure no one tried to force him into matching the name on that paper. She had cut into pieces the net Aracely had woven for all of them. The ache in her wrist, like Ivy was pressing the point of those brass scissors into her, would not let her forget.

The tap of knuckles struck Miel's door, the soft rhythm she recognized.

"Come in," Miel said without moving.

The thread of Aracely's perfume snuck into the room ahead of her.

"Are you hungry?" Aracely said. "I was thinking of making something."

Miel shook her head, cheek still against the bed.

Aracely sat on the edge of her bed, the slow lowering of her weight buoying Miel a little. It had always been a comforting feeling to her, the sense of another person sitting near her, especially Aracely. Now it sharpened the truth of how little they'd talked.

"I'm sorry I yelled at you about Emma," Aracely said.

"I deserved it," Miel said, her voice coming out hoarse without her meaning it to. Not a crying sound. More like her voice, within the country of this house, had fallen out of use.

"No, you didn't," Aracely said. "And I went over there and made it right. She's cured. At least until the next time around."

"Great," Miel said, and the word came out so soft even Aracely missed the sarcasm.

"You can't do that again," Aracely said. "If you're not really here, you can't help me. I'd rather you tell me that."

Miel nodded, her cheek rubbing against the quilt.

"I know I've expected a lot of you," Aracely said, and the lowering of her voice made Miel know what she meant, how Miel had been handing her eggs and lemons and glass jars since she was six, her small hands holding them up. "But you're not gonna disappoint me by telling me you can't do it. Everybody has bad days."

Miel shut her eyes, guilt braiding thick in her wrist and snaking deeper into her.

Aracely ran a hand down Miel's hair. "Do you want to talk about what happened?"

She almost asked what she meant, the night Aracely had to bring her home, or the lovesickness cure Miel had wrecked when she did not open the window fast enough.

But it didn't matter. The answer was the same either way.

"No," Miel said.

A knock echoed up from downstairs. Sam's mother. She was the only one who never used the doorbell. She thought it was too formal when the four of them were so much like family.

Aracely went downstairs. Miel pulled herself off the comforter, tripping over clothes she'd left on the floor yesterday and the day before, and followed her.

Sam's mother stood in the front hall.

"Have either of you seen Samir?" she asked.

Aracely's eyes crawled over to Miel. "You were supposed to meet him somewhere, weren't you?"

She could see Aracely holding her back teeth together. Her eyes flinched a little wider. Miel could almost hear what she was thinking. *Yes, Miel. Say yes.*

"Yes," Miel said, letting her gasp sound like a sudden realization, as though she'd forgotten and now remembered. "Yes." She glanced toward the watch Sam's mother wore on her left wrist. "I'm late, but I'll make sure he's home early."

Sam's mother looked between the two of them, her gaze careful and considering.

She did not believe them.

Miel knew how tall Sam's mother was, taller than Sam or Aracely. Her long skirts, skimming the floor, made her look even taller. But she never seemed this tall when she laughed, or when she taught Miel the difference between sweet basil and tulasi. She had a tulasi tree on the side of her house that she never cut or picked from, and its green and purple leaves seemed to give off a stronger scent for being left alone.

She seemed this tall only when Sam and Miel brought home grass snakes. Or when the parents of one of the girls she looked after did not notice that their daughter was so nervous so often she bit her fingernails to bleeding.

Or when she wore this kind of worried look. It was those moments, and this look, that made Miel hesitate to call Sam's mother Yasmin. It didn't matter that she'd told Miel to. This woman was so much a mother, so much an adult, and any reminder of that made addressing her by her first name feel strange and irreverent.

"Do you want to stay until he comes back?" Aracely asked. "I'll make café de olla."

Of course Aracely would think the answer was coffee mixed with cinnamon and piloncillo in a clay pot. It made their lies feel as weak and thin as skim milk.

"No," his mother said. "Thank you." She nodded at Aracely and left, turning toward the door.

She must have been willing to believe them, or pretend she believed them, for now.

Aracely leaned into Miel. "Find him."

Sam mother's had barely left, the sound of her steps on the front walk just faded, when Aracely reached for her keys.

"Are you gonna help me look?" Miel asked.

"No," Aracely said. "I'm gonna check on Emma Owens."

"Now?"

"You better believe now," Aracely said. "Your boyfriend"—she shrugged into her coat—"in case you haven't noticed, isn't ready to have this whole town know his legal name. The last thing we need is to worry about that woman keeping her mouth shut. I'll let her talk all night if that's what it takes." She sighed. "And God knows it probably is."

She was out the door before Miel could tell her not to, that there was no reason, and no use.

ocean of storms

)

The surface of the river was as dark as juniper berries.

All the stories were lies. His mother's fables about chukar partridges and women who disguised themselves as lynx. Miel's fairy tales about stars falling in love with moons.

What had his great-grandparents' stories of stars and moon bears gotten them? It hadn't let them stay in Kashmir with their countless saffron crocuses. It hadn't saved their family trade, built of the delicate work of bringing those flowers to life and then slipping the rust-colored threads from their centers.

What had Miel's fairy tales gotten her? This town didn't love her the way they loved the Bonner girls, even if they feared them. They didn't gather to protect her and Aracely when strangers threw empty bottles at the violet house, calling them witches.

To this town, Miel was as dirty as the water that had spilled from the rusted tower, and as strange as the roses that grew from her wrist. When she was a child, they thought the hem of her skirt, never

drying even in full sun, meant she was possessed. Now they considered it the sign of some sin that lived as deeply in her body as her
roses.

But if the moon in the sky could move whole oceans, then maybe,
if he wanted it enough, every moon he'd made could pull at this
water. It could draw it into the sky like a ribbon and turn it to ice
crystals and clouds.

Sam stared down into the river. If he gave himself up to it, maybe
it would do to him what it had done to Aracely, turning him into
what he truly was. Maybe it would give him a body that matched
this life he had built. Or maybe it would make him want to be a
woman called Samira.

And if it did neither of these things, maybe it would have enough
mercy to just take him under and turn him into water. Maybe there
was enough force in him to fill in this river, drive all the water out
like he was a meteor, so there'd be nothing left. Just a wetland, a damp
crater in the earth.

He could not guard Miel against nightmares rooted so far into
her they walked with her like shadows. But he could destroy this
one thing Miel feared.

He waded down the steep bank until he found where the river
dropped off to its full depth. The force of his body cutting through
the water pulled him down. Almost warm near the surface, the
river turned cold the farther he sank.

He lost the moon and the stars. He lost the clouds turning the
sky to silver.

He drifted down, letting his body go, not fighting the dark. He
shut his eyes and saw the blink of Miel's eyes, like candied ginger,
and how her eyelids were a little darker than the rest of her skin.
How her fingernails were short from her biting them, how she always
smelled like whatever rose her body was growing, even when it hadn't
yet broken through her skin.

She was amber and last light. The moment between summer and fall. The honey she ate off spoons in Aracely's kitchen.

This was one of the things he loved about her, that they called her Honey, and she was so quick to eat her own name.

He would never be free of this. Of any of it. How he wanted Miel in a way that hurt as much as the tightening of his lungs against the cold water, a desperation for a breath in matched only by the impossibility of taking one. How he was losing the feeling that one day, he could live the life that matched the name his mother had given him.

The day he needed to be a girl, a woman, had once felt so far away for so long that he believed he'd be ready. The time when he'd be as old as when a bacha posh cast off her boy's clothes and ways had seemed such a great stretch of time away from where he was that the impossibility of reaching it exceeded the impossibility of him wanting to be a girl.

He'd been pushing it for years, pretending that day was still far off. He'd pretended even when he'd started bleeding. Even when he had to start wearing binders under his clothes.

But for this moment, his body was not his. It floated and hovered. It belonged to the water, the current holding him. Its pull made him understand why he had gone into the river in the first place. It wasn't just this rage in him, or even Miel.

It was that raw hope that maybe the water would not only take him and turn him into something else, but that it would decide for him. Maybe, the way it had for Aracely, it would see him for what he really was, and make him into it. If he was meant to be a girl, maybe it would make him want to be a girl. If he would never grow out of being a boy, maybe it would spin the raw materials of his skin and muscle into a body that matched.

He wanted, more than he wanted a breath, for the water to take this decision from him.

He opened his eyes, and thought he caught the shape and light of every moon he'd ever made, faint as the reflection of fairy lights in a pond. The faint rings of violet and blue-green and gold floated around him. But the heaviness in his forehead made him shut his eyes again, and he lost them.

Arms wrapped around his waist, pulling him.

He recognized her touch, the way she dug her fingers into his sides. He tried to fight her, to let her go like she was a moon the sky could take. He didn't want to be the thing weighting her to the earth.

But his arms and legs felt no warmer and no more alive than the water. His fingers filled with a numbness that made him wonder if he was disappearing.

As long as he'd known her, she'd never gone into water so deep she couldn't see the bottom. Even when they swam together, she stayed in the shallows.

They broke the surface, and the thin chill of the air hit him.

His breaths were short. They sounded like the fast, hard winds that pulled through the trees on fall nights. He felt like he should have been taking in the whole sky's worth of air, but he was still gasping.

"Sam." She yelled at him, held on to his arm even when he broke away from her.

He treaded water to keep himself up. He reached out for her, worrying that as soon as she settled she'd panic and stop swimming. But she kept her grip on him and dragged him toward the bank, scrambling like the water had fingers that would draw them both down.

She clawed her way up onto the bank, pulling him with her.

He knelt with his back to the river, forearms pressed into his thighs. Water from his hair dripped down the back of his neck, and his jeans stuck to his body.

"Sam," she said, her voice quieter, wavering.

His shoulders hunched forward, curving around the pain that flared through his sternum.

She knelt in front of him. Her wet hair splayed out over her shoulders. Ribbons of water fell down her body. "Sam." She grabbed his upper arms.

In that moment of her skin touching his, her looking into his face, he saw it. The spark of recognition, like the static off a doorknob shocking through her.

Her lips parted. Her eyes opened so much that even in the dark, he could see every shade of brown and gold. A small gasp matched the rhythm of his next breath.

She understood. She'd caught the defiance and the rage in him.

Each drop of water off his hair drummed against his skin like a needle.

He hadn't slipped, or fallen in, or been dragged in by hands that hated him. He'd gone in on purpose, and she knew it.

At first, he did not register the shape of her hand. It flew quickly, a brown-winged bird with an underside covered in tiny, pale feathers.

He didn't recognize that flash of lighter and darker brown as part of her until it struck his cheek. It pulled from his lungs what little air he had left, enough for a blunted sound at the back of his throat. And the force of her, the weight of how badly he'd wanted her to touch him even if it was this, to slap him, made the rain feel as distant as the stars.

bay of billows

)

They had never hit each other before, not once. Miel hadn't hit him when he reached out to touch a baby rattlesnake they found twirling through the grasses. The sun turned it into a ribbon of pale bronze, and Sam had seemed like he wanted to pet it, like it was an animal in one of his mother's stories.

And Sam had never hit her, never even come close. Not even when a boy at school called him the worst word Miel could think of anyone calling Sam, a word his mother had once, in their old town, found painted on the side of their house. Sam went at him, the closest she'd ever seen him to getting into a fight. But Miel grabbed him, hooking her arms through his, holding him, and she'd felt the rage in him. How he could have overpowered her, but didn't because he wasn't willing to hurt her.

Now Miel had reached across the space between them, breaking that seal on the years they'd known each other. Years of nights together, a few times fighting enough to stop talking to each other, and they'd never struck each other. And now she'd hit her best friend, the boy who came near her when to everyone else she was strange and made of water.

But she had gone into the river after him, thinking he needed her to save him, watching him and worrying with each second he stayed under. She'd hesitated by the edge only long enough to see his shape, the light flash of his shirt, the dark blur of his hair, his arms slack near his body. Then she'd let the water take her.

There was no joy in having covered herself in the water she was so afraid of. Its current called to her, reminding her that it had taken her brother, and her mother, and now it had almost taken her best friend. Its beads covered her skin, like fingers needling her. If she had stayed in that water a second longer, she would have felt the film of her mother's dress brushing her shins, or her brother's fingers grasping at her wrist, trying to save her.

Then Miel had seen Sam's face, the lack of panic, the reckless edge in his expression. And she knew. The water hadn't tried to steal him.

He'd let it have him.

Now they knelt facing each other, his hands on his knees, her arms crossed and held tight against her.

He hadn't broken eye contact with her, even when she slapped him. It frightened her. And it made her want to brush his wet hair out of his face with her fingers, put her mouth on his hard enough that she couldn't tell if she was kissing him or biting him.

"What are you doing?" she asked.

He didn't answer. He didn't look away either.

"Why did you . . ." She could not say the words. She could not speak the truth that Sam had gone into the water, in all his clothes, in weather cold enough that he couldn't pretend he was swimming.

"Sam," she said, making the syllable sharp enough that he'd have to look at her.

A sheen of water made his eyes look like hot glass.

"Where are you?" she asked. "Where did you go?"

Sam's breathing deepened but didn't even. One inhale was slow and paused, the next sharp and broken.

"Why are you shutting me out?" Miel asked.

The change in his stare was so small it was almost invisible, but she felt it as clearly as the border between sun and shade.

"I'm shutting you out?" he asked. "Do you know how much I don't know about you? What happened the other night? Why were you out there?"

Miel got to her feet.

"Where the hell do you get off saying we know each other too well?" he asked.

She wasn't listening to this. She turned her back and started walking.

He stood and followed her, his hand flying out toward her.

"No." He grabbed her forearm. "You are not walking away from me. I didn't ask you to come here, but you did. So you are not leaving."

His grip pushed the thorns of her newest rose into her wrist. The pressure of his hand burned into her, her skin red and sore. The bud crushed against her.

She blunted her gasp so it was no more than a sharp breath in.

But Sam felt those thorns.

What he didn't know was how fast this one was growing in. Half because Miel wanted him and her body felt it. Half because the Bonner girls wanted her roses as fast as her wrist could grow them, and her skin and muscle knew enough to comply. The pain meant that, every minute, she had the feeling of those tarnished scissors held against her forearm.

He drew his hand away, and held it out in front of him, studying his scratched palm. Even through her wet sleeve, the thorns had drawn blood in lines as thin as strands of her hair.

He cupped his hand under the back of her wrist, his hold firm, but lighter than when he'd grabbed her.

A flinch ran down her arm. But she gritted her body still. Moving now would be worse than hitting him.

He folded back her sleeve.

Drops of blood stained her wrist. Water had glazed the leaves, turning them almost translucent. The bud, a breath from opening, had grown round and swollen as a bulb on a string of globe lights. A shell of grass-colored petals covered the violet flower, a little of the pink at the center showing.

His breathing and her own heartbeat kept her from hearing the night birds.

"Sam," she said.

He eased her sleeve back down. "You're so many questions to me," he said. "And you always will be." He said the words without admiration. They were bitter, resigned.

He let her go, put his hands in his pockets, his fingers sliding against the river-soaked denim.

She could see the things living inside him, dragging their sharp edges.

"You don't want me," he said. "So what do you want?"

"Sam," she said. She wanted him, and he knew it. He had to know it. How much she wanted him hardened the air between them.

She took a step toward him, so slow she hoped he wouldn't notice her narrowing the distance between them. She was as unanchored as she felt on the nights when she and Aracely would lie on picnic tables, looking up, imagining they could fall into the sky.

He turned his back to her, and started walking.

Anger flared through her fingers and spread through the rest of her body. He'd stopped her from leaving, and now he wanted her to let him go.

"You know what?" she said. "You say you don't know me, but you don't know yourself."

He half-turned, hands still in his pockets, the muscles around his eyes tensing.

"Tell me something." She came toward him. "Did you ever really want me, or was I just the one you wanted because you knew I'd keep your secret?"

Now he looked as startled as he was angry, like the acknowledgment of things they never spoke of would make them float into the sky, that they would stick like stars and be declared to everyone on the ground in points of light.

"Don't look at me like that," Miel said. "I'm not gonna tell anyone and you know it."

His expression shifted again, angry and injured, the tension in his eyes softening but his jaw held tight.

"I know this hasn't been easy for you," she said. "I'm not gonna pretend I have any idea what this is like for you. But it hasn't been easy for me either. I can't ask you anything. I can't ask what you want. I have no idea if it's okay to kiss you. I have to guess which parts of you I can touch and which ones I can't. We can't talk about any of it because I don't want to push you or confuse you or make you face anything you're not ready for."

"I am not confused," he said.

"Then what do you want?" she asked.

His eyes flicked over the ground, the milk thistle and lamb's-ear leaves crowding their ankles like pieces of worn silver velvet.

She'd never tell him what the Bonner sisters wanted, that piece of paper and that name they threatened her with. But it didn't stop the anger from rising out of the center of her, turning her lips hot and making her speak.

"You have no idea what all of us are willing to do for you if you just let us," she said.

Sam looked up. "One thing, Miel. One thing I didn't want to talk about. I've given you all there is of me. You have it. How much of you have you kept back?"

She had held nothing back just because she wanted to keep it from him. His was a world of painted moons and feather grasses and trees that bloomed in autumn. She didn't want to bring into that world the awful, half-remembered things she grasped at when she had a fever. She wanted to be the girl who belonged under his moons, the girl whose skin he'd set foil stars on in constellations that mirrored the sky.

Maybe she'd kept more from him than he had from her. But he was still as unfamiliar as the valleys of vapor on the moon. She didn't know the safe ways to touch him, or whether she should say his name, let the word *Sam* off her tongue when he was touching her and she barely had the breath for it. She didn't know if it would remind him that she wanted him, or if it would just remind him that he did not want to be a girl called Samira.

She knew him no better than the landscapes in those library astronomy atlases. He was as distant as the lake of summer and the marsh of sleep and the ocean of storms.

"I can't map you," she said, and the choked laugh in her own voice surprised her. That resignation, the giving-up, made her body feel light, unmoored. "I've tried, and I can't map you."

"I don't want you to map me," he said. "I want you to . . ."

The sound of his voice cut out. He winced harder than when she'd slapped him, his slouch so hard and fast she thought he was doubling over. She stepped forward to catch him, hold him up. But he straightened, pulled himself back.

Even through this, she caught his mouth slipping into the shape of the next word, a word his voice gave no sound. His tongue flicked against his teeth, but then he bit it, stopping himself.

It was still enough to let her guess what he didn't finish saying.

I don't want you to map me. I want you to love me.

The unsaid words clung to her like foil stars. She felt the light from his moons tracing them, the shadows of lunar seas leaving their outlines on her skin. She would wear this night—those words, said and unsaid—on her body. Whether the points of those stars would cut into her hinged on whether she answered what he could not say.

"I love you," she said, the words said so softly they didn't feel tethered to her. "I've always loved you. You know that, right?"

She meant it however he wanted to take it. That she loved him as the boy who'd first been willing to come near her. That she loved him as her best friend. That she loved him in a way that made her glow with the memory of every moon he'd ever painted and every time he'd spread his hands over her back.

"Yeah, great." The sarcasm in his voice was sudden, as sharp and narrow as an icicle, and she felt the rose stem dragging its thorns against her skin. "But you know what? I don't love you. Because I don't know you." He turned his back to her and the river. "You never let me."

lake of sorrow

)

They had said so many awful things to each other, but this was what echoed in her head like the sound of glass breaking. *I don't love you. I don't love you.*

She had loved him since they were small, when they'd met on feral land among the brush of feather reed grass. They had spent nights pretending the stars were things that could be lured to earth. That the fairy rings thick with white-capped mushrooms were the light of the moon seared into the ground.

A little more of the rose slid out of Miel's wrist. It made her bite down on her tongue, the faint taste of blood slipping down her throat.

She knelt next to the water and plunged her hand in, her palm still hot from hitting Sam. The first cord of gold was tracing the hills, but she hadn't gone home, knowing Aracely would probably still be sitting in Ms. Owens' kitchen. If she went home, she'd take Sam's words home with her, and they'd rattle around in that empty house, barren and cold without Aracely's noise and laugh.

Miel beat her hands against the water. Her fingers clawed at the current, even though she knew it wouldn't feel it, that she never hurt it the way it had hurt her. She could never take from the river as much as it had taken from her.

And now she couldn't even give her mother the offering of her roses. She couldn't cut them away and force them down into the river that had stolen her mother. The Bonners demanded she surrender those petals, or they'd spread lies about her mother and what they thought was the truth about Sam.

The blood and muscle holding her together felt like a cast iron pan left out on a stove, barely cooled. The autumn air around her felt like ice that might crack just from touching her skin.

A thread on her forearm, hot and damp like a trickle of honey, made her open her eyes.

She looked down at her wrist.

A trail of blood dripped onto her palm.

The rose was gone. There was nothing but the stub of a stem, the wood rough from being snapped instead of cut.

"No," she said.

She grabbed at the water, reaching out for the rose she'd broken off. Her fingers clawed for the flower head, her eyes scanning for the violet petals, the pink center.

"No," she said, the word splintering across the flickering water so she couldn't tell if the river was echoing it or if she was saying it, over and over.

They'd never believe her that she hadn't meant to.

"No," she said, and this time she could hear her own voice, repeating it.

She'd lost something the Bonner girls considered theirs. She'd lost the only thing protecting her mother's wandering spirit, and a secret rooted so deeply in Sam that if anyone tried to tear it out of him he'd break apart.

She saw the flash of copper in the same second she felt Ivy's hands on her.

"No." This time the word hardened and turned to screaming. "No."

Ivy had seen her. Of course Ivy had seen her. Miel had been kneeling here long enough that the she could smell the faint warmth of the sun, and there was nothing the Bonner girls did not know.

Ivy was pulling her to her feet, gripping her on the sorest point of her wrist.

Miel kept screaming, twisting out of Ivy's hold.

Ivy dugs her nails into her. "Stop," she said, the word hot in Miel's ear. "Or I'm telling everyone about her."

Her. That one word, that word that did not belong to Sam, worked better than all the threats the Bonner girls could have made.

Miel could have begged, could have sworn that she didn't mean to lose the rose. But she owed this to Sam, and to his mother, and to Aracely. She owed them whatever compliance would satisfy the Bonner sisters. As long as it wasn't forcing Sam into the light, she would accept the consequence of not handing over that rose.

Miel went slack, and let Ivy take her.

She let her pull her deeper into the woods, toward the stained glass coffin. She let Ivy force her inside, accepting this punishment decided by these four sisters and given under their watch.

Ivy shoved the lid closed, and the latch clicked.

Miel tensed, trying to breathe in the little ribbons of air from the holes in the stained glass.

She looked through the side panels, wondering who would stand guard. She searched for the color of Peyton's hair, that orange that looked softened by sun and dust. The almost-auburn of Lian's, even the red-blond of Chloe's. Though she doubted Chloe was made to do such chores as watching defiant girls. Chloe no longer led her sisters, but she had once, and even to Ivy, that must have counted.

Miel looked again for Peyton and Lian, for their hair standing orange against the gold trees.

But all Miel saw was that bright fall of copper.

The back of Ivy's hair.

Ivy was walking away from her, leaving her, and none of her sisters were here. There was no other red. Just the yellow of hornbeam and hickory leaves.

Miel threw her hands against the lid, screaming into the small space between her mouth and the stained glass.

Without the other Bonner girls keeping Ivy in check, Miel was locked away, unseen and easy to forget. There was no one watching to make sure she was still alive and breathing.

There was no one waiting to let her out.

Miel rammed her hands into the stained glass above her. "They're not gonna give you what you want," she screamed.

She wished, as hard as she wished to be out of these walls of stained glass, that the Bonner girls knew how little her roses could do for them. If they did, they couldn't still demand she give them up. They couldn't want them for the simple reason that they could take them. The roses weren't some much-loved cat, and Miel hadn't refused an invitation to a birthday party.

But Ivy was so desperate to believe the rumors that the petals could cast a kind of love spell. She wanted four of them so she and her sisters could slip them under pillows or bake the petals into vanilla cake.

They were grasping at anything that could show they had no less power than before Chloe had left them. A point they wanted to make with four roses and four stolen hearts.

They were lashing out at Miel, because she had seen what no one ever should have, Ivy and an uninterested boy, a boy who did not matter except for the fact that a Bonner girl had bored him.

But understanding this would not crack these glass walls. It would not make the Bonner girls hear her.

Miel's hands stung from the impact, but she kept throwing them at the glass.

"You don't need them," she called out to the space between trees. "They won't help you."

But Ivy was gone, and the trees didn't answer.

sea of the edge

)

*M*iel wasn't in their first class of the morning. He hadn't seen her in the halls, or on the walk to school he'd taken fifteen minutes early, both trying to avoid her and hoping he'd see her.

Mr. Valk called on him just before the bell rang. "Samir," he said.

Half his teachers called him Samir even when no one else did. Maybe they thought it was more formal. Or they meant to command his attention, like calling a child by both first and middle names. Or they wanted to be sure he never forgot that he was different from his classmates. The Henrys and Christophers. The Lilys and Julias.

Mr. Valk tipped his pen in the direction of the empty desk next to Sam's. "Where's Miel this morning?" he asked, as though Sam was responsible for whether she showed up to class.

Sam opened his book to the page chalked on the board. "I don't know."

At the end of the fifty minutes, Ivy Bonner ducked into the class-room, saying Miel was sick and that she was picking up her assign-ments.

So now Ivy was Miel's best friend. That hadn't taken long. That made sense though. Miel was their kind of pretty. Not perfect and polished, not like Nina Chan, one of the girls who knew as well as Sam that if they wanted this town to love them, they'd have to give themselves nicknames; Nina had been crowned Pumpkin Queen last year, her curls so coated in hairspray they looked varnished. Or even like Adair Lewis, who always danced the part of the sugar plum fairy at the community theater each Christmas; she stood up straight as a cypress tree, and had her hair, almost as pale as her skin, always rolled into a bun with no stray pieces.

No, Miel was like the Bonner girls. She was dark where they were pale, her hair brown-black while theirs came in all shades of red. But they were both a little careless, unpolished, half the time without their shoes and half the time wearing their good shoes into the dirt. No makeup except for some brushstroke of bright color, the Bonner sisters' pine-green eyeshadow or the plum-colored lipstick Miel sometimes wore.

It made him wonder how many other best friends Miel had on standby. Maybe it'd been all four of the Bonner sisters the whole time, and he'd just been too dense to notice.

Outside Mr. Valk's room, his classmates lined the hallway, boys mostly, watching Ivy and probably trying to work out if she'd gone up one or two cup sizes since she'd gone to this school.

That was a difference between Miel and the Bonner girls. Miel had shed her baby fat a little at a time, like each season was water, wearing her down, cutting her into a different shape. But the Bon-ner girls started out bony, all jutting elbows and knees so skinny the sharp round of the cap showed, and each year filled out a little more. Boys had already been looking at Ivy when she left school, but those who hadn't seen her up close since then wore their wonder on their faces, their shock at how her hips and her breasts now seemed as round and soft as her face.

Two seniors—Sam thought one had the last name Reese, but the second was a transfer he didn't know—stood against the lockers. They didn't hide their survey of Ivy's sweater and skirt and tights as she made her slow walk down the hall.

"Is she registering?" the transfer asked Reese.

"She's picking up stuff for another girl," Reese said.

"Another girl who looks like that?"

That. Sam felt the first flick of anger clawing its way down his arms.

"No," Reese said. "Miel."

"Who?"

"You pay attention to anything I say?" Reese asked. "Miel. The girl with the wet skirt."

"Huh?"

"Her skirt," Reese said. "It's always wet."

For the first time since Sam noticed them, the transfer looked away from Ivy and at Reese.

"Look sometime," Reese said. "Been that way since she came out of the water tower."

The transfer held his tongue against his bottom teeth, and Sam looked away. The gesture repulsed him, and at the same time seeing it felt like the breach of some rule, like walking in on a guy masturbating and then not backing right out of the room.

Reese's laugh was low, a half-grunt.

"What?" the transfer asked.

"Nothing," Reese said. "Just makes you wonder if she's always wet anywhere else, doesn't it?"

Sam felt the part of him trying to hold him back. He registered it, like the brush of fingers on his shoulder. But it couldn't stand up to that clawing feeling that now made its way up to the back of his neck.

He grabbed Reese by his jacket, shoved him against the locker hard enough that the back of his head hit the metal.

"What the hell?" the transfer said, grabbing at the back of Sam's shirt.

Sam jerked out of his hold.

Reese looked scared for a second. Then his lip drew back, and he looked more offended that Sam was touching him.

Sam pressed his forearm against Reese's throat, and the fear rushed back into his face.

"Take it back," Sam said.

The transfer caught the back of Sam's collar and pulled him off Reese. Then there was the shout of a teacher, pulling them all apart, and then walking them to the vice principal's office with everyone watching.

Then everyone in the hall scattered. That left nothing but the transfer's insistence that Sam had attacked Reese, out of nowhere.

Mr. Woods, the vice principal, dismissed everyone except Sam.

For the most part, Sam had managed to stay out of Mr. Woods' way. He only knew him by the way he wore a different pin on his tie each day of the week, and by the stories about how, at the start of each year, he held a lawn games party half the teachers looked forward to and the other half felt obligated to attend.

Mr. Woods steepled his hands. "This is serious. You know that, don't you?"

Sam crossed his arms. He just wanted it over with. The detention if he was lucky, suspension if he wasn't. Maybe even a threat of expulsion that he'd need his mother's calm, friendly voice to smooth over.

That was the worst part, the thought of them bringing his mother in, calling her away from watching the children she'd been hired to teach and look after.

The doorknob clicked, and then the hinges of the door whined open.

Peyton Bonner was standing in the doorway.

"I just want to say that this is why my mother doesn't want us going to this school," she said, in a nasal, indignant voice she'd probably grown out of years ago but dredged up to make a point with anyone more than twice her age.

Then she started into some story about how she'd heard Reese making racist comments about Sam's mother, and that Sam had just been responding. She wasn't making it all up; if there was a new slur running around the school, there was a good chance everyone could thank Reese and his friends. But what was she talking about?

"That's not what happened," Sam said.

But Mr. Woods wasn't even looking at him.

Who was he going to believe? A dark-skinned boy who'd just had his arm against his classmate's neck, or this freckled girl with curls the color of the construction-paper pumpkins six-year-olds cut out at the grade school?

For once, that was working in Sam's favor.

Mr. Woods looked between both of them. Then he landed on whatever conclusion he'd been scraping toward, and his eyes stayed on Sam.

"Detention," he said. "After school. One week."

"You can't do that," Peyton said. "My father needs him."

Now Mr. Woods looked annoyed, like he just wanted them both out of his office.

"You can serve it out after the harvest," Mr. Woods said. "Whenever Mr. Bonner says he can spare you. Understand?"

"Thank you," Sam said, biting back any other words so hard the two syllables came from between his clenched teeth.

He caught up with Peyton in the hall.

"What are you doing?" he asked.

"I don't like having debts," she said. "Now we're even."

Before he could ask her anything else, she was halfway down the hall, toward Ms. Owens' office, where her sisters were probably waiting.

"Samir." Mr. Woods stepped into the hall.

Sam's back grew hot under his binder.

"I think you should go home," Mr. Woods said. "Just for the rest of the day."

Sam opened his mouth without knowing what he'd say.

Mr. Woods held up his hand. "It's not a suspension. It's a suggestion."

Sam swallowed a laugh. *A suggestion.* That was vice principal for *demand.*

"I think you and Mr. Reese both need some time to cool off," Mr. Woods said.

Sam saw the look on his face. He knew he couldn't take back his proclamation, couldn't decide now that he'd changed his mind and that Sam was suspended. This was how he could feel less like he'd been herded into doing what a fifteen-year-old girl wanted.

"I know your mother's working today," Mr. Woods said.

As opposed to any other day? Sam almost said, but held it back.

Everyone knew Sam's mother because she looked after the children of a few wealthy families. She coaxed them into practicing the violin or flute with promises to tell them more about Laila and the boy who loved her so much he was called Majnun, because people thought his own heart had driven him mad. Brothers and sisters fought less when she was around, reading together instead of grabbing at each other's hair. To them she was magic and warmth, and they did as she said. She cleared their cupboards of oversalted and sugared food, and taught them the sweet bite of parsley, how lemon juice brightened the flavor of cucumber and yellow tomato. Daughters declared artichoke salad their favorite food. Boys came to love the sharp tang of onion and sesame seeds.

When they did not want to eat their soup or practice their music, she bribed them with stories about goats whose wool changed color with the seasons. A moon bear appearing to travelers who'd lost their way, the white crescent on its chest bright against its fur. Banded peacock butterflies granting wishes to children who freed them from spiderwebs.

Those children loved her, and Mr. Woods wasn't willing to cross their parents by pulling Sam's mother away in the middle of the day.

"Do you have someone who can pick you up?" Mr. Woods asked.

Sam let out a breath through barely parted lips. "Yeah," he said. "I can probably think of someone."

sea of tranquility

)

Once they were out of sight of the school, Aracely pulled over. Mr. Woods hadn't been willing to let Sam just walk home, so he'd had to let Mr. Woods call her.

She set the car in park. "What happened?"

Sam slumped into his seat.

She turned and faced him, one hand on the driver's-side headrest. "Anyone ever tell you that you make one hell of an unresponsive seventeen-year-old?"

"Thanks," Sam said. "I work at it."

"Look," Aracely said. "I know what you're going through."

"No, you don't." Sam sat up. "I still have to live like this. Nothing is gonna fix me. There's no water that's gonna make me into something else."

"And I'd start from where you are if it meant what happened that night didn't have to happen," Aracely said. "We don't get to become who we are for nothing. It costs something. You're fighting for every little piece of yourself. And maybe I got all of me all at once but I lost everything else. Don't you dare think there's any water in the world that makes this easy."

Guilt crept over his skin like the wisp of cold air from the cracked window.

He sank back into his seat. "Thanks for picking me up." He meant it, but it came out bitter, almost sarcastic.

"This is not okay," Aracely said. "This is not an acceptable way to handle what you're going through."

"Are you gonna tell my mom?" Sam asked.

"No," Aracely said. "You are."

"Fine." He unbuckled his seat belt. "Can I go now?"

"Is that what you want?" she asked.

The thoughts of everything he wanted were so bright and numerous, like threads of sun coming through at the edges of his mother's curtains. He wanted to be a girl who wanted to be a girl, or a boy who was, in a way no one could question, a boy.

He wanted to be able to hang his moons in the trees without having his name stripped down to Moon. He wanted to remember if he'd asked to be called Sam or if his mother had decided this was his nickname, if she worried that Samir was a name that would, to everyone else, make him even more different than he already was.

He wanted to know if Miel had chosen him, or if she'd just fallen into the familiar rhythm of their nights outside because he was the first one to be unafraid of her.

He wanted not to want the girl whose attachment to him had been so tenuous that the Bonner girls had stepped into it as easily as Adair Lewis turned across a stage floor.

"No," he said, looking up at Aracely. "I want you to cure me."

She dropped her hand from the back of her seat. "What?"

"Is that a *what* like you didn't hear me or a *what* like I need to say it another way?" he asked.

"Sam."

"Please," he said. "Don't treat me like I'm still five. I'm not. I can pay you, same as anyone else."

Aracely looked at her lap. "I don't want your money."

"Then whatever you want, I'll give it to you," he said. "Just cure me."

"Why?"

"Because I don't want to feel like this anymore," he said. "And I don't think she wants me to either."

"Which of those is more important to you? Because . . ."

"I want you to cure me," he said. "I want you to fix me."

"I can't fix you," she said. "And you don't need fixing."

"Fix this," he said. "Fix this one thing for me."

"Think about this." Aracely leaned over the gearshift. "Really think about this."

"I am thinking about it." He raised his voice enough that he could hear it coming back to him off the car windows. "This is my body. It's my heart. It doesn't belong to anyone else. I say what I do with it."

Aracely gave him back a startled look, her fingers resting on the steering wheel.

"So cure me," he said.

She opened her mouth, but then it fell shut again. Her polished nails scratched against the steering wheel. "Okay."

lake of summer

☽

She tried to tune in to some feeling in her body. Anything that would keep her from falling away from the golds of the trees, and into the memory of the river.

She tried to shut her eyes and feel the dryness on her tongue, but she felt both thirsty and choked with water. Her stomach should have clenched, but her whole body seemed weightless, floating. She'd been in here long enough that she should have felt pressure against the fly of her jeans and the hard seam between her legs. But even that she didn't feel. She'd been sweating too much, even with the chill of the glass, and she felt nothing but the clammy layer of wet salt coating her skin.

It had been the water that killed them all, but it had started with there being so little of it. There had been a drought that year, and summer had left the river low, braided with undercurrents her mother did not know about until they took Miel, and then Leandro, and then her. The roots and stones and contours of the riverbed made whirlpools and riptides that, in most years, more rain and greater depths smoothed out.

Her mother had thought the lower waterline would make the water safer, easier to wade through even in the dark. She had no idea that the drought had given what little water was left claws.

Her mother did not guess that water could be more dangerous when there was less of it.

The memory of her mother's screaming rang through her head. It splintered into each trembling note, and then resolved into a clear, haunted sound. And the silence, the lack of her father's voice, the wondering if maybe the water had taken him too, turned each of those sounds jagged.

Her mother had only done what the priests told her to, holding Miel in the river. But Miel fought so hard as her mother kept her underwater that her mother took it as proof that these roses had cursed her, that her daughter was pure and good and just needed to be saved. Whatever petaled demon made her grow them was leaving her body.

But Miel fought so hard she broke out of her mother's hold, and the current, with its hands grown from the dust and cloudless skies of this drought, swept her out of reach. It took her down so far she lost the moon, and all its distant light.

The space between the stained glass panels turned dark as the river. It was swallowing her.

The memory of her mother holding her down forced away the feeling that she had her own body. She was turning to water.

Her mother's voice echoed in her head, her insistence that all Miel had to do was stay still, give in, and she would be cured. Her mother had repeated the priest's words. *The difference between baptism and drowning is a few faithless breaths.*

Miel threw her hands against the glass, banging her palms against the dyed stars and planets not just because she was trapped but because being among the blues and greens plunged her into that night years ago, that night that had made her water. The memory was floating back, a distant air bubble at the bottom of the river, making a slow ascent.

She was hitting the glass because her brother was gone, her brother was dead, and she could hear the echo of him calling her from the river, looking for her, realizing there was none of her left to find or save.

She was hitting the glass because, years ago, when Sam had first knelt in front of her, the rust-dirtied water soaking the knees and shins of his jeans, she had thought he was her brother.

Later, when Miel looked at Sam, she didn't understand how she could have thought this. Sam looked so little like Leandro. He did not have Leandro's arching eyebrows, and Sam's lips, compared to Leandro's, were thin and tinted almost purple. His hair fell in loose coils instead of half-straight and half-curly like Miel's and Leandro's.

But no matter how many years she put between her and that moment of mistaking him for someone else, it stayed.

She drove her hands hard into the top panel. The skin on her knuckles broke and bled, and the pain made her shut her eyes. But she still shoved her hands against the glass, because her mother was dead too, and Miel could hear her cry on the wind.

Her mother had died not just in the water, but in a way only a broken heart could kill. Not with the kind of lovesickness Aracely cured. Not longing for a lover. Her mother's heart was the kind of broken caused by children, one who grew forbidden petals from her skin, and the other who lost his life trying to save her.

Miel's roses had cost her both Leandro and her mother. And the memory, inside this small space that would not let her get away from it, drained away the daylight. The silver between the trees turned to gray and then deep blue.

She was screaming and sobbing even knowing that no matter how much noise she made, even if her voice could tear the gold leaves off the hornbeam trees, it would not bring back her mother and Leandro. Here, within this narrow space, covered in stained glass light, she could not forget. The air around her, hot as her skin, and the glass, cold as the river, would not let her go.

unknown sea

☽

 am watched Aracely pick through her store of eggs, all those colors she could get only from the Carlsons at the edge of town. Theirs was the only farm that had so many kinds of chickens their egg cartons held every shade from mint green to pink to dark brown.

Sam glanced toward the ceiling. "Is Miel gonna hear us?"

"No." Aracely weighed each egg in her hand, pale blue and rich olive green, deep copper and peach. "You know why? Because she's at school." She side-eyed him. "Where you should be."

So Miel wasn't sick. He'd never known her to cut class, but if anyone could get her to do it, it was the Bonner sisters. If they could get Mrs. Galen to tell their parents they were in Sunday school when they'd really snuck off to try nail polishes at the drugstore, then they could get Miel to skip school. She was probably somewhere looking through magazines with Lian while Chloe braided her hair. The ways in which girls made formal their friendships, the ways they declared and solidified that yes, they belonged to one another, were as foreign to him as the ice-covered fjords in his geography textbook.

Maybe they weren't friends anymore, but he wasn't turning on her, not even for Aracely. If Miel wanted to cut class with the Bonner girls, it was her call, not his. If she was willing to have Ivy come in and lie for her, and the teachers were stupid enough to believe everything Ivy said, it was none of his business.

Aracely had narrowed her choices down to three eggs, one blue, another brick red, another dark brown. "And where you would be if you hadn't punched some guy in the face."

"I didn't punch him in the face," he said.

Aracely took the sheet and unfurled it, letting it spill over the table like milk. "Lie down."

Even through the sheet, he felt the grain of the wood. In a few minutes, he would look like Aracely's other visitors, calm, as though they could see the stars on the walls of the indigo room.

From this angle, he saw a flash of green.

A sweater the color of clover hung over a chair. Sam's heart pinched. He recognized it as Miel's, remembered unfastening each button as they climbed the stairs, eyes shut, his mouth on hers. It had ended up draped over the edge of his bed.

So many times, he'd found a scarf she'd left behind in a classroom. Halfway through their study sessions, she'd take down her hair, and then she'd forget to pick up the hairpins. He had learned, early on, that Miel was both clean and sloppy. She left her clothes strewn over the floor of her room. But when she came over, and Sam left her alone for more than a minute, she would start doing any dishes in the sink. "Will you stop that?" he would say when he came back into the kitchen. "What?" she would ask, and then say, "It's here, and I'm bored."

He had spent the last ten years making sure he pushed exactly as hard against her as she did against him, so that everything they had built would stay standing. If he either let up or gave it more of his weight, it would fall.

And until the night he ran the pollination brush over her arm, this kept him still, the possibility that if she did not feel how he felt, it made no difference, unless he put her in the position of having to tell him.

This was what they had created, a place where she was more than the girl the water tower had spilled out, and he was more than a boy painting a hundred moons, a boy who knew *mare nectaris* and *sinus roris*, the sea of nectar and the bay of dew, and every other lunar feature better than his own body. As long as he didn't question it, prod it, it stayed. But now he had, and he was losing her.

It's here, and I'm bored. The words came back to him. Maybe why she once met him on the open land every night was that simple. He was here. She was bored. And now she wasn't. But he was still stranded in this world that only half-belonged to him.

Aracely considered a blood orange but then set it down, and chose a bergamot, the kind grown in the place that made the father he had never known.

The warm scent of cloves and the honeyed acid of the bergamot orange wafted over him. He opened his eyes just enough to see the pair of eggs Aracely had chosen, one red, the other copper.

Her hands settled on his shoulders. He tensed, then reminded himself that this was how the lovesickness cure worked. He had to let himself take it.

The room turned into a whirl of scents, cloves and cardamom and laurel leaves. The walls took him into their blur of indigo. Aracely whispered a prayer under her breath, keeping her hand on his chest. Not off to one side enough to touch either place his binder flattened. But in the center, below his collarbone.

The rhythm of her hushed words cut through him. Her hand hovered over his body.

The perfume of the spices, the calcium of the eggshell, the sweet acid of the bergamot left his forehead throbbing. Under the pressure of Aracely's palm, he felt his love for Miel turning over and pulling away from the places it hid. It had woven itself into his veins, as much as the stem of her rose had roots under her skin.

He felt the sting of the lovesickness dragging away, like tearing the weft out of a woven cloth. His body resisted, but Aracely kept him still, pinned like a butterfly under glass.

With one hand, Aracely cracked the first egg into a jar of water. She held the jar up to study the pattern of the yolk.

Sam set the heels of his hands against his eyes. He would not give in to the jagged breathing that rattled his lungs and throat. But he blinked, and tears dropped from his eyelashes, first the left, then the right.

He brushed them away. He knew what Aracely thought of crying. She once caught Miel sobbing because the pain of a new rose, hours from bursting through her skin, would not let her sleep. She stood near her bed and said, "Stop it, mija, you're gonna turn yourself to salt." When she found Sam crying over a stray kitten that had died despite him and Miel feeding it eyedropperfuls of milk, she said, "And you think this will bring it back to life?" Not harshly. The truth ballasted her words. It kept them straight and tall.

Crying was a waste, she told them.

But now Aracely whispered, "Get it all out of you," neither kind nor reprimanding, a recommendation no different from another curandera's prescription for curing nightmares. "It'll make everything inside you softer. This'll go easier."

He kept his hands on his eyes as Aracely swept the bergamot orange over him. It hurt, the lovesickness coming unanchored and drifting from the edges of his body, his fingers and his toes, his lips and the ends of his hair. It drained toward his heart, the gathering weight pinning his rib cage to the table.

But it was as much relief as pain, the shock of relaxing a muscle after keeping it tense. Aracely's hands were sharing the weight, luring it toward her palms and out of his body.

Aracely had left the window open, knowing that he didn't care how cold the room got. He was not some lovesick woman or man who expected his money's worth, who would complain if the indigo room had chilled, making it necessary to keep the window closed until the last minute. Aracely would draw out his lovesickness, and then throw the nervous, feathered thing, no bigger than a thrush, out the open window. She would launch it like a dove, a barely visible wash of peach or blue Sam never would have caught if Miel hadn't taught him to watch for it flying out the window and vanishing.

Aracely set one palm on his heart and the other on his throat until the lovesickness rose to her hands.

In that moment, he was thirteen, and Miel was wearing her favorite dress, the violet-tinged blue of a cloudless sky. The thin ribbons of the dress's straps kept loosening and falling down her arms, and each time he helped her tighten them he peeled a gold foil star off a sticker sheet and pressed it onto her shoulder or her upper back. She asked him why, and he told her to trust him.

And she had. She had left them there the whole day, while they let the sun heat their backs. When they ran, her perspiration made the foil shine damp, and it wore the edges of the adhesive, but the little stars stayed. And that night he had lifted each one off her, slowly, so they didn't pull at her skin. When he was done, she laughed, mouth open, to see that each foil star had left a lighter cast of its shape. In that first blazing day of summer, her skin had tanned enough that she was covered in constellations.

She had wanted to name every one. She named one for Aracely, one for Sam's mother, and then she told Sam he had to pick one, the one she would name after him. He had brushed his fingers near one at the base of her neck, the shape small but the edges clean and sharp.

He had mapped her body like a new sky. He had known even then that this night was something perfect, without jagged corners to catch themselves on. But it was only now that he knew why. That day, with the foil stars, there was both a reason for him to be touching her, and no need for a reason. They were younger. She didn't hesitate before she pulled leaves from his hair, and he hadn't paused before reaching out and placing one of the foil stars on her shoulder.

Sam sat up, pulling away from Aracely's hands.

"Sam," Aracely said, his name emerging from one gasp and falling into another.

The lovesickness rushed back into him. It stung every corner of his body. He was a river caught between water and ice. Frozen too much to move. Not enough to stand solid against the wind and the pull of the moons he had made.

His body felt heavy with the lovesickness that had almost gone. Now it hooked into him, its hold deep and firm. It was an animal nearly torn from its nest, and he was the tangles of twigs and thread and grass where it made its home.

If anyone tried to tear it away again, its claws would rip him apart.

"I can't," he said, the words choked and small.

Aracely's eyes flashed red brown. Her hands still smelled like laurel and cloves. "Why?" she asked.

"Because it's mine," he said.

It was his. All of it was his. His body, refusing to match his life. His heart, bitter and worn. His love for Miel, even if it had nowhere to go, even if he didn't know how to love a girl who kept herself as distant from him as an unnamed constellation.

These things belonged to him. They were his, even if they were breaking him.

He slid off the table.

"Sam," Aracely said, more concerned than calling him back.

"I'm fine," he said, not turning around. "I'm fine."

He left the wisteria-colored house, and crossed feather grass fields toward the woods.

The feeling of Miel's mouth on his turned so solid it felt like the chill of metal. It grew from the brushing of her rose petals to the sting of how the winds blew on the shortest day of the year. It took root in him, digging itself in harder for having almost been torn out. He felt her, warm and alive as the roots of a yew tree.

The way he loved her was his, even if she wasn't. His names were his, all of them.

The moons he'd made were his, to hang or hide or wreck.

From a scarlet oak tree, he took down one that was the dark blue of an indigo milk mushroom's gills, the slice of a crescent moon almost lavender. From maple trees, he took down another the gray of an overcast but rainless day, and another the soft gold of the beech tree outside Miel's window. He found the lilac and pink moons of late spring, the green and yellow ones of the planting season, the amber of fall and the crisp, pale blue of winter. He found ones so small Miel could have hidden them in drawers, and others big enough that he'd forgotten how hard the metal or glass had been to take up the wooden ladder.

There were so many moons. So many lunar seas and shadowed valleys. When they filled his arms and he could not carry any more, he clustered them together at the base of a tree, trying to remember where he'd set each one down so he could come back for them.

The ones near houses he'd leave, so sons and daughters could fall asleep sure the tinted light would keep away their nightmares. But he'd tear down every one he could find in the woods. They cropped up like the eggs he and Miel dyed at Easter and then hid in the church grass for children to find. The only time of year Aracely bought white eggs. One moon reminded him of the ones they colored green with yellow onion. One was the dusk color that came from blueberries. Another was the gold and soft brown of the eggs they dyed with cayenne and turmeric. The next was the deep turquoise that came from red cabbage so purple that the work of the dye seemed like a magic trick.

The woods were grass and leaves, and he was a child trying to find countless eggs. He found one moon, and then spotted another, the trail of them leading him deeper into the trees, until the reds and rust colors were so thick he could barely tell it was daytime.

lake of softness

)

She fell deeper under the water. She was losing not just the bright gold of the trees outside the glass, but every light Sam had ever made. Those moons were how she knew him. Each year on his mother's birthday, he hung a moon the yellow of wild marigolds. The greenish cast of a corn moon told her he couldn't sleep. And a plain white moon, like clean linen, meant he was ready for a new year, breathing out the last of the December air.

He spoke in the light that slipped in through windows. It was his language, his tongue. On her last birthday, he'd left a moon painted dark gold, a honey moon so amber that the light it let off made her sure she had woken up in autumn, months after she'd fallen asleep. When she had a cough so deep in her lungs Aracely would not let her leave her bed, Sam had brought one that looked like sun through lilac blossoms. And each year, during the season when the farms took in their harvest, he hung one that cast a blush over her whole room, to keep away her nightmares of the pumpkins' vines and ribbed shells.

Those moons had been his way of calling her outside. They'd slipped out of their houses each night to find each other. But now the air between them prickled with warning, and she was losing him. He was every light in the sky, and she was losing him.

Cold air swept through the stained glass, and Miel surfaced to it. She floated toward it, the scent of damp leaves and earth flooding away the salt on her skin. She gasped and coughed like water had filled the panels. Inside these walls, she was, in every moment, slipping from her mother's grasp.

But now she was finding her breath.

The lid struck the side of the stained glass coffin, and the impact rattled the frame.

She thought she had made him up, this boy she had imagined out of shadow, the difference between dark and moonlight. His hair, so dark that at night it looked like blue-violet ink. The brown of his forearms and the back of his neck, the color of the cinnamon fiddle-head ferns his mother grew along the side of the house.

But then the dark flash of his hair and his hands turned to the warmth of him. It turned to him setting her arms around him when she couldn't feel them enough to do it herself, and him pulling her out. He had the gravity of the moon in the sky. He could pull on oceans and rivers. He could drag lakes across deserts. There was enough force in him to turn the river that held her to light. He drew the water out of this place where she was forever slipping from her mother's hold and drowning in the dark.

"What happened?" he asked.

She breathed in the warmth that clung to his skin, her forehead on his shoulder, her cheek against his shirt. If she stayed this close to him, he was the whole world. There was no stained glass, there were no pumpkins turning clear and brittle, no gradations of red sweeping through the dark. There was no lost moon, not when he remade it so many times. There was just the strength in him from all those nights taking the wooden ladder from his mother's shed and into the trees. She could feel it in his hands and his arms. She could feel it when she slid her palms over his back.

"Who did this to you?" he asked, his arms crossing her back.

But she only half-registered his words. Her body was sore from fighting the glass, and her skin was stinging with dried salt, and she held on to him hard enough that she felt him startle, his breath catching between them.

"Hey," he said. "It's okay." And for the space of his words, they were small again, her soaked in rust-darkened water, and him, the one boy she didn't scare.

She set her mouth against his cheek, kissing him where she'd slapped him, her grasp at taking it back. She would let her whole body turn to roses in exchange for making those few seconds disappear, how she'd struck him when he was hurting.

The steadiness came back into him. He understood. Her hands in his hair or clutching the back of his shirt, the *I'm sorry* folded into how she touched him. And she felt it, how him holding her, his palms making her feel her own body again, this was his *I know*, his *so am I.*

There were apologies too heavy for their tongues. Even too heavy for any one set of their hands. So this one, they shared. They carried it together. They interlaced their fingers, hers against his, and held it in their palms. They wore it on their skin. They guarded it in the breath of space between their bodies.

And this, their first apology in a language they were still learning, was a thing they stammered and halted through. But it stopped them from spinning out and losing each other. It kept them in each other's fields of gravity, finding each other.

lake of dreams

)

till holding on to him, she'd begged him not to take her
home. "Please," she said. "I don't want her seeing me like this."
She didn't want this to be the way Aracely thought of her, shaking
and still trying to get her breath back, her skin pale with salt.

She'd already wrecked everything with Sam. He'd seen the
worst, cruelest places in her.

But with Aracely there was still a little left to salvage. She was
still the girl who handed her blue eggs and lumia lemons. They were
still something a little like sisters, standing at the stove together,
melting the piloncillo into their coffee.

So now she lay on her stomach on a sofa in Sam's living room,
her cheek against the cushion.

Sam sat next to her, his hand on her back as he asked her, "What
happened to you? Who put you in there?"

She couldn't drag her eyes up to him. She stared at the woven rug under the coffee table, the knotted wool in reds and creams and deep blues.

It was so quiet in this house, empty except for them, and the two of them barely talking, that Miel could hear Sam's next breath out.

He pulled his hand back, and Miel couldn't move enough to tell him she wanted it.

His fingers slid off her. "What I said . . ."

Don't, she tried to say. They had settled things, made their apologies, with their hands and their bodies. *You don't have to say anything.*

"What I told you," he said. "I didn't . . ."

She heard him blow a slow, soft breath out between his lips.

Her heart felt like a thing becoming glass, its flesh turning hard and fragile. She'd wanted this since the day he turned her skin into a brown sky dotted with pale constellations. But now she was too broken and brittle to take it. She wasn't a soft place he could fall. She was all edges, all fierce rivers and panels of stained glass. Only joints of rose brass held her together.

He sighed, standing up. Out of the corner of her eye, she saw him slipping his hand into his pockets.

"Do you need more water?" he asked.

She shook her head. She'd already stood at the tap, drinking out of her cupped hand before Sam could hand her a glass.

"Are you hungry?" he asked.

She shook her head.

"Miel," he said, and heat pinched the wound where her roses burst from her skin. "Miel, please say something."

She needed to think about Sam's hair and skin, instead of the deep colors of that stained glass.

She needed to think of Aracely's soft gold hair instead of the brazen yellows of those trees.

She needed to think of her father's hands cutting a length of bandage, and not her wondering about where he'd gone, the hesitation that tinged her memories of him. She needed to remember her mother's laugh instead of her screaming, her soft voice instead of the rush of water over stones in a drought-stripped river.

That last one, her mother's laugh and voice, sparked a memory so strong Miel felt the air around her turning, everything becoming the flowered wallpaper of her mother's kitchen. She remembered the pattern even better than her mother's face, the flowers that must once have been yellow but that had faded to cream. That kitchen had held more of her mother's laughter than anywhere else in the world. It was where her mother sugared violet petals with fingers as skilled as a silversmith's. She added cinnamon and cayenne to mole. She let Miel and Leandro cover their hands in flour and powdered sugar when they made alfajores, the shortbread they spread with dulce de leche.

Finding that memory was as bright as catching trees bursting into bloom. It was a memory from when Miel was barely old enough to make them. After that, she would turn three, and four, and the roses would come, and they would take everything. But she could hold on to this, her hands and Leandro's pale with sugar and flour.

Alfajores de nieve, coated in powdered sugar so each looked made of winter.

She didn't have Leandro anymore, or his hands, smooth and dark as finished wood. But she had Sam, this boy, and his brown hands.

Miel pulled her eyes from the knotted carpet, and looked up at Sam. "I think I am hungry."

"Yeah?" Sam's smile was slight, but without caution. "Anything in particular?"

Miel pushed herself up on her hands, her body stiff as if she'd slept on it wrong. "Have I ever shown you how to make alfajores?"

The way his smile shifted, she knew he didn't know the word. He probably thought she'd made it up, like one of her stories about stars. He'd had the alfajores she and Aracely made and brought over on New Year's Eve. But they'd never made them together, not like she'd shown him how to make recado rojo from achiote seeds and cloves and a dozen other spices. He didn't even recognize the name *alfajor*.

She slid off the sofa, and the air felt thin and yielding, like she'd been walking in waist-deep water and now crossed dry ground.

She and Sam both knew where to find anything in each other's houses. He knew how Aracely arranged her spice cabinet. Miel knew the patch of the side garden where Sam's mother let borraja grow wild, the starflowers blooming pink and then turning deep blue. She picked handfuls, and hundreds of five-pointed blossoms still brightened the green leaves and wine-colored buds, covered in what looked like a coat of white down.

Sam followed her like they were dancing and she was leading him. He held the starflowers in his hands, and brought them inside with her. She pulled down flour, and he brought out the eggs. She looked for milk, and he set out the vanilla.

They washed the borraja flowers, patted them dry, brushed them with egg white and covered them in sugar. They mixed butter and flour until it formed into dough, soft and pale.

"What were you doing out there?" Miel asked, adding cinnamon and ground cloves like her mother had, not just to the dulce de leche but right into the dough. "Shouldn't you be in class?"

Sam worked in the dark threads of spice with the heels of his hands. "Woods sent me home."

"For what?" she asked.

He cringed, his shoulders rising. "I might've gotten into a fight."

"With who?" she asked.

"Does it matter?"

She touched the candied borraja flowers, checking if they'd dried.

The sugar gave the pink and indigo petals the look of unpolished crystal.

"What were you fighting about?" she asked.

"Forget it." Sam folded the dough over onto itself. "Point is, I'm supposed to be cooling down."

Miel stirred the sugar and milk on the stove. It started off pale as the moon, and the longer they let it cook the darker it turned, deepening to gold and then amber. Aracely let hers cook for hours, until it was brown as hazelnuts.

Now heated, it let off the scent of the vanilla seeds she'd scraped into the pot, warm and sweet. She couldn't remember if it had been Sam's mother or Aracely who'd first taught her how to slit open a vanilla bean. It hadn't been her own mother. She'd been too young to hold the knife.

Miel's thoughts had barely flitted toward Sam's mother when they landed on three words, said in her voice. *He'll get there.* Those words had done nothing but frustrate Miel. His mother's calm and patience had not made her calm and patient. They'd made her unsettled, more in a hurry for Sam to see that *bacha posh* were not words that would make him something other than what he was. They were not a spell in a fairy tale. They would not make him want to be a girl once he was old enough to be a woman.

He'll get there. Miel could still remember his mother's face when she said those words, her pale, dark-lined eyes full of a concern that was more care than worry.

He'll get there, Sam's mother had tried to tell her. But Miel hadn't let that calm and that patience find its way into her.

Instead, when she and Sam had fought, she'd thrown it all at him. She'd forced him up against things he wasn't ready to look at.

She was no better than Ivy, no better than the Bonner girls sliding Sam's birth certificate across that wooden table.

"I'm sorry," she said.

Sam looked up.

"I shouldn't have . . ." She stopped. She didn't know how to apologize without doing the same thing again. Bringing it up enough to apologize meant shoving it all toward him again.

Sam didn't move. He just watched her, his face open but a little tense.

"I shouldn't have pushed you that hard," she said.

His jaw tightened, the way it had by the river.

"If I ever don't tell you something, it's not because I don't want to tell you," he said. "It's because I don't know."

Maybe no one else would've caught it, but in that flinch, she saw it, the fact that all this was breaking him.

The truth slid over her skin, that if she loved him, sometimes it would mean doing nothing. It would mean being still. It would mean saying nothing, but standing close enough so he would know she was there, that she was staying.

Sam took his mother's wooden rolling pin from the freezer, where she always put it, a trick she swore by for rolling out roti, but that Sam said his aunts considered just shy of sacrilege to the family recipe.

Miel felt the conversation evaporating, like water vapor boiling off the milk on the stove. She let it. If Sam didn't want to talk about this, she wouldn't force it. Maybe there was nothing else she could do for him right now, but she could do this, be there whether he wanted to stay quiet or wanted to speak.

He leaned over the counter, sleeves rolled up to his elbows, putting the weight of his shoulders behind his hands. The line of the muscle in his forearm stood out as he worked the rolling pin.

He caught her watching him. "You'll never look at me the same way after this," he said.

"Are you kidding?" she asked. "There's nothing more alluring than a guy who knows how to work a rolling pin."

He laughed without looking up.

Her own words, said without thinking, brushed over her, prickling her. Even with his laugh. Worse, because of his laugh. Was she flirting with him? She couldn't flirt with him. He was Sam. Even after they'd slept together, flirting felt distant, almost formal, the act of a boy and a girl who'd just met. He knew all the things about her that made flirting impossible. There was only so much she could flirt with someone who knew that eating casaba melon made a rash spread across her stomach.

A flash of color made her check her hands.

A sugared starflower petal had stuck to her palm.

The rough, shimmering surface, edges deep blue, made her wonder how much she could touch Sam without him flinching away.

There was no flirting. They were years past that.

She came close enough to make him look up.

He took a step back, startled by the small distance between them. But she set the starflower petal against his lips, touching only the sugared surface, not his mouth, until he took it onto his tongue.

He shut his eyes, letting the petal dissolve.

Miel pretended, for that one moment of him closing his eyes, that the petal had come from one of her roses, that he was taking onto his tongue a thing she had grown from her own body.

She turned back to the milk and sugar simmering on the stove. The thought of being in bed with him, how his mouth had felt when she brushed her thumb over his lower lip, made her feel like the powdered sugar in the air, floating and shimmering.

The wooden spoon slipped against the bottom of the pot, and a slick of hot dulce de leche sputtered onto the heel of her hand.

She pulled away from the stove, a gasp whistling across her throat. The coin of heat burned into her palm.

Sam grabbed her hand and set her palm against his lips. His

tongue licked away the dulce de leche, already cooling enough for his mouth when a few seconds before it had scalded her hand.

In that second of his tongue on her palm, she felt the new rose-bud pressing out of her wrist. Even with the pain cutting through her forearm, she thought of kissing him until it was a full rose, bursting open.

She thought she felt his lips pressed against her hand, the place where the sugar would have worsened the burn if he hadn't taken it into his mouth. But he did it so quickly. Before she could be sure, he set the cold rolling pin against her hand.

Her fingers trembled from the dulce de leche's heat and the sudden chill of the wood.

She would never be Aracely. Fearless charm would never flow from her body like yards of chiffon. But Sam looked at Miel as if all her sharp edges and cursed petals, everything she'd tried to keep in shadow, were the glinting facets of unpolished rose quartz.

What Sam had told her the time she first kissed him, about pollinating each pumpkin blossom by hand, she knew it was true. He hadn't made it up. But now it felt like something he'd invented, a fairy story about an enchanted paintbrush that shimmered with pollen like gold dust. It covered her in the feeling that his fingers were brushes, and under them she was growing into something alive.

She stayed still a few seconds too long. A stricken look crossed Sam's face.

"Sorry," he said.

He looked down at his hands like he didn't recognize them, like they were not his to move.

"Tell me to let go," he said, his hand still on the back of hers, still pressing her palm into the cold curve of the rolling pin. She could feel the ridges of the calluses on his fingers. "Tell me to, and I will."

He kept his eyes on hers, and she could feel the hum of life in his heart like a dragonfly buzzing by her ear. His heart was not a dead thing, not weak from lack of use. It was hard and tight, a muscle that would not give.

"Do it," he said, and now the edge in his words sounded like a challenge. But under it was a hitch in his voice that sounded like he meant it, that he wanted her to make him let go. "Tell me not to."

In this second, she was not the child from the water tower. She was a girl noticing, for the first and for the hundredth time, that her best friend's hands were warm as birch bark on summer nights. That his forearms were the brown of a yearling buck's coat. That at the outer edge of his brown-black eyes was the thinnest ring of what looked like purple. The color of the saffron crocuses his family once farmed thousands of miles away, the men harvesting the cupped blossoms, the women picking out the thin rust-colored threads.

"Show me again," she said.

"What?" he asked.

"How you make sure the pumpkin blossoms grow into something." She felt the shiver of remembering the pollination brush on her skin, and he got it, he understood so fast that he shared it.

"I don't want to do this," he said. "Not now. Not if you're gonna regret it."

"I won't," she said. "I never did."

She came toward him at the same time he pulled her into him, her mouth reaching his so fast her teeth nicked his lower lip. She tried to pull away, to tell him she was sorry, see if they could laugh about it. But he didn't let her. He put his hand on the back of her neck and kissed her harder, a drop of the blood off his lip finding her tongue and turning to salt.

This was the boy who'd made her unashamed of how the bottom edge of her skirt was always damp, when everyone else thought it was a sign that she was odd or cursed. It had bothered her enough that she wore jeans most of the time, not hemming them, the bottoms dragging through mud and fallen leaves until they were frayed and dyed dark and it was impossible to tell that, like her skirts, they were always wet.

But with Sam, there was nothing she wanted to hide. Not the wound on her wrist that would not close even between roses. Not the petals she drowned in the river. Not even the way she could not sleep during the pumpkin harvest season without the light on.

His breath feathered over her mouth. His fingers caught in her hair. He kissed her so quickly that his tongue parted her lips before she thought to do it herself.

First he tasted like the sugared starflower petal she'd set on his tongue, and then the dulce de leche from the heel of her hand.

People here argued about what the moon smelled like. Some said it was a crisp scent, like pressed linen or new paper. Others said no, it was sweet and alive, like night-blooming jasmine climbing on the first warm night of spring. Others swore it was new and silvery, like just-washed spoons, still warm from a sink full of hot water and lemon soap. But to her, it was Sam. The metal and paper of his moons, the rosewater from his mother's kitchen, the sharp trace of paint and turpentine she only ever picked up when she was this close to him.

Her hands slid down his back, her palms catching on his shirt. Her lips found flecks of paint that didn't come off in the shower, the blues and whites and golds he had not yet managed to wash off his skin. A thread on his upper arm, a patch just above his elbow, a constellation on the back of his wrist.

They shut off the stove, not caring that the dulce de leche would turn to crystals, that it would take them an hour to wash out the saucepan.

This time, instead of climbing on top of him, she pulled him onto her. She wanted him covering her, soaking her like the light from his moons. She wanted her skin taking in as much of his scent as it could hold. And when he touched her, she wondered if this was how he touched himself, if this was how he'd figured out what felt good.

In the years since she'd walked in on him changing, there had been so many times she had turned off her bedroom lamp and slid her hand under the quilt, trying to imagine she was touching him, that the place she had set her hand was not on her body but on his. But even if they were the same inside their jeans, he was so different from her that she could not imagine his body as her own. Even his underwear, the plain gray cotton, was so different than the yellow and blue and pale green ones Miel bought in packs of three colors.

No matter what their bodies had in common, she and Sam were not the same. So the feeling of touching him had always slipped from her fingers even while her fingers were still against her. The closest she'd ever gotten was imagining her hand belonged not to her, but him.

Now, his fingers traced her, and the shudder up through her body made the small of her back curve away from the sheet. Her hair spread out, trailing off the edge of the bed, her neck so exposed to him he set his mouth against it, and stayed.

With his weight on her, she was water and he was a moon, his gravity pulling her closer. He was a world unmapped, a planet of valleys and vapor seas no one but he had a right to name. If he let her, she would learn the bays and oceans of him. She would know him as well as he knew the *maria* in the moon atlases.

She grabbed his belt and the waist of his jeans and pulled them away from his body enough to get her hand in. First her fingers were grasping at his boxers, feeling him through the thin cotton. Then her hand crawled up to the elastic band and found its way in, and she took hold of him, hard, like there was a single shape of him to be grabbed. She put her hand on him as though he had a body that would let him be called *he* and *him* without anyone ever daring to question it.

He didn't pack, didn't stuff a pair of socks into his underwear. Didn't fill a condom with dry grain or hair gel or any of the other ridiculous ideas they'd considered before he figured out that working on the Bonners' farm could get him out of PE, out of changing in a locker room. And that was something she loved about him, the fearlessness, how he simply wore jeans loose enough that no one would ask questions.

For one pinching moment, Miel wondered if that was what had made the Bonner girls suspect, if they'd looked at him close enough, seen how the shape of him did or didn't push up against the crotch of his pants.

But she wasn't letting them in, not this time. She was shutting every window in this house and scaring them off with the light from Sam's moons. It was just him, and her, his fingers flicking against her like the hot light of falling stars, her touching him in the best way she knew to remind him there was no distance, no contradiction between the body he had and a boy called Samir.

lake of joy

☽

The first thing Aracely must have wondered, seeing Miel in the doorway, was why her hair was wet from the shower. Why she smelled not like her own soap, but like the kind Sam used. Why she was wearing not her own clothes, but one of Sam's flannel shirts over a pair of his cuffed-up jeans, the hems damp because even if they were his, they were on her body.

But before Aracely could ask about any of that, Miel spoke.

"I want a pumpkin," she said.

Aracely set down the glass jar she was refilling with dried rose-buds. "What?" she asked.

"I want us to carve pumpkins," Miel said. "You and me."

They would go to a farm other than the Bonners'—any farm but the Bonners'—and they would walk through the rows of curling vines. They would pass Rouge Vif d'Etampes, and yellow-and-green-striped carnival pumpkins, and the round, orange kind called a jack-o'-lantern because it was a favorite to hollow out and fill with candles.

Aracely would bring knives for both of them, and they would cut shallow ones to leave on their doorsteps, maybe an Autumn Crown pumpkin or the pale blue-green kind named Shamrock.

And they would bring home others wide and round enough to carve. They would sit at the kitchen table, newspaper spread over the wood, and they would hollow them out. They would set the seeds in the oven, drying out the pepitas and then sprinkling them with salt and chili powder.

Miel would not think of her mother, frantic and clawing the flesh out of a pumpkin big enough to hold Miel. She would blot out that memory with the yellow of the kitchen table, and the shades of the pumpkin rinds, and the smell of dark sugar in the air as she and Aracely passed each other spoons of sage and fireweed honey.

There would be no glass pumpkins. Everything would be damp and warm and alive. Miel and Aracely would paint their lips to go out, and while Aracely touched up the edges of Miel's color, she would remind her that the achiote Miel loved for its earth and pepper and flower taste came from a plant called a lipstick tree.

Aracely was still staring.

"For the lighting," Miel said. They would use the smallest blades in the knife drawer to carve patterns in their pumpkins. Then they'd set candles inside, and they would bring them to the river. The water would carry them alongside all the other pumpkins the rest of the town had brought, all those carved, floating lanterns.

Aracely's laugh was not unkind, but disbelieving. "You want to carve pumpkins for the lighting?"

Miel still tensed with the thought of holding the cool shell of a pumpkin. But she didn't want to live fearing the way they swelled and grew on the vine, never falling, just settling into the earth. She wanted to find the beauty in the cream Luminas, and the blue-gray Jarrahdales, and the deep-ribbed Cinderella pumpkins that looked as soft as the throw pillows on Aracely's bed.

She didn't want to fear anything. She wanted to be as fearless and generous as the woman who stood in this indigo room, for her laugh to be like Aracely's, both reckless and kind.

"Yeah," Miel said. "Can we go buy some?"

Aracely shut the wooden cabinet. "I'll get my coat."

small sea

☽

He was already fake-tutoring Peyton. Mr. and Mrs. Bonner trusted him with so little reserve they had no idea how bad he was at math, or that he and Peyton had never even opened a book together.

Sam had first offered to help Lian with her reading when they went to school together. Every time he caught her in the hall when no one else was there, he told her that he or Miel would go over the English and history assignments with her. Miel probably wouldn't have been so happy about him volunteering her, but Lian was so used to her sisters' company he couldn't help wondering if she'd say yes to help from another girl.

The first time he'd asked, Lian had been polite, the way she always was. "What are you talking about?" she'd asked, her smile still in place. A little shake of her head.

"You're not stupid," he said.

He knew she wasn't stupid. He'd seen her in math class, drawing

the kind of tessellations and polyhedrons that could have been il-
lustrations in the textbook. She could be a designer or an architect.
The fact that she struggled in English class to turn in one-paragraph
in-class essays, that she'd given up on doing the reading, didn't mean
she was as slow as everyone thought.

It wasn't his business. He knew that. But he hated seeing it, her
bowing to the way other people saw her, her sinking beneath the lie
of what everyone else thought. So if he could say enough to remind
her that she still existed, that she was both other than and more than
what everyone else assumed she was, maybe she would lose the truth
of herself a little more slowly.

Lian didn't see it that way. He'd said, "You're not stupid," and her
expression had shifted, her green eyes half-closing, the smile turning into tension in her jaw. "Fuck off."

But Lian was the one he went looking for today. He found her
on the brick path that ran in front of and then around the side of the
Bonners' house.

She blinked at him, waiting for him to speak.

"I quit," he said.

That blank expression slipped from her face. "What?"

"I'm done," he said.

Lian's stare flashed toward either side of them. She was looking
for the shine of glass among the vines. He could tell from how her
eyes were moving.

Her face tightened, filling with a look both offended and injured,
as though she was taking this insult on behalf of her family. Who
was he, she must have thought, to judge anything that happened
here? How could the strange boy who painted the moon over and
over say anything about these fields turning to glass? And what right
did he have to quit?

"It has nothing to do with the pumpkins," he said. "Look, I don't
know what you're doing with Miel."

He could still feel Miel's hands spreading over his back, her body pulling the heat out of his. How he'd put his mouth not against her forehead the way he had so many times but to her mouth. She'd tasted so much like honey, like sage and wildflowers.

He looked up at the house's windows. "All of you. But whatever your game is, I'm not gonna be part of it. I quit."

Lian set a confused look back into place, blinking in multiples.

Even now that Mrs. Bonner taught her daughters at home, Lian showed no sign of shaking away the act she'd fallen into, the role of the slow sister. In summer, when the Bonners kept all the windows open, Sam had heard their lessons through the screens. Mrs. Bonner never asked Lian to read out loud, which must have seemed like a kind of cruelty, a way to point out that which her second-oldest daughter could barely do. During their discussions of books, Mrs. Bonner moderated Ivy and Peyton's debate over whether Pip from *Great Expectations* was a romantic or a sap, while Lian sat staring out the holes in the lace curtains.

"Why are you telling me?" she asked.

"Because you're smart," he said. "And you'll tell anyone who needs to know."

He took the brick path back to the edge of the Bonners' yard.

At the corner of his vision came a flicker of movement, like the ribbons of foil dancing on wooden posts in strawberry fields.

Peyton Bonner stood, elbows cupped in her hands, the wind puffing up her curled hair. She pressed her lips tight, a worried look on her face. He knew she was wondering if he'd still be her excuse for Jenna Shelby.

"Don't worry," he said. "We're fine."

Peyton nodded, her lips still pressed together. She looked younger, the way she had by the water tower, holding that gray pumpkin.

Sam couldn't remember when she'd stopped carrying it around.

He'd never wondered until now. One day it had just been gone from her hands.

"You remember that pumpkin you had when you were three?" he asked.

Her mouth broke into a smile. "Lady Jane Grey?"

His next breath turned into a laugh. "You named it?"

"*Her*," she said, prim as a teacher correcting a mispronounced word. "I named *her*. And yes."

"What happened to her?" Sam asked. "You took that thing everywhere."

Peyton sighed, but not without humor. "Lady Jane Grey, like her namesake, was beheaded after a tragically short reign."

"What are you talking about?" he asked.

"The pumpkin was turning, and my sisters were afraid I was gonna carry it around until it rotted," she said. "So they convinced me she wanted to be part of a pie."

Convinced. Three Bonner sisters against one. They'd probably cut the pumpkin open without Peyton's permission, and had to talk her down from wailing by telling her this was an end worthy of Lady Jane Grey.

"You know, I never meant to scare her," Peyton said.

Sam shook his head. "What?"

"The night at the water tower." Peyton's eyes drifted toward the place on the horizon where the old water tower used to stand, a silhouette against the sky. "I never wanted to scare Miel with the pumpkin. I just thought she might want to hold her. I thought it might make her feel better."

Peyton's face was so open, almost apologetic, that Sam felt like they were at the water tower again, Peyton standing with her sisters, Sam slipping his jacket onto Miel. They had all been children then, so he'd never considered just how young Peyton was, the smallest of four sisters. A girl offering to share her favorite thing with a girl she did not know.

It wasn't Peyton's fault, how much Miel feared pumpkins. But with the four of them all lined up like that, it was no surprise that Miel had seen Peyton's first step toward her as a threat.

Maybe if Peyton had just been Peyton, instead of one of four bright-haired girls, she would have seemed more like a friend and less like a force. But they would always be the Bonner sisters, a truth that both guarded and isolated them.

"You don't have to tell her that," Peyton said. "But I wanted you to know."

lake of goodness

)

Tonight, half the town was putting pumpkins into the water, the way they did every year. They had hollowed out pumpkins they'd bought for the occasion. Dusky orange Estrellas. Deep blue-green Autumn Wings. Gray that was almost violet, and the off-white Luminas. They had emptied their shells of seeds and flesh, and then carved patterns of leaves and lace lattices. When they set candles inside, the cuttings glowed. One by one, they let them float on the water, the wide, slow current reflecting the light.

A little farther down the bank, Miel saw Sam's mother, watching the same children she persuaded to practice their euphoniums and cellos. Her skirt almost swept the ground as she bent to talk to them, the glimmer of her eyes and her slight smile drawing them as if she were about to tell them a secret.

Sam had to be around here somewhere. He usually helped his mother keep track of the sons and daughters she'd been charged with taking to see the pumpkin lanterns. Miel looked for him, but even when she didn't see him, she felt the pull of him, the certainty that he was close. That they would touch again before the heat from their hands faded off each other's bodies.

Miel stood with Aracely at the edge of the river, unashamed of the wet hem of her skirt. She let it brush her knees, and did not try to hide it.

The weight of pumpkins filled their hands, the candles inside them warming the shells. The one Aracely held, round and green, she had carved with swirls like the tops of fiddlehead ferns, the shapes traced in light. Miel's, a cream Lumina, glowed where she had cut out little rounds for the light to come through. It looked like one of Aracely's favorite dresses, pale fabric dotted with coins of gold dye.

A few old women, the ones who argued about whether milk helped pumpkin vines grow bigger fruit, the same ones Miel thought would have been first to gossip about her, watched her, and smiled.

Miel thought her rose would burst into petals. They would spill from her sleeve and cover the ground. The whole town knew she was afraid of pumpkins. But she never thought these señoras would be proud of her for carrying her own floating lantern.

She had never thought this town held even a handful of people who cared if she was afraid.

"You ready?" Aracely asked.

Miel nodded. Aracely crouched alongside the river, and set her pumpkin on the water. It drifted into the dark, the current carrying the swirls of light.

Then Miel knelt, looking into the water, and watched the pumpkins floating down the river. A pale one dotted in light spun near the bank. One so dark green it looked blue bobbed along the current. A flatter orange one with the billowing shape of a fairy tale pumpkin looked like its rind was glowing.

Miel let the Lumina pumpkin go. The cream-white round floated, casting coins of light on the water. It rode the current and joined the clusters of other pumpkins, bumping Aracely's so their light flashed and skittered.

But the soft rush of the river was sharpening, deepening like a knife cutting down through the earth. It held the thread of her mother's screaming. It cupped the small breaking of Miel's sobs, her begging her mother to let her out, or not to hold her under. The sounds swirled through the water like the hem of a dress.

Part of Miel was still in the water.

Both she and her mother and Leandro were lost down there.

So many women had given her mother advice on what to do with her. *Draw a star on her forehead every Sunday. Mallow tea at sunrise. Say the prayer of Nuestra Señora de las Nieves, and then, when she is older, buy her a dress as blue as the Virgin's veil.*

The history of Miel's family had said that, one day, she would turn on her mother, the roses growing from her body a warning of her treachery.

Held within all those sounds was her father's voice, a memory of him yelling that existed only in the distance. When she tried to look at it straight-on, it vanished.

Her unease broke and brightened in her stomach.

She was inside one of those pumpkins. Her body, small as when she was five, was inside one of the bigger ones floating on the water. Or maybe she was in the smaller ones. Her hair in a white one. Her rose in one as orange as Ivy Bonner's hair. Her hands in a blue-gray one. She was in pieces.

Miel waded into the river, the water splashing up to her waist. She pulled the lids off the carved pumpkins, grabbing at every one she could. But she found each one empty except for the candle set inside.

Even within the walls of the stained glass coffin, she'd been able to keep away the truth of why her mother did what she did. Even when she remembered the small space inside the pumpkin, or the wide, rough river, she kept these things as far as her hands could push them.

But now, surrounded by all this water and all these pumpkins, her memories shook off the film and haze of so many years.

Her mother had put her inside a deep gold pumpkin, the biggest she could find, to try to make her good.

Miel's roses were proof of what her mother already knew. Miel's brother, Leandro, had made her mother beautiful and happy. But Miel had made her mother ugly. Her mother had been beautiful since she was a girl, looked at by men years before she was old enough to marry. And Miel had not turned out the same. Miel had left her mother's body misshapen from giving birth, her face tired and worn, and Miel had not stolen that beauty for herself.

And her mother had forgiven her for that, for stealing her beauty and not even taking it for herself.

But then the roses had come. They had declared that Miel was not a daughter but a possessed creature. And all those voices, the priests and the señoras and the gossips, had told her mother what heartbreak those roses, and any child who grew them, would bring her.

Her father's yelling, the only memory she had of him raising his voice, spread out through the dark. She caught just enough of his words, the sound like clouds tumbling over, to understand.

You don't know what she'll do to you when she gets older.

I'm doing this for you, don't you understand?

She'll turn on you.

The words came with a pain in Miel's wrist, small but deep. It felt like the point of a hot knife, held against her skin.

Miel's father and mother had argued, about her roses.

He had left, because of her roses. He was gone, because of her roses. The things that grew from her body had scared him off, driven him away.

Now there was nothing left of Miel but her roses.

Miel threw the lids off more of the pumpkins, freeing their light to spill into the air. She had to be in one of these. There had to be somewhere she could find the body that had been hers. The more she heard her mother's wailing, the faster she worked.

Miel had not only cost her mother her beauty, and her husband. She had cost her Leandro. Her mother had lost her son all because he'd tried to save Miel.

This was the brittle core of how her mother had died. She was looking for her son, always looking for her son, and when she knew she'd lost both Leandro and Miel, she must have stopped fighting. She must have given up, stopped kicking and grabbing at the current, and let it have her.

Miel only registered the flash of Aracely's hair before Aracely grabbed her arm.

"You're fine," Aracely whispered. "You're fine."

But Aracely shouldn't have touched her. Anyone who touched her, she would take down with her. If Aracely held on to her, if she tried to save Miel, she would die like Leandro. The river may have saved Miel but it did not save Leandro. She could still hear her brother yelling, looking for her.

Miel elbowed Aracely in the ribs, and broke away from her.

Sam caught her upper arms.

"Hey," he said. "Come on. Let's go home."

Miel stilled, his touch bringing her back to the first day she met him. The feeling that she was small made him seem the age he'd been when they met.

That day, Miel had come back to life. Her eyes felt new and raw. They stung with all the minerals in the water, dimming everything she saw so that everyone watching her looked like a nightmare creature.

Sam's voice had been so gentle, his hair black and his skin dark enough that she mistook the blur of him for her brother. But the moment her vision cleared, letting her see his unfamiliar face, she heard the echo of her brother's voice in the water, and knew he was gone.

This was the worst thing, the thing she could never tell Sam, that this was how Miel thought of him, always. Even before she thought of him as Sam, or Samir, or Moon. The first one willing to touch her, and the one who had slit her open with the truth that he was not her brother. The first one who did not recoil, thinking she was the cursed child of a river spirit or the omen of a coming drought, and the one who made her realize how much she had lost.

A hundred eyes shone in the dark. The air vibrated with whispers. Miel felt them wondering, out loud but in hushed voices, if she was the witch who had turned those pumpkins on the Bonners' farm to glass. They had already ruled out the Bonner girls, who exonerated themselves by being afraid to touch those glass pumpkins.

But Miel and Aracely wore the name *bruja* on their skin.

Now everyone watching wanted to know if the girl with the roses had turned those pumpkins hard and translucent, if she had left some curse that would spread across the fields, chilling the flesh of every vine and its fruit.

Next those eyes would sweep over to Aracely, blaming the woman who pulled lovesickness from weary hearts. Aracely would have to hide in the violet house, fearing who might be waiting in the side yard or at the edge of the road, and Miel would carry with her the truth that she ruined everyone she loved.

Miel looked from Sam to Aracely.

In Aracely's face, she found the things that had been missing from Sam's, the absences that had told her Sam was not Leandro. Aracely's arched eyebrows. The smooth, unbowed line of her lips. The hair that was straighter than anyone's in their family; Miel saw it now, even though it was gold instead of dark.

Aracely half-parted her lips. She looked caught between speaking and deciding not to.

Miel fell back toward every moment she'd thought Aracely might ask her where she had come from, or why she feared pumpkins as though they had teeth. Every time, Aracely had opened her mouth with a kind of hesitation that made Miel wince, and then had shut it.

Aracely had never been trying to ask Miel anything.

She'd been trying to tell her.

But she hadn't told her. All those times, and she hadn't told her.

Miel had never been able to figure out why this woman had loved her when she was a strange girl made feral by water.

But Aracely cared because she knew the dark places Miel had been.

She remembered them better than Miel did.

Miel looked back at Sam. In his face was sadness. Not confusion or shock.

What she'd just realized, he already knew. The regret on his face was so settled.

He'd known all this for so much longer than she had.

The boy she loved and the woman who looked after her had told her so many lies.

Miel looked at Aracely, her face stricken, eyes frozen wide.

"You are my blood," Miel said. She turned to Sam. "And you . . ."

His eyes fell shut. He was surrendering to what she knew, not defending himself.

She wrenched her arms out of Sam's hold, and ran.

"Miel," Aracely called.

They tried to go after her, but she lost them. She slipped away from the river and into the trees, cutting through farms and skimming dirt paths.

Her wrist stung and throbbed. Her body took in all this brokenness, all the lies, and through her roses released it, so the weight of it wouldn't break every one of her ribs.

sea that has become known

☽

He painted *mare frigoris*, the sea of cold, and then *lacus somniorium*, the lake of dreams, sure he felt Miel across the open land, sure he could find the perfume of her roses. Just a thread of it, carried by the wind. It made him brave and reckless. It drove him to cover every brush he had in color, flicking them over metal and glass. He wanted to send out into the night his apology, made of paper and paint and light.

An old tarp and newspapers covered his bedroom floor, brushes and paints scattered over the canvas. He wanted to hang a dozen moons, each painted dark, nothing but a slash of light at the edge. One covered in deep violet, edged with a rose crescent. Another hunter green, with the grass-colored thumbnail of a corn moon. Some smaller than young Lumina pumpkins, and some big enough that Miel couldn't pretend she didn't see them.

This was the one thing he was good at. Painting moons, leaving them in trees where they shone gold or silver, the night sky claiming them like stars. This was the only way he knew to tell her that without her, he wasn't Moon. Without her, the girl they called Honey, the girl who licked her own name off knives when Aracely wasn't looking and off spoons when she was, he was as diminished as an almost-new moon.

He was nothing but a young moon, the thin thread of light that clawed its way along the edge of a dark new moon.

The moons had always told her what he did not know how to say. When he was too much of a coward to tell her he loved her, the blush of a rose moon, or the washed-out red of a strawberry moon, or a pinkish purple of a flower moon, spoke for him. And now these dark moons, edged in light, were his weak try at an apology.

But there was no true apology in telling her that even though he was sorry, that he wouldn't have done anything differently. He knew that.

If all this had been his, if it had belonged to him, he would have told her. He'd given her his hands, his real name, every story his mother ever told him about Kashmir and Peshawar and even Campania, even the clan of fishermen who'd made the father he did not know. He'd given Miel his family's fairy tales about banded peacock butterflies, and he'd given her a body he wasn't even sure of possessing.

He gave her all of it. If it belonged to him, it was hers.

But this hadn't been his secret to tell. Even if Aracely and Miel belonged to each other, even if they were sisters in a way Miel did not yet understand, he could not have made this his choice. It had never been about him. It had been about so many secrets Aracely kept unspoken that Sam wondered if she would burst into a hundred thousand butterflies.

If he didn't want everyone in this town knowing that his mother had given him the name Samira and that underneath his clothes he had a body that matched it, he couldn't tell anyone, not even Miel, that the woman named Aracely had once been called Leandro.

But Miel was hurting too much to see that. She hated him. She hated Aracely.

Now he'd worn himself out painting, sitting on the edge of his bed with his head in his hands, fingers combed into his hair. Every free paper and glass globe he had, he'd covered in color. Paint smudged his forearms. He'd brushed his hair out of his face, and left an arc of dark blue on his forehead.

Her words still spun through him. *And you . . .*

Even when he shut his eyes he saw her glaring at him.

His fingers left streaks of paint in his hair, but he didn't move them. Painting another moon, and another, hadn't made him forget. Ink blue and pale gold only reminded him of the nights he'd snuck outside with her.

The smell of turpentine made him remember being in bed with her, the self-consciousness of wondering if his skin and his sheets smelled like it, that bitter smell like new leather.

A soft but sure knock clicked against the door.

He got up and pretended to blend a dot of umber into yellow. "Come in."

His mother had barely stepped into the room when she had the heels of her hands against the window, easing it up. "This paint. You're going to give yourself a headache."

The wind rustled the edge of the newspapers.

She clicked on a lamp. "And you're going to make yourself blind."

Sam squinted against the light. He painted with as little electric light as possible, seeing by candles in tin holders, or the moon itself when enough of it flooded through the window.

"Come downstairs," his mother said. "You need to eat."

He didn't have it in him to argue. He followed her down to the kitchen, where blood oranges, stems on, clustered on the counter next to a bowl of olives.

It had been one of his favorites before they moved here, orange and olive salad. Once it had made him think of his father, of the little town he came from on the Gulf of Salerno. The stories his mother passed on. Groves of hundred-year-old olive trees and orchards of figs that smelled of caramel when they fell. Lemons in blue-glazed bowls. Hillsides so steep that from the water they looked like straight drops into the sea.

He wondered how his mother thought of his father now, maybe as some vibrant, shimmering visitor who stopped by a few times for dinner and then disappeared. A man who belonged to them so little she did not miss him.

But then that wondering got crowded out, and all he could think of was the whispers in their old town. Even if he was so small he only half-understood what they were saying, he caught the tone. The glances toward him as if he could not see them looking, even when he was staring back.

His mother snapped the stems off the oranges. "Are you going to tell me or are you going make me ask?"

Sam pushed at one of the oranges, letting it roll away and then back.

"Something happened with Miel," his mother said. "At the lighting." No hint of a question in her voice.

The lighting. He wondered how much of this town was whispering about Miel rushing into the water, tearing the lids off the lanterns, or if they had been too busy helping their children give the current the pumpkins they'd carved together.

Whenever the weather turned cold, people grabbed at gossip quicker, as though they could spin it like wool, wrap themselves in it. Back in their old town, it had been a bare-branched winter when his mother had made the mistake of talking about Sam's father. With a trusted friend, she'd shrug off the story like flicking cigarette ash away from her fingertips.

But that friend couldn't resist telling a few of her friends, and soon the town had hummed with whispers.

"I don't think Miel and I are friends anymore," he said. "I don't think we're anything anymore."

His mother snapped off the last stem and set down the orange. "I doubt that."

She cut the tops off the oranges, and set each one on its flat base.

"Your father taught me to make this," she said.

"With fennel," Sam said. "I know."

Most of what they made in this kitchen was from his grandmother's recipes. Aloo baingan made with almost-blue eggplant. The warmth of a half-dozen spices lacing under the saffron and rose in Kashmiri chai. But a few his mother had learned from his Campania-born father. Dishes with lemon leaves, and wild arugula so sharp it felt cold on his tongue. They set their peaches and plums in a bowl Sam's father had given his mother, ceramic glazed as deep blue as a cloudless sky. His mother hadn't wanted to accept it, this piece that had been in his family for three generations. But his father thought it was meant to be with her, that blue he considered a darker shade of her eyes, so he'd hidden it at the top of her closet, knowing she'd find it only after he'd gone.

But the gossip in their old town had reduced all this to something as cold as trading olive oil or raw marble. *You want a green card, and I want a baby.* They called it a bargain his mother made to sleep with a man she didn't love, as many times as it took to have the child she wanted. How they were married for only a couple of years, how she was the only divorcing woman who, seven months pregnant, wished her husband well as he left her.

How Sam existed because his mother and his father thought little of trading things others considered sacred.

By the time they moved here, his mother knew better. She kept quiet about a story she always considered proof of how much she loved Sam, how much she had wanted a child even if there was no man she wanted as her husband.

But he never forgot. He existed because his mother set out to make him exist.

Sam turned one of the oranges in his hand. The flush of deep red thinned along the peel, and then faded.

"I made a mistake, didn't I?" he asked.

"Probably," his mother said. "We all make them every day."

"No," he said. "I mean, coming near her that day. When the water tower came down."

His mother ran her knife over a row of olives. "You don't really believe that."

She held out a knife, her fingers cupping the blade, handle toward him.

As a child, this had been one of his favorite tasks, the first thing his mother had let him do with a knife on his own. Slicing away the pith. Using the tip of the knife to nick the seeds away. Making rounds of deep red fruit so thin they were almost translucent, while his mother sliced olives as purple as tiny plums.

"Do you know what kind of child you were?" his mother said, a laugh under her words. "To say there needed to be a man of the house and that you were going to be that man? To declare you were going to be a whole new person so that everyone would know there was a son taking care of his mother?"

Sam set the knife against the orange. He could do this. If he could do nothing right with Miel, at least he could do this for his mother. Slice perfect rounds of blood orange. Arrange them on the plate like the bright tiles of their roof, and know he had managed this one small thing.

"And just think." His mother smiled, and the wrinkles around her eyes looked as fine as the silver necklace his father had given her. She wore it only with her good dresses. "You wouldn't have existed if it weren't for that squid."

He offered as much of a laugh as he could. When he was seven or eight, it used to make him laugh every time, the reminder that his father had wanted to come to this country because of the squid that defied him. He'd been born into a family of fishermen famous for their skill catching squid as red as wine-colored velvet. They rose close enough to the surface to catch only when the moon was a dark ring in the sky, and his father's family was known throughout Campania for night fishing, filling the hulls of their boats before sunrise.

But not his father. When his father went out with his brothers, the squid scattered like minnows. The brothers returned at dawn, their boat light and bobbing, to the taunts of other fishermen.

Sam used to think that was a stupid reason for his father to leave where he was from. But then he thought of his great-grandparents, their fields, the skill it took to plant the corms. This had been their family's trade. There would have been shame in their brothers or sisters lacking the skill to grow those crocuses, or having hands too clumsy to pluck out the saffron threads that cost more for their weight than gold.

His father had come to this country both to escape from what he was not and to discover what he might be.

"What if . . ." Those two words, and Sam's mouth felt as dry as when he woke during a fever, his tongue parched. He had to force the words out.

His mother looked up from the olives.

Her gaze, neither indifferent nor intent, made him look down at his shirt.

Bacha posh were words he'd first heard from his mother's mother. If he didn't follow the path set out by those words, he might forget

her drawings of saffron crocuses, or how sure her hands looked sep-
arating mint leaves from their stems, the green never bruising. He'd
been so sure he could become Samira if he gritted his teeth hard
enough, wished it hard enough, pressed his fingernails into the heels
of his hands so hard his knuckles paled. And now, if he didn't, he
might forget how his grandmother sat with him, spread out his set
of crayons on the kitchen table until she found the deepest gold and
purple, showing him the shape and color of those crocus petals.

He would have to admit that whenever his grandmother told him
the story of the two lovers at Saif-ul-Malook, he'd thought more often of being the prince than of being the fairy.

He wondered if it would be a kind of betrayal to his grandmother,
shrugging away the name she had asked his mother to give him. If he
lived his life without it, if he altered it even by one letter, he worried
that part of him would disappear. He would become someone his
grandmother would not recognize. The blood he shared with that
old woman he loved even though he barely remembered her might
drain away like dust and ice and light stripped away from a comet.

But he wouldn't know unless he said it. His grandmother wasn't
here to listen, but his mother, his grandmother's daughter, was.

"What if I"—his breathing was turning shallow—"wanted to"—
now it was stinging his lungs—"stay"—the words would come only
one or two at a time—"this way?"

"What?" his mother asked, those fine wrinkles appearing again,
this time with wondering instead of smiling.

He tried to even out his breathing. But it stayed quick and
gasping, and he had to tear the words out. "What if I wanted to stay
this way?"

The words came out in a rush of air, and he started coughing.
His mouth felt like orange pith, bitter and wrung-out.

He folded his tongue against his teeth, bracing for her questions.

Her asking what he meant, and him having to tell her that he wanted not to go back to being Samira, but to go forward as Samir. That being a bacha posh had been a lie he told himself to pretend he was like the girls whose mothers and fathers dressed them as boys, but who then grew up to be women. That he had made the mistake of believing his discomfort would be like theirs; theirs was less often a wish that they could be boys, and more a longing for the way boys were allowed to take up as much space as their bodies could fill.

But he wanted both. He wanted to be a boy who grew into a man, and for there to be space in the world for him.

His mother set down the knife. "Is that really what you want?"

Sam's mouth was still too dry, his breath too used up from saying the words all at once, to answer. The inside of him was cracking and crumbling like the glass and paper frames of his moons.

Later, they would have to talk about this. They would have to talk about how he did not know if he wanted to change his body but he knew he wanted to change his name. How they would have to change his papers to say what they had made everyone believe they already did.

How there was no letting go of Samira, because now she felt like a friend he had imagined to fill the empty space before Miel. But he could not be her.

There was still a part of him, spinning and wondering, that wanted to know how long his mother's calm and patience would stand, how long until it fell or crumbled beneath everything he was. Would it hold if, one day, he drew closer to the faith of her father's family, or her mother's, both these faiths she'd rejected because she was so sure God was bigger than religion? Would it stay if, one day, he left this town to hang moons every place on earth there were trees, or if he never lived anywhere but this place his mother had given him? Would it stand no matter what he became or did not become?

But for right now, that one sentence—*What if I wanted to stay this way?*—was all he had in him. He'd used up all his words.

So he nodded.

"Good," his mother said.

With that one word, the space around them felt lit with the violet petals and gold threads of all those crocuses. He couldn't see them, not straight on, but he could sense their shape, the soft lines of the flowers and the wisps of glowing orange. They were halfway between living blooms and the arcs of colors his grandmother had drawn him so many years ago.

His mother's nod looked like a surer, quicker version of the one he'd given her. That was his mother, forever taking hesitation and making it into something clean and finished.

"People should know what they want," she said.

bay of dew

)

$\mathcal{M}$iel was on her knees in Aracely's closet, pulling at her clothes. Aracely's favorite nightgown, black velvet trimming copper satin, heavy and long enough for fall nights. The linen of her morning-glory-purple skirt, the hem stained from how she wore it to work in the garden. The skirt she put on to go out, covered in so many glass beads it looked jeweled with sprays of seawater.

But Miel could not find Leandro. She could not find any trace of her brother. Instead of the pressed clothes their mother always put him in, there were these twirling skirts. Instead of the way he smelled, the strangest mix of wood and powdered sugar from their mother's kitchen, there was the amber of Aracely's perfume. There was none of Leandro left, not because Leandro had become Aracely, but because instead of choosing to be Miel's sister, Aracely had chosen to be a liar.

Everyone called Aracely the kind curandera. Other curanderas made the lovesick drink flaked deer antler, obsidian dust, and batata. That black milk would leave them sick for hours, making it easier to pry the lovesickness loose.

But there was nothing kind about Aracely. Her gentleness was as much of a lie as her name. She could have given herself their mother's name, so Miel would know her. She could have told Miel the day she slipped from the water tower.

She could have been the sister who took her home, put a kettle on the stove. They would have passed back and forth aster honey crystallizing in its glass, the kind Aracely liked as much as Miel. She ate it like candy, and they shared a jar when they stayed up late talking.

Even that memory wasn't soft anymore. Now it was as rough as the crystals along the edge of the aster honey jar.

Aracely's perfume crept into the room, as strong and deep as aged whiskey.

Miel didn't look at her.

Aracely, like Leandro, was the beautiful one of the two of them. Aracely was tall the way Leandro had been tall, even as a child. Aracely glittered with wry mystery the way Leandro glowed with kindness. But instead of Leandro's dark hair, Aracely had so much gold flowing over her shoulders it looked like the crown of her head was spinning it.

Miel knew Aracely as well as she knew the crescent whites of her own fingernails. She knew Aracely's eyes, dark as Spanish molasses. But now Aracely was someone else. She was a woman holding the heart of the brother Miel thought she'd lost.

She remembered the sense of Leandro, how he felt and how he laughed, the softness in his hands. But she didn't remember him well enough to account for all of him. She could not number all the pieces that made him, and then find them all in this woman.

"Do you remember the town we lived in?" Aracely said. There

was a sigh under her words, like she didn't know where to start and decided this was as good a place as any.

Miel didn't remember. She remembered more about their family's kitchen than the place she was born.

"It was further up the river," Aracely said. "That's why no one here recognized you."

"How did we end up here?" Miel asked.

"It's where the river widens and slows," Aracely said. "The calmest point before it gets to the sea. Everything stops here."

Miel felt the flinch of wanting to argue with everything Aracely said, but she knew Aracely was right. The bottom of the river here was cluttered with old nets and washed-away branches and even little boats that had sunk and bobbed along the bottom until they rested here.

"It's where we washed up," Aracely said.

Now Miel remembered Leandro calling her name, looking for her, and then their mother wailing, screaming when the current stole Leandro, and he could not fight it.

"I know you were trying to save me," Miel said.

Aracely stepped to the threshold of the closet. "But you don't know how I lived."

The smile in Aracely's voice—she could hear it—made Miel look up.

"The water took me," Aracely said. "It saved me." Her face was full of a soft peace that made Miel think of the few minutes before the sun set. Aracely looked like she was talking about a lover she had parted from, but still thought well of. "It took me. And then it gave me back this way."

"What do you mean, this way?" Miel asked.

"It let me die as a boy," Aracely said, "and it gave me back as a woman."

Miel set her folded hands against her chest. The depths she feared most had given back the brother she lost.

If Miel shut her eyes she could see it, the water stripping her brother down to his heart and building him back up as this woman. It took every part of Leandro, and gave him the body that would become Aracely, building her out of the cold and the dark and the things she had once been.

The water had finished her, spun her into a grown woman during the years she had belonged to it. It had been her cocoon. It had made the raw elements of Leandro into this woman.

There had been so much more to the appearing of this beautiful woman than a summer of gold-winged butterflies.

The butterflies had not brought her here. Yes, they might have turned her hair a color to match them. But they had not given her to this town the way the water had. They were a celebration of her emergence, a sign of her appearing.

Leandro had reappeared as Aracely, an event marked by countless wings.

Miel had fallen out of a metal tower filled with dirt- and rust-darkened water.

"It's not fair," Miel said.

"What isn't?" Aracely asked.

Miel couldn't remember those years in the water. She couldn't remember the rush of the water that held her being drawn from the river and into the tower. She felt only the dim light of knowing she had half-existed, not breathing because, for that time, she had no heart and lungs. They, like the rest of her, had been folded into the river.

For a while, she had not had a body but had been made of water, before that water gave her back.

"It made you older." Miel had stayed the same as when the water took her, a little girl who did not grow until she again had her body and breath. "It didn't make me older."

"It wasn't about it making me older," Aracely said, though the tightness in her face told Miel there was more than she was willing to say. But this, unlike everything else, was Aracely's business, not Miel's. "It just gave me back as what I was meant to be. And I was glad you were still little. I was glad the water kept you the way you were, that you didn't lose any time."

Miel searched Aracely's face, the understanding spreading inside her. "You knew I was in there."

Aracely pursed her lips, looking caught but not ashamed. "There were only so many places you could be. I couldn't find you in the river. But then I stood under that water tower one day, and I could feel you. You were so close I kept thinking I could take your hand."

"Then you just waited for them to take it down?"

"That water tower was a storm hazard," Aracely said. "They should've torn it down ages ago. All I had to do was flirt with the right people, and its days were numbered."

Miel cringed thinking of her brother—no, not her brother, this woman—recognizing her in that stale water. She tried to remember what it felt like to be in there, and couldn't.

She felt hollow with the understanding that her brother, the boy named Leandro, no longer existed. His muscle and bone and heart had been repurposed into making this woman.

"You should've told me," Miel said.

"When?" Aracely asked. "When would have been a good time to tell you? When you were a little girl, and I looked this different from the brother you knew? When you were a little older? Last week? When was the right time?"

Miel's memory slid back over every time Aracely had opened her mouth, pausing before speaking, and Miel had braced so hard she felt it in her body. Each time, she'd thought Aracely was about to ask her questions that would land too hard for her to catch them. Each time, she'd hoped Aracely would say nothing.

And each time, Aracely had.

Miel had given off such raw fear, such apprehension, that Aracely had never been able to say the words. Miel's panic had scared her off. Miel had startled Aracely with the force of her conviction that for things to be good, they had to stay as they were. They had to be two women who knew just enough but not too much about each other.

In so closely guarding her own secrets, Miel had forbidden the possibility of Aracely ever telling hers. "Please don't blame Sam," Aracely said. "Be mad at me all you want, but I asked him not to tell you."

"Why?" Miel asked.

"Because I didn't want him telling you what I couldn't figure out how to tell you myself."

Aracely sat down on the floor next to Miel, her dark red skirt fluffing like the edges of her zinnias. Her sigh sounded like a breeze wisping at the petals.

Aracely reached for Miel's hand, then hesitated, letting her fingers pause halfway between them. "Do you remember our family?" she asked.

"Not a lot," Miel said.

"We're a lot of brujos and brujas."

Miel laughed then, but it came out strained and short.

"We come from a family where everyone has a gift," Aracely said. "Do you think I just learned how to cure lovesickness? It's in my blood. It's my gift. We all have them. Our great-uncles with broken bones. Our cousins with susto."

Miel reached out for what little she remembered. In the presence of Aracely's voice, it bloomed like a bud opening.

Their relatives had gifts that were useful, without thorns. Miel's great-uncles could cure joints that had gone stiff with age and the ache of old injuries; she had watched them rub chili powder into bent fingers until they came back to life. Her second cousin could bring down any fever, cutting it with the tea of young blossoms.

Her great-grandmother could drive away even the worst nightmares, her garden full of marjoram and moonflower. Miel had been two, maybe three, when her mother had taken her and Leandro to their bisabuela's house; she did not even remember what the old woman looked like. But she remembered that the house had smelled so much like vanilla that the air went down like syrup.

"We're curanderas," Aracely said. "And curanderos."

"I'm not a curandera." Miel turned over her arm, hiding her wrist. "I don't know how to cure anything."

Aracely folded her hands and set them in her lap, her dark fingers disappearing into the fabric.

"It had been so long," Aracely said, eyeing Miel's forearm. "Everyone thought the roses had just died out."

Miel's mother and aunts must have sighed with relief at that, celebrating the other gifts that blessed the family.

"When your first one showed up," Aracely said, "it'd been a hundred years since anyone in our family had grown one."

Miel turned her wrist on her lap. The appearance of these petals must have been as sudden and unwelcome as a bat emerging from a dark attic.

"Our mother," Miel said. "Did she have them too?"

Aracely's mouth paused, half-open for a second, before she said, "Our mother?"

"Did she have the roses?" Miel asked, wondering for just that minute if this was why her mother was so set on ridding her of them. Maybe her body had grown them too. Maybe they sprouted from her back or ankle, and she veiled them under her clothes. "Did she have them and hide them?"

"No," Aracely said. "The curanderos and curanderas weren't in her family. None of this was."

"What?" Miel asked.

"The roses," Aracely said. "The curanderos. They were in our father's family, not our mother's."

The possibility of her mother having the same roses drained away, like wind stripping the petals off a bud.

Her father.

"What happened to him?" Miel asked, but even through her own words, she felt her center humming with the understanding that she already knew.

She heard more than her father shouting. She heard his whispers. She heard her own screaming. She heard the crying and pleading of a boy named Leandro.

She heard everything.

It must have taken a few seconds. But in all that noise, she felt like she'd been sitting in this closet, beneath the sweep of Aracely's skirts, for as long as she'd been in the water tower.

"You remember," Aracely said. At first it had the ring of a question. But then it echoed. *You remember. You remember.* No question. Only the understanding that Miel was sliding into the same memories Aracely must have had this whole time.

bay of mists

☽

"Miel," Aracely called after her.

But Miel ran from the room. She tried to leave behind each dim memory that caught fire and lit a dozen more.

First, she heard all those stories, her father warning her mother in a voice low enough that he thought their children would not catch the words. But Miel and Leandro were pressed against the hallway wall. They were there for every story about how children born with roses turned on the women who'd borne them. Either by bringing curses on their families' farms, or by confessing their mothers' sins, out loud, in church, or even by killing their mothers. The sharp memory of her father, telling the story of his great-great-aunt who poisoned first her mother and then her whole family, came back. That girl had drawn the toxins from the white trumpets of moonflowers, and slipped them into her family's tea.

All of them, her father had said, his whisper rasping at the edges. *She just killed them. Do you understand that?*

She heard her mother and father arguing, still in those whispers so strained they turned to hissing. Her mother saying, *She won't be like that, she's our daughter.* Her father saying, *And you don't think every mother before you said the same thing? I don't want her turning on you.*

And all this had alternated with his sobbing apologies for bringing this curse on her.

Aracely called Miel's name again.

Miel's steps struck the hallway floor. These things she remembered were swirling, forbidding stars. If Miel ran fast enough, she could break out of their gravity.

The roses had come from her father's side of the family. Miel remembered that now. He had carried them, unseen, like passing a sickness with no sign of it. *I didn't know it would come back,* he'd told Miel's mother. *I'm so sorry, I didn't know it would come back. We thought they were gone. I never would have done this to you.* And her mother telling him there was nothing to forgive, trying to convince him, in whispers, that this petal-covered curse was a ghost that would go silent if only they found the right way to quiet it.

But her love only made him set on making sure Miel didn't hurt her, that she didn't betray her mother as so many rose-bearing girls before her had. So when he inspected her bandage one afternoon, and found that three green leaves had broken through it—not slipped from the edge, but grown straight through the bandage—it must have felt like her roses defying him. Miel remembered his face, his anger not at her but at these blooms. They had not only possessed his daughter. Now they were mocking him.

Miel's bed took the force and speed of her body. She set her face against the blanket, trying to press herself down into the dark, where she was nothing but a girl who spilled from a water tower.

But what came next, what she remembered now, brought with it the same pain in her wrist that had kept her awake so many nights.

Her father, holding the rounded end of a butter knife's handle into the blue flame of their gas stove. Her asking what he was going to do with it, him telling her not to worry, and didn't she want to be a good girl for her mother.

Her running to Leandro when her father took a few slow steps toward her, the hot glow just fading out of the metal.

Her father yelling for Leandro to hold her down, Leandro saying no, her father leaning down and shouting at him that if he didn't do this, it meant he didn't love his sister, or her mother. If he didn't do this, it meant he wanted to lose them both.

She remembered Leandro crying, the resistance leaving him, him doing as his father said.

The hot metal had burned the opening on her wrist, pain spreading down to her hand and up her arm. Her own scream had ripped against the back of her throat. Her father explained, his voice low even through her screaming, that this would seal the wound on her wrist, cauterize it, stop the roses from growing again. *It will be over in a minute, mija. All over in a minute.*

Now Miel folded her hands under her, palms against her sternum. Her thumb found the hard knot on her wrist, like a pearl buried under her skin.

The knot of scar tissue, the one she'd let Sam touch. The wound her roses grew from had been there for as long as she had memory. But this knot hadn't been there before that afternoon her father had turned on the gas stove.

This knot was her body's response to that metal searing her wound.

But even touching her own wrist, seeing that her body was no longer a child's body, didn't stop her from hearing her mother's voice. How her mother grabbed the butter knife out of her father's hand so hard and fast that the dull teeth cut his palm. She shoved him away from Miel and Leandro. *What are you doing to her?* Her mother's voice had sounded like the shriek of the wind.

They'll destroy us all, he'd said. She still remembered that, how he never blamed Miel for the roses, how he spoke of them like something apart from her. Even with that curse running through his family, he could not imagine his own daughter being intertwined with those stems and thorns.

Leandro had held ice to the burn on Miel's wrist, sheltered her in the loose cover of his body while she cried with her eyes shut tight, and their mother's and father's voices swelled to screaming.

Miel's shoulders tensed, like her body jolting awake after half-falling asleep, at the memory of the door slamming.

In that door slamming, Miel understood, for no longer than it took to remember the sound, what betrayal he must have felt. How hurt that Miel's mother could not understand he was doing this for her, out of fear that they would lose their daughter to those roses, that she would turn on her mother. He had wanted to protect his wife from his daughter, and his daughter from herself, and his only thanks had been the screams of his wife driving him from his own house.

But then the sound faded, and Miel was that little girl again, crying at the pain and heat that encircled her wrist.

Not like this, her mother had yelled after him. *We don't do this to our children.* And he had left them.

The pumpkin. The baptism.

Her mother had never disagreed with their father that their daughter needed to be cured. She'd just disagreed on the method. She would not go as far as he would go. The handle of the butter knife in the gas flame was cruelty she would not allow, not even from a man known for tending wounds and setting bones.

Her mother held to her conviction that she could cure Miel without hurting her. To her, sealing her daughter inside the hollow of a pumpkin, or holding her in water still a little warm after a long summer, was so much gentler than the pain of hot metal. These were cures blessed by the priests and the señoras.

The warmth of a palm landed on Miel's back.

"I'm sorry," Aracely said.

I'm sorry. Leandro had whispered those words as he held her down, baring her wrist to the hot metal. He had clenched his back teeth to keep from crying. But he'd blinked, and a tear had fallen onto her forehead, hot as the spray off the kitchen sink.

Miel shook her head, face still pressed against the bedspread. But the dark didn't take her.

"Miel," Aracely said.

Aracely's voice was calling her back, pulling her from deep water toward the surface.

"I'm so sorry," Aracely said, and Miel broke into the light.

Miel turned onto her side, palm on the bedspread, her elbow pressing into the mattress.

Aracely's eyes looked dark and wet as the river that had taken her, and their mother.

Whatever guilt Aracely had inherited from Leandro, it seemed so small compared to Miel's. Her roses had cost them everything.

"I killed you," Miel said. "And then I killed her."

Aracely grabbed Miel's hand, her palm warm but her fingers cool. "Don't you say that."

"You had to go in after me because I fought, and she couldn't hold on to me. And then she had to go in after you."

Miel couldn't say the rest. The unexpected currents. The drag to the bottom of the river. How she imagined her mother swimming against the pull of the water, and then realized both Leandro and Miel were gone, and there was nothing to swim for anymore.

That was the part that Miel couldn't let her thoughts land on, that moment of her mother giving up and letting the water take her.

"She loved you," Aracely said. "But she got lost thinking that your roses were something outside of you . . ." Aracely stopped, her mouth half-open, her eyes skimming the floor. "She got so caught up think-

ing she could save you from them better than our father could, that
if she loved you she had to . . ."

She stumbled again, stopping. But this time she looked up, meeting Miel's eyes. "She never wanted to hurt you."

Those memories had left in Miel a fear of her mother's hands,
the pinch of those desperate nights when she sealed Miel inside
that pumpkin and, later, held her underwater.

"You really believe that?" Miel asked, and she heard in her own
voice both skepticism and forgiveness. A suspicion both that her
mother had been trying to hurt her and that she had been justified
in doing it.

"Yes," Aracely said. "I've always believed that. But just because
she loved you doesn't mean you deserved what she did. Or what
he did."

The knot of scar tissue in her wrist felt hot and tight. It stung
with wondering if maybe her father wasn't wrong, that these roses
were things to be killed. How could Miel think anything else now?
Her roses were the reason the Bonner girls knew what Sam needed
so badly for no one to know.

"I should have let her," Miel said. "I should have just stopped
fighting."

Aracely squeezed her hand. "Never stop fighting."

That water, that river that did not save their mother, had adopted
them. It had found her and Leandro when their mother couldn't. It
had kept them until it decided it was time to let them go. Miel hated
it, wanted to turn it all to ice too solid to get lost in, while knowing
that she owed it her life and her brother's.

Her sister's.

Miel looked down at Aracely's hands. Those long fingers. Leandro had long fingers, and small palms. Miel remembered them even
when she couldn't remember the rest of him. And now those hands
belonged to this woman.

"Do you ever hear her?" Miel asked.

She expected Aracely to ask, *Who?* And Miel would have to explain that sometimes she heard her mother's murmuring, not crying but mournful, when the winds grew deep and loud.

But Aracely's mouth pinched. Her eyes fell shut, and she nodded.

Miel couldn't help looking over Aracely's body. Maybe there was some of Leandro in her. Maybe her shoulders that made dresses hang so well. Or her feet, the left foot a half-size bigger than the other. She couldn't remember if Leandro's had been the same way.

Miel's envy turned the back of her throat bitter. This woman in front of her had been so good at being Leandro. And now she was so good at being Aracely.

Miel had never been good at being anyone.

But she couldn't be mad at Aracely for that. She couldn't even be mad at Leandro, a boy who did not exist except for how Miel remembered him and Aracely remembered the flinching discomfort of being him.

If Miel hated Aracely for not telling her, she was little different from the gossips in this town, those whispers that would call Sam a liar for not telling them the truth of a body that was not theirs to judge.

That little splinter of guilt, catching in Miel's palm, made her understand that there were things to be angry at. She could be angry at the river, the drought, the undercurrent that year. She could hate the fears that ran through her family like blood, the unquestioned faith that all girls who wore roses on their skin would turn against their mothers.

She could rage into the whole rainless sky, without hating Aracely, this woman who had both been born her family and become it.

"You're smart," Miel said. "Hiding like this."

"What are you talking about?" Aracely asked.

"If you're trying to hide from what happened, this is how to do it," Miel said. "Becoming someone else."

"Miel," Aracely said. "This isn't me hiding. Me trying to be her son, that was hiding. This"—the tips of her nails, painted the color of champagne, grazed Miel's forearm—"this is me not hiding."

lake of spring

)

Maybe she still hated Sam for lying to her. But his life, his names, all of them, did not belong to the Bonner girls.

Neither did Miel. She left her wrist bare, so the Bonner girls could see how she'd cut away her latest rose. It had never been theirs.

She found Ivy on the side of the Bonners' house.

For a second, how nervous Ivy looked stilled her. Ivy had her arms crossed, each palm and set of fingers spread just above her elbow. Barefoot on the cold brick, but wearing a scarf. One of a thousand Bonner-girl contradictions that played in the imagination of every boy in this town.

She was looking at the pumpkins, the vines that crept closest to the Bonner house. A few more had turned to glass. One a dark blue-green. Another red as the skirt Aracely had been wearing on the floor of the closet. A third as purple as the violet house, if the color had been distilled and darkened like vinegar reduced down in a pan.

Each one, once dull orange or an almost-blue green, now caught the sun inside its shell, lighting up gold.

Miel stepped onto the brick path that hugged the house. "This ends now," she said.

Ivy turned, and in this light her eyes shifted to a darker gray. "Excuse me?"

Miel stepped forward. The windows above them were cracked but not lit. She still came close to Ivy, and kept her voice low.

"Do you want your mother and father to know what Peyton does on Thursday afternoons?" Miel asked. "I'm sure they know, in their own way. But no one's ever really made them think about it."

There was something almost like pity in Ivy's laugh. "You think I'm afraid of my parents?"

Miel took another step toward Ivy. "How about how Lian passed her classes? I'm guessing no one's ever put that in front of them." Now she was so close to Ivy she could see the faint tint of blue in her gray eyes. "Or you. Maybe nobody knows your secret, but they will. Whatever you're hiding, I'll find it."

Ivy's smile had that same pity, without being unkind. "You can't."

The softness didn't deter Miel. She leaned in close enough to whisper.

"Try me."

At the corner of Miel's vision, the last of the light flashed off those glass pumpkins, deep and shining as the tumbled stones Sam's mother wore.

"You don't own any part of us," Miel said.

Ivy studied the reddened skin on Miel's wrist, the small wound.

"I could tell everyone about her," Ivy said.

Her. That one word made Miel press her feet harder against the brick path, trying not to show Ivy that this one syllable touched her.

The thought of what it would do to Sam dragged over her skin like a safety pin.

"Everyone'll think you like girls," Ivy said.

Miel hated Ivy for everything she assumed she knew about Sam, her implication that his body made him a girl. But a ribbon of admiration tainted Miel's rage. That Ivy could protect Peyton so fiercely and still talk about girls liking girls spoke of something fearless in her. Loyal to those other three girls, who were as much part of her as her own body, ruthless to everyone else.

"I don't care if they do," Miel said. She wanted Sam, both what he was with his clothes on and what he was naked. She didn't care what that made her. "They can call me whatever they want. But he's not a girl."

She thought of Sam, of the smell of paint on his skin and the scent of black cardamom on his clothes, and the smallest movement twitched under her skin.

She felt a new burst of growth breaking through to the light. She held her gasp in her lungs, and glanced down at the green shoot, the new leaves.

Ivy did not see. Miel kept her arm at her side, stopping herself from wincing as the thorned stem inched out of her skin.

"You really want everyone knowing your mother tried to drown her children?" Ivy asked, no taunting. She laced the words with neither coaxing nor threatening.

Miel bit back every *that's not true.* Her tongue wanted to let go of the words *that's not what happened.*

Instead, Miel whispered, "Just try it."

Ivy took hold of Miel's elbow. Not a reflex of being angry, lashing out, but the slow wrapping of her fingers around Miel's arm.

"You really want to take us on?" Ivy asked. "You sure about that?"

Miel leaned back to pull her arm away, but stopped.

Ivy looked so tired, wrung out by all that blunt determination.

"No," Miel said. "I don't want to do anything with you."

Miel glanced down at her wrist. A new bud looked red as the center of a blood orange. The more she thought of the brown of Sam's hands or the amber of Aracely's perfume, the more leaves twisted out of her. The leaves turned such a deep green that they looked like the blue of sky lupines. Flashes of gold streaked the petals like candle flames.

Ivy saw the flick of Miel's eyes. Miel was gritting her teeth to keep from crying out with pain and relief.

"I'm walking away, Ivy," Miel said. "You're letting go of me, and I'm walking away. And if you threaten anyone I love again, I will take you down. All of you. I will find every secret you ever tried to hide, and I will make sure everyone knows."

They both looked down at Miel's wrist, where the rosebud swelled like a bulb of blown glass.

"What do you want with them?" Miel asked. "They're not gonna get you what you want. And they're sure as hell not gonna make it so Chloe was never gone." Miel could almost smell the warmth of her own roses drifting out the cracked window and into the chilled air, the stems still inside, in that blue vase. "So what do you want with them?"

Ivy lifted her gaze.

A sheen crossed her eyes, like a slick of oil on water.

That passing light, the slight opening wider of her eyes, sank into Miel.

Fear. That was the plain, unadorned reason Ivy wanted Miel's roses.

It hadn't been about power. It had been about fear. And it hadn't been about what they could get everyone else to give them. It had always been about them, just them.

They had almost lost Chloe. They had splintered and then tried to fit themselves back together, even if they could not control how they all had grown edges and corners, how they might scrape against one another.

Instead of twisting like the smooth green of morning glory vines, they were wearing one another down like brambles rubbing away the thorns of other brambles.

And Ivy must have thought that if she could control this one thing, she could keep them together, interlocked instead of breaking.

With those roses, she believed they could have any boy they wanted. If their charms failed on a boy with glasses who played the violin like it was part of his hands, or the tall one with crooked teeth but perfect blue eyes, they could call on these roses.

But it had never been about any one boy, or even a string of them. As long as they could have anything they wanted, they were still the Bonner girls. They were still one force in four bodies, in four shades of red hair.

Miel didn't care. That force, those shades of red, weren't moving her wherever the Bonner girls wanted. And they weren't threatening Sam.

"If you try and hurt anyone I love," Miel said, "I will make sure everyone in this town knows you and your sisters can't do anything. The famous Bonner girls can't get what they want. You can't even get boys to fall in love with you anymore. Why don't we ask Aracely? I bet she could tell you there's not a single heart in this whole town that's lovesick over any of you. The magnificent Bonner sisters? They don't exist. You don't rule this town anymore."

Miel's own venom spread over her tongue like melted sugar. It was dark and unfamiliar and so smooth she felt like she was drinking it. Ivy's flinch only thickened its sweetness at the back of her throat.

"You leave me alone, and you leave Sam alone," Miel said. "Or everything I know, everyone will know."

Ivy leaned into Miel, her mouth near her ear. "You don't know anything."

She grabbed Miel's rose by the stem and pulled.

Miel screamed, the ripping of the thorns through her skin like having a vein torn out. Her scream sounded not like her, but shrill and wild, the shriek of a downed bird.

The thorns dragged through Miel's muscle. They sliced across her veins. They turned the small opening in her wrist into a wound, and it throbbed like a burn, a hot coin searing her skin.

The last of the stem flopped out, the end limp as a wet rope.

Ivy pinched the rose stem between her fingers. The streaks of yellow on the red petals looked like bands of light crossing a blood moon.

Blood flowed out over Miel's arm. It salted the back of her throat. Her wound dyed her shirt, the rose's pine and amber scent raining down from her wrist. She was a lipstick tree, blooming with red so bright it did not look real.

A sweep of auburn burst into the darkening air.

Lian Bonner's eyes flashed green as a wet pumpkin vine. She wore a heavy sweater, cable-knit in a thick yarn, but like Ivy, she stepped onto the brick path in bare feet.

Miel's scream had called her out. Soon Peyton and Chloe would come out too. They would pull Miel into the pumpkin fields and quiet her. They would hold her down so that when Mr. and Mrs. Bonner came out asking what on earth was going on, they'd keep their hands over her mouth and her limbs, and the green of the vines would hide her.

They would pretend they were crouching in the pumpkin fields looking for an earring Ivy had lost. They would tell their mother and their father that Lian had seen a mouse, or that Chloe had been trying to scare Peyton with a grass snake. And the weight of their hands would press more blood from Miel's body, until she could not bite Ivy's palm or fight against Peyton's and Lian's fingers on her ankles and wrists.

Miel grabbed a glass pumpkin and wrenched it. The stem snapped and let off a spray of blue glass splinters.

If the Bonner girls would not face these fields, if they did not understand the force spilling out of their windows, Miel could make them. She could break it open and put it between her and them.

She shut her eyes and threw it at the brick path. It shattered, a million little clean, sharp noises. Like rain hitting the different-colored tiles on the roof of Sam's house, sounding like handfuls of sewing needles.

Miel opened her eyes, holding her wrist against her chest to slow the bleeding.

Shards of blue littered the brick path and the dirt. Pieces had skittered into the rows of pumpkin vines. They looked like a hundred blue glass flames, a forbidding river between Miel and these bare-foot girls.

And she ran.

sea of showers

)

The inside of him was as frozen as winter ground. He'd gotten so used to telling Miel what he would tell no one else. Now that impulse to find her, tell her that he'd done it, he'd said the words he didn't even know were true until he heard them in his own voice, left his heart held tight. It was the hollow echoing of an instinct he could no longer lean against. Now she wouldn't let him near her, and he was all ice and cold earth. Everything felt as sharp as frost flowers, cutting him even though they had come from him.

He always tried to stop Miel from touching frost flowers, those curls of ice that grew from the weeds on the coldest December mornings. He searched for them for her, spotting the violet-tinted white in the undergrowth. But he warned her that even though they looked soft as petals, they were sharp.

She always touched them anyway. Those petals, looking so much like spun sugar or the tongues of irises, lured her. She touched them, and they drew blood from her fingertips.

Every time, those frost flowers left her bleeding. Every time, she cut her fingers, and for that moment of her blood coloring the ice, he hated those petals for being sharp and beautiful.

Tonight he'd hang every moon he had. To give this town all the light that was in him, even if all he was to them was this paint and paper. To get Miel to hate him a little less. To show her that every moon he'd ever made her was not a lie.

So many times, he had told her in light what he did not know how to tell her any other way. Now he needed these moons to tell her why he'd done what he'd done, why he'd kept from her what he'd kept from her. That he could not betray a secret so much like the one he was keeping himself.

If he tried to turn all this light into words, he would catch himself on them. What could he say? That he hated the way he'd hurt her, but that there was no other choice, no way he could live with the decision to give up what did not belong to him? Those words would be thorns snagging his skin and clothes.

The closest he'd ever gotten to telling Miel what he could tell her in light was with his hands. His palms on her waist. When he flicked the pollination brush over her arm, and her eyes moved between his fingers and his mouth, and he touched her in a way he'd convinced himself he never could unless she moved toward him first.

But now she wouldn't let him near her, so all he had was the moon, this light in the sky he knew as well as his own body. He knew where it glowed brightest. Where its reflected sunlight vanished into craters and seas. The starburst of lighter contouring. And the shadowing that children in this town were taught to see as a face, but that Aracely had taught Miel to see as a rabbit.

As a child, Sam had stared up at it, imagining the moon's light spilling over him in a rush of cool air, the opposite of the sun's warmth. But he had not truly learned it until he painted it, mixing the gradations of colors for *mare cognitum* and every other crater and valley, brushing on the darker shade of the vapor seas. He had done it so many times he could paint freehand now, no sketching, no outlining.

He'd start with the trees that shaded the wisteria-colored house. Outside his mother's house, he'd hang a blood moon and a mead moon, to match the different-colored roof tiles. He'd light up the beech tree outside Miel's room with a rose moon and a flower moon. A grain moon and a hay moon would light the way between here and the wisteria-colored house. He'd spread the light of every lunar sea and valley.

The shift away from the world he'd built with Miel, the knowledge that she now hated him, was so sharp, he could taste it on the air, like a salt crystal. The world they had between them was both brighter and softer than everything else, cast in deep blues and golds. It swept away the muddy haze that settled around all other things. It dulled the way Sam had to keep his eyes down if he wanted to be left alone at school but had to look up at the right time to scare off anyone who would not leave Miel alone.

A knock clicked against his bedroom door.

"Come in," he said, expecting his mother, ready to show her what he'd finished so recently the paint hadn't dried.

It wasn't until the door hinge's soft creak that he realized that hadn't been his mother's knock.

Aracely stood at the threshold.

"Have you seen Miel?" she asked.

Sam let out a curt laugh. "What do you think? She doesn't want to see me."

"She didn't come home," Aracely said. "I'm worried."

He grabbed the edge of the drop cloth on the floor and rubbed paint off his hands. "She's upset," he said. "Did you think she wouldn't avoid us for a few days? She's probably not coming home until she's sure you're asleep."

"I don't think that's what's going on," Aracely said.

He folded the drop cloth in on itself. "Why not?"

Aracely held out her wrist.

A trickle of blood striped the inside of her forearm. It came from an unseen wound; Sam could not find the cut. But that thin stripe, that cord of red, looked the same as when Miel bled from the place her roses grew.

lake of time

)

The moon came through the ceiling of cloud cover, the reds and golds brightening the woods like the trees were catching fire.

The rush of breaking the glass pumpkin and running had worn away, and the pain had forced her onto her hands and knees. She crawled deeper into the woods, her skin so hot with pain that the cold felt faint as the brush of a leaf. Her blood spilled on her jeans, the stains deep as the gems on one of Aracely's necklaces.

She was losing the feeling in her fingers. She couldn't have screamed if she wanted to. All that came was the wet sound of her breath against the back of her throat. She lost the feeling in her wrists and ankles, the numbness opening her.

Miel raised her head and spotted a glimmer of purple and red. The shapes of planets and constellations resolved, cut and engraved in panels.

The stained glass coffin.

She scrambled away from it, crawling under the ceiling of gold leaves. Under her breath, she whispered Aracely's prayer of Santa Rita de Cascia, saint of impossible causes. But she did not know if the impossible cause was her life or her thorn-covered soul.

Pain anchored her, keeping her down. She clutched her arm close to her body, pressing her wrist against her chest to slow the bleeding. The knot of scar tissue in her forearm felt heavy as a metal bead. Crawling with both knees but one hand slowed her down, putting too little distance between her and the stained glass coffin.

The woods seemed endless, a whole world of green and gold. She didn't know them like Sam. The fields of feather grasses were their place, but the woods were his. Branches offered places to hang his moons that fallow fields didn't.

But she crawled. She dragged herself across the ground, understanding now that nightmares were weak, silly things that would scatter in the light. They were made of dyed glass and river water and lies that grew even sharper when the truth lit them up.

Dirt coated her clothes and her skin. She left a streak of blood on the ground, and was too weak to kick at it and cover it over.

They were too much entangled, Miel and her roses, like two trees that could not be pulled apart without killing both. Ivy had pulled a rose from her by its roots, and enough blood came with it to dye her clothes, to turn every breath into a gasp. She was bleeding out so much red her skin looked like countless petals, enough for a wide, endless garden of scarlet roses.

She wished her roses were the magic Ivy thought they were. She wished a cup of fluffy petals, their bay-laurel-oil-and-lavender smell, could make a woman realize she was in love with a man who sold las flores de calabazas at the market. She wished its perfume could make that woman brave enough to tell him that the soft pumpkin taste of the blossoms he grew was forever making her think of kissing him.

Her poor mother. All the stories Miel's father told her, those tales about the treachery of those roses, how they would turn Miel against her, how they would make her nothing but a creature possessed by the things that grew inside her. Her mother was right to try to save Miel from those petals. Because those petals, and the fact that Ivy and her sisters had wanted them, were killing her now.

Light swam through her vision, like gold glitter from the cascarones they broke at Easter. Blood slicked her collarbone as she held her forearm against her chest.

Her body was not a garden. It was not earth waiting to be rid of brambles and weeds. Ivy had bled that rose out of her body, and now her life was coming with it.

She raised her head, hoping to see the road, or the edge of any farm except the Bonners'.

But her eyes found only the shine of stained glass, those etched stars and planets, brightened by flashes of moon that slipped through the trees.

She could not get away from it. She'd thought she was crawling and dragging herself away, when all she was doing was dragging herself back. No matter where she pulled her body, it would wait for her. She was too lost to find a straight path away from it, and all those stars and planets of jewel-colored glass would draw her back.

The Bonner girls would make the moon—the one in the sky and every one Sam had ever painted—disappear. They would take all that light into their skin.

Miel resisted the feeling of her body going limp, but she was collapsing onto the ground. Her hands were too weak to do anything but open and close her fingers. The blood and air went out of her, and there was nothing but those whorls of green and violet.

sea of cold

☽

The truth—Sam wasn't afraid to admit this, and he doubted Aracely would've been either—was that this town liked his mother better than they liked him, or Aracely. Even though his mother was a generation closer to not being from this country, even if they would count that against anyone else, she charmed them. She laughed easily. She enchanted children into practicing instruments and trying foods and reading books their own parents couldn't convince them to.

That made her the best choice to ask around if anyone had seen Miel. Aracely took the farms, the orchards where she bought bergamot oranges and the families that sold her Araucana and Faverolles eggs. And Sam searched the woods, these trees he'd mapped with the light of his moons.

He carried with him a moon, cold and blue as the one in the sky. It lit the ground as he walked. It chilled the warmth of the rust-colored trees.

It found a ribbon of deep red cutting through a carpet of gold leaves.

The thought of Aracely's wrist, bleeding the same as Miel's, made the leaves look like they were turning to blades, each branch covered in knives.

"Miel?" He held up the moon, following that band of red.

A soft gasping sound pulled him deeper into a grove of yellow trees.

He stopped. In front of him was the stained glass box he'd found her locked in.

The gasping sound flared again, pulling his eyes down.

He dropped the moon. The candle flame flickered before the wick caught again.

She was a dark shape, clutching her arm to her chest, her hair fluttering with how hard she was trying to breathe.

"Miel." He knelt next to her, saying her name again, and again.

His body felt like it was turning into one of his own moons, his skin and muscle a frame of paper, his heart a lit candle.

Her eyes were half-closed, her shirt and jeans patched with stains that were drying red-brown. A slick of new red, wet and bright as pomegranate seeds, covered her forearm.

Her rose. It had been pulled out by the stem, and its absence was costing her all this blood.

"What happened?" he asked. "Who did this to you?"

She opened her mouth like she was trying to answer, but there was no sound except her breath rasping against her dry lips.

He saw his hands doing the things he knew to do. Unbuttoning his shirt, wrapping it around her forearm, tying it to slow the bleeding. Taking her arm, the one not coated in blood. Putting it around his shoulder. He felt her damp skin, sensed his hands moving.

But the candle at his center had turned cold, a wick darkening to an ember and then going out. And all that cold pulled so deep into the core of him that he didn't even feel the bite of the air against his bare forearms. He didn't feel the chill of the earth against the shins of his jeans, or through his undershirt and his binder.

"Hold on to me, okay?" he said, and the words were as unsteady as his breathing. There had to be a way to move her without hurting her more. They had to be able to help her before the empty place in her forearm gave up all the blood she had.

Her body trembled against him, the movement slight as her petals underwater. Sam held on to her, trying to steady her, her wrist held between them. The wound let off water and blood. It soaked through the shirt he'd tied around her forearm.

Sam found the recognition in her eyes. The hollow in his chest turned tight and hot.

Her roses were as much the life in her as her heart. And the way she bled was killing her.

Miel grabbed Sam's other hand, the blood on her palm slicking his. She held on so hard her fingers trembled.

He tried to ease his hand out of hers. "You've got to let go, okay?"

She didn't loosen her grip.

"Please don't leave," she said, the words dry and wrung-out.

She put all the force and will she had into holding his hand, hard enough that he could feel her slowing pulse against his palm. Hard enough that he was losing the feeling in his fingertips.

"I'm not leaving you," he said.

But her eyelashes flickered, the recognition leaving her. Her skin felt damp, fevered. She was too far away to hear him, but close enough to hold on to his hand so hard he couldn't get his fingers back without hurting her. He needed both his hands to help her, but she held on so tight he felt it wringing the blood out of her. She was giving what little strength she had, the force left in her heart and her breathing, to keeping her grasp on him. And if he waited until she was weak enough that it slackened, he'd lose her.

He was losing her, this girl who built with him each night a world so much softer and more beautiful than the one he woke to in the morning. She was the wild blossoms and dark sugar that spoke of what the world could be. She was the pale stars on her brown skin.

She was the whole sky.

That was the cruelest thing about losing someone. In being lost, they became so many different people, even more than when they were there. To Aracely, she would be the lost sister who had only begun to understand that the woman she lived with was made of a boy name Leandro, and a hundred thousand yellow butterflies, and the bright, wild wish to be as she really was.

To Sam, she was the girl who gave his moons somewhere to go. She was the dark amber of beechwood honey, the caramel of sourwood, and the bitter aftertaste of heather and pine. She was every shade of blue between two midnights.

And she was slipping from his grasp because she would not let go.

lake of perseverance

)

The world darkened and brightened. The wind cupped the thread of her mother's crying, weak and soft.

Only the slowing rhythm of her pulse in her wound made her sure she was still alive.

His hands on her took her out of these woods, back to a night when he left a rose moon in the beech tree outside her window. And she let herself slip out of the feeling of bleeding from her wrist, and into that first rush of light that had made her wonder if it was spring. It had brought the sudden feeling of being in a different month. Thinking winter was months away and realizing it was October.

This pale, rose-colored light had made her expect to look out her window and find all the trees blooming. A million blushing petals against a midnight sky. Spring descending over fall in countless pink blossoms. That blush on the whole world had turned her next breath into something between a gasp and a laugh. She could almost feel it in her mouth now, almost laughed like that again, but the salt at the back of her throat choked it out of her.

She sank under the memory of finding the trees outside not in blossom, but all amber and gold, tinted with that rose light. Instead of disappointment, it made her feel covered in the sound of his name. *Sam. Samir. Moon.* All the names she knew for him. Only one of his moons could make the world slip into another season.

Miel opened her eyes as much as she could, her eyelashes shading her vision. She slipped her fingers tight between Sam's.

She felt his heartbeat in his chest. She heard him saying her name over and over, the two of them breaking against each other.

Her eyes stung, and stayed dry. She had nothing left but the will to hold on to his hand, not to lose him. The water had taken Leandro. It had almost taken Sam. She wasn't letting go. All the strength in her body she let pour toward her fingers like sand. The night would not turn to water and tear his hand from hers. No matter how much the dark became a river and the wind a current, no matter how much blood Ivy's pale fingers had taken from her, Miel would not let go of Sam.

Through the slow, loud rhythm of her own pulse in her temples, she heard him sobbing into her hair. The sound was so low, it disappeared. He was holding it tight in his throat, like he meant to stay quiet. His breathing was hard enough that she felt it staggered with his heartbeat.

She wanted to lift her hand to his cheek, to still any drops on his face before their salt reached his lips or his neck. There wasn't a reason to cry, or be afraid. She wasn't letting go, wasn't losing him. If her lips had given up any sound, she would've told him.

A lock of his hair brushed Miel's cheek, like a whip of cool air. But her skin was so hot she barely felt it. He was holding her so close his eyelashes feathered against her cheek. And she meant to hold on to these things, not lose them like silver charms slipping from her fingers and falling into dark water.

The soft brush of something small and wispy grazed Miel's cheek. She thought it was his eyelashes, or another lock of his hair, but then she felt it again.

The cool film of petals.

She looked up at Sam.

Instead of the salt of his tears, tiny rose petals, red as the blood she was losing, clung to his cheeks. One had caught on the inner corner of his eye. Another had stuck to his lower lip, a third on his temple.

He blinked, and another fell from his eyelashes.

A flicker of movement tilted inside her forearm. She felt a new burst of growth breaking through to the light. She held her gasp in her lungs, and glanced down at the green shoot, covered in tiny new leaves.

It was curling out, taking on the woody look of a rose stem. Then it uncoiled, turning green and pliable, like a morning glory vine.

One thorn snagged the fabric of Sam's shirt, pulling it back enough to find its way out of the cloth he'd tied around her arm. Then it unfurled and reached Sam's bare wrist, pressing into him. He flinched but then relaxed, and for that second she thought she could feel what he felt, the pain clean and sudden as a needle.

Then Miel felt the pull, a shift between her veins.

Red lit up the stem, the leaves and thorns tinted gold like sun on a dragonfly.

The stem was drawing blood out of Sam. Miel could feel it dripping into her.

She tried to twist away from it, to stop taking from Sam when she had already taken so much from him.

But now he held on to her, his fingers sure. Before his hand had been tense and twitching against hers. Now it kept her still.

The glow traveled from his wrist to hers, like the stem was pulling from his body not blood but light.

He held his wrist closer to hers, giving his blood to the lit-up stem. She didn't want to take it from him, to strip from him something that belonged to his body. But now he held on to her harder than she'd held on to him. Now he wouldn't let her break away from him any more than she'd let his hand go.

The few petals clinging to his cheek rained onto her neck and collarbone. The stem curled away from Sam's wrist, drawing back so close to Miel's that it tucked under the fabric of Sam's shirt around her wrist. And her body began to feel like a living thing again, her heart no longer shuddering.

The world came back to her in time to hear the Bonner sisters, their voices twisting in the air like strands of a braid.

eastern sea

☽

Giving her his blood had left his wrist sore, a good kind. His body felt that way after he'd spent the afternoon hauling in the biggest field and Cinderella pumpkins. The stem had pulled back toward Miel's wrist, and the cut from the thorn felt clean, already healing.

He felt Miel shifting her weight.

"Can you help me get up?" she asked.

If she hadn't been so streaked in her own blood, her shirt so dyed red, he would've laughed. She couldn't stand on her own. The flush had come back into her cheeks and her lips, but she was still shaking enough that he was ready to carry her if he had to.

She was already leaning on him, trying to get to her feet. He steadied her, standing with her, holding an arm around her waist.

"You have to leave," she said, but she wasn't looking at him. She was watching a point between the trees, a dark space among the fingers of yellow leaves.

It wasn't until the wind calmed that he heard why.

The sound of the Bonner girls' voices, the mingling of higher and lower pitches, their shared cadence. But instead of reckless and laughing, their voices sounded taut and pressing. They hushed each other.

"Did they do this to you?" he asked. Every time he'd covered for Peyton, every time he'd tried to remind Lian that she was not as slow as everyone thought, each hour he'd worked for Mr. Bonner, stuck him like the thorns on his mother's Callery pear tree. Not the short, clean thorns on Miel's roses. The Callery pear's were little daggers, rough, and each as long as Miel's fingers.

He felt the warmth of Miel's palm on his collarbone. Her blood had stained his undershirt, and her hand left a soft imprint of red.

Now she was looking at him. "You have to leave."

"Miel," he said, their faces close enough that he could see her pupils spreading and contracting. "Are they the ones who did this to you?"

"Go," she said. "You have to leave."

"So do you," he said.

"I'm not backing down on this," she said, looking toward the trees. Fear cut into the resolve in her voice. "I'm not backing down from them. Not anymore."

"And I'm not leaving you alone."

"Dammit, Sam." She broke away from him.

The sudden movement must have hurt her. She clutched her wrist against her, rubbing the back of her forearm with her other hand. Her steps wavered, and he set a hand on her back.

Her eyes were so coated in tears she was a blink from them spilling over. She stared, her mouth half-open.

The trembling in her eyelashes and lips was more than pain. It almost looked like pity. Her pursed lips, the slight tilt to her head, the cringe of a lost cause. Like Sam was a child trying to bring back to life a bird fallen from a nest.

"They know about you," she said.

Each word was another thorn off that pear tree. Their points didn't slide all the way into him, like the thought of the Bonner sisters hurting Miel. But they pricked him, left him scratched.

"What?" he asked.

"They saw your birth certificate," she said. "They have a copy."

Now those thorns were shredding his clothes, cutting them away from his body.

"They could out you to everyone," Miel said. She stumbled forward, away from his hand. That film of water spilled over and fell down her cheeks.

He could not shrug away the sense that his shirt, his binder, his jeans, were all turning to pieces. They were falling away from him, leaving him naked to the night and all these trees.

But it was his body. It was his to name. And he was under this roof of gold and darkness with a girl who would learn to call him whatever he named himself.

He would never let go of Samira, that girl his mother imagined when he was born. She would follow him, a blur he thought he saw out of the corner of his eye when he stood at the counter, making roti with his mother. Or he would see the silhouette of Samira crossing the woods, wearing the skirts that fit her but he could never make himself fit. Maybe one day he would see her shape, her dark hands setting the lantern of a hollow pumpkin into the water, candle lighting the carved shapes.

But this was what she would be now, his shadow, an echo of what he once was and thought he would be again. She would be less like someone he was supposed to become, and more like a sister who lived in places he could not map, a sister who kept a light but constant grasp on both his hand and his grandmother's.

No one could make him be Samira. Not him. Not the Bonner sisters. Not the signatures on that piece of paper.

The girl he needed did not hide and wait inside him. She stood with him. She always had, this girl of wildflowers and feather grass, this girl he'd painted a thousand lunar seas, a hundred incarnations of *mare nectaris* and *sinus iridum*.

Sam pulled Miel into him, her forearm the only thing between them. "I don't care what they have," he said.

"Sam," she said.

He held on to her, keeping her up. "If you're doing this, we do this together."

"Sam." His name broke into pieces on her tongue.

"Samir." He put his hand to her face, his thumb grazing her damp cheek.

She pressed her lips together, blinking against the tear caught at the inner corner of her eye.

He set the pad of his thumb against it, and she shut her eyes.

"You can call me whatever you want, but my name is Samir."

The crushing of leaves announced the Bonner sisters. They emerged from the yellow leaves, the shades of their hair like the different colors in a bloom of flame. They wore sweaters as deep and vivid as the panels of stained glass. Dark green and purple. Blue and red.

Their eyes, two sets of brown, the others green and gray, met on Sam and Miel, their bodies crushed together.

Sam pressed his hand against the back of Miel's neck. But he didn't look away from the four of them. He met as many of their eyes at a time as he could. First Peyton's and Lian's, his stare straying to Ivy and Chloe.

He straightened his back, trying to stand as tall as his mother. The soreness in his arm felt like a charm, a coin Miel had slipped into his hand. A reminder.

"I'm a boy," he said, because the rest did not matter.

He felt Miel watching him. Her whispered *What are you doing?* warmed his neck.

The lies, the rumors that might touch him tomorrow, did not matter right now. The truth was currency, new and shining. It let off light, glowing like the moon he'd set on the ground.

"I'm a boy," he said, "and I always have been."

The Bonner girls blinked at him, staying in their line, a row of vivid hair and sweaters.

Then a splintering sound, like a sheet of ice giving beneath too much weight, cut through the air.

Sam and Miel and all four of the Bonner sisters turned their faces to its source.

A crack, thick and deep as a line of paint, crossed the stained glass.

bay of rainbows

☽

$\mathcal{T}$he six of them were watching that crack crawl across the green and violet.

Samir. He was calling himself Samir. And he was looking the Bonner sisters in their faces—their faces that seemed like different panes in the same sheet of stained glass—and telling them that he knew what they knew, and he didn't care.

One set of eyes at a time, the Bonner girls were looking from the cracked stained glass to Sam and Miel. Brown and green and gray all swirling and settling on them.

Their stare was heavy as a coating of snow. It felt colder in contrast with the warmth of Sam's body, his lack of hesitation when Miel dropped her forearm from between them and he let his chest touch her. He didn't flinch away or twist his shoulder so he would not feel the front of him, would not remember what he had under the shirt that bound him down.

She thought of Aracely, coming out of the water soaked and a stranger to her own body. Surfacing as someone older than when she'd gone in, while the water had kept Miel the same age. Back then, Miel had the sorrow of a child. But Aracely's heart carried the sadness of the woman she would become.

Sorrow kept Miel still, but had aged Aracely. And that same sorrow was keeping Miel still now.

Her mother hadn't hated her. She knew that. She'd feared for her. She'd loved Miel, seen her as a daughter she could lose to petals and thorns. She'd been a young mother little older than Aracely, panicked and desperate to hold on to the children she'd made.

What mother could resist a hundred tales of roses that had stolen the souls of sons and daughters? What mother could stand against her husband's insistence that their daughter was sick, and needed to be cured, and not want to find a gentler way to do it than the sting of hot metal?

What woman could ignore the warnings of señoras and priests who said they knew how to save her child? How could she not bring her daughter down to the river when they promised the current would take this curse from her?

Miel could not choose if Ivy or the other Bonner girls or anyone else told lies.

But she could tell the truth.

Miel found Ivy's eyes.

"My mother loved me," she said. Maybe her father had too. Maybe all he did—the bandages so tight her fingers turned numb, the end of the butter knife in the gas flame—was the form his love had taken. Maybe fear had twisted it, leaving it threadbare.

But this was the thing she could remember, the thing she could say out loud.

Miel couldn't tell for sure from the faint light, the glow of the moon above them and the moon Sam had brought with him. But Ivy's eyes looked slicked wet like silver.

"My mother"—Miel said, letting each word fall with its own weight—"loved me."

She felt the sky taking the words, singing them back, like thunder echoing between clouds. They were the scream of the wind.

They were the sound of another crack snaking through the lid of the stained glass coffin. The faint light of stars and the sickle moon shining off the glass, showing how the crack had cut it in half.

A flare lit in Peyton's eyes.

She took a step back from her sisters, her glance skittering between them and the stained glass coffin.

"I like girls more than boys," she said, and a set of cracks snapped through the stained glass, with as many branches as a bare winter bough.

The rest of them flinched, drawing back.

Lian's posture rose, making her look almost as tall as Chloe.

Her irises took on a brighter color, like the green of spring leaves warming and lightening to the green of tart apples.

"I understand more than any of you know," Lian said, and another set of branching cracks frosted the glass.

These were the truths they had to tell. And Ivy looked like each one was crawling along her shoulder blades.

Chloe did not move. But the breath she drew in sounded like a finger of wind. Wisps of her hair softened her braid, the moon making the edges look almost white. Her stance looked so upright, so much like a dancer's that Miel could imagine her twirling through the pumpkin rows barefoot.

"Clara," Chloe said, landing on each of the syllables and letting her weight fall on the balls of her feet. "Her name is Clara."

Her voice was trimmed with not just defiance, but correction, as if she'd stepped in after overhearing someone telling a lie.

Even through the pain in her wrist, Miel felt a flare of guilt, shared with the rest of the town.

That baby had a name. She wasn't *Chloe Bonner's baby*, the way Miel always thought of her. She wasn't *that baby the Bonner girl had*, the words the gossip called her.

She had a name. Through all the glances and whispers, she'd had her own name, a name Chloe had given her. And until tonight, Miel had never known it. Worse, she'd never even wondered.

The cracks in the stained glass branched into smaller cracks, whitening the panels.

Their secrets were killing them. They knew it. Speaking them gave the power of those unsaid things back, but it broke them into pieces like the stained glass.

Miel had never noticed how different, how much more pointed, Chloe's chin was than the rest of them. Or how Lian's eyes were not just greener but darker, closest to Mr. Bonner's of the four of them. Or how Peyton's nose made her look so much like their mother.

Now they were all watching Ivy. Sam was watching Ivy.

Ivy, who had taken the weight of deciding when the four of them moved and breathed, the single living thing they were together. Ivy, whose secrets were so buried they didn't even ride the current of whispers in the halls.

Ivy, whose lips trembled with the tension between wanting to speak and staying quiet.

Miel almost lifted her hand, stopping Ivy from speaking.

She understood.

The woman Miel had lived with for years she had once known as her brother Leandro. Now she was Aracely, and she and Miel were two halves of a matched set. The day and night girls. Aracely had hair as gold as late afternoon, her eyes the deep brown of a wet, fertile field. Miel's hair was dark as a starless autumn, a night made brown by fall leaves, and her eyes matched the gold of low twin moons. Without each other, there was neither night nor day for either of them.

Without each other, neither of them existed.

Without her sisters, Ivy Bonner did not exist.

Ivy hadn't just wanted Miel's roses, convinced her sisters that they needed them, because she thought they would earn them the love of any boy, any heart they faltered in winning. She hadn't just wanted them because if they could have any boy they wanted, they were still the Bonner girls. And she hadn't just wanted them to be the Bonner girls so everything would go back to how it was before Chloe left them.

She had wanted them because if they were not still the Bonner girls, there was no Ivy.

If she did not live as part of the life that spread between the four of them, she did not exist.

Their mother and father, so tense with fear for and of their own daughters, had already sent Chloe away. Now Ivy would always worry over the four of them breaking apart, becoming a fraction of a life in each of their lonely bodies.

The rest of them had secrets. As much as they each existed as one Bonner girl out of four, Chloe and Lian and Peyton all had enough of lives and breaths outside of that dark blue house to have their own secrets.

But they were all Ivy had.

Ivy's mouth wavered, her lips pursing shut and then parting again. "I have nothing that's mine."

The brass hinges and joints groaned, and the glass shattered. The milky stars and blue-green sky exploded. The curves of the red and violet planets broke into pieces. The clusters of stars burst into shards, and the blue whirled in on itself like the curves of a nautilus shell. Each panel splintered like ice, spraying into enough pieces for a whole sky of constellations.

Miel and Sam shielded each other's eyes as the pieces flew. The Bonner girls crowded together, protecting each other from the glass slashing their skin, until their hair became one mass of auburn and copper and rust. The air turned to cold and glass. The wind had teeth and nails.

Sam held on to Miel tighter, their hands in each other's hair.

The echo of the glass falling faded, letting them breathe. The scent of every rose Miel had ever grown found her. Winter pine and wildflowers, cinnamon and Meyer lemons. The clash of seasons was so sharp that when she breathed it in, it traced the lining of her lungs.

They turned, all of them, to look at the broken glass. Sam and Miel tipped their faces toward it. The Bonner sisters unfurled from their huddle.

The pieces of stained glass were breaking away from the frame, not falling onto the ground but streaming up into the sky. Those tiny shards shimmered and glinted as they rose into the air, the night drawing them up. Streams of glimmering blue and violet mixed with ribbons of red and green, like the coins of sun on the surface of a river. Each piece winked with moonlight, reflecting back the gold of the birches and hickories.

Then the rose brass frame sat bare as a forest in January. There was no more locking Miel in there. No more sealing each other in to make sure they were all neat and the same as the letters in Chloe's handwriting.

They had all given up their truths, things they guarded more closely than their secrets. The words they'd spoken were streaming toward the sky with all that stained glass. None of it was any of theirs to tell unless it belonged to them.

The Bonner sisters left not together, but peeling away one at a time. First Chloe, then Lian, with a look over her shoulder. Then Peyton, hesitating and tipping her head before she spun in a half-circle and started walking.

Ivy's eyes looked wet and faceted like cut stone. Her face said words Miel knew she would never hear. *I'm sorry. I shouldn't have taken what was not mine.* Her eyes strayed to Miel's wrist, like she was wondering if she was still bleeding.

These were girls so unused to apologizing that they could not knit these unsaid things into words.

The Bonner sisters did not stay in their cluster. Instead, leaving the woods, they were red-winged birds among the yellow trees.

But they kept close enough together that they could hear one another. Sisters, four of them, instead of one organism in four pretty, blurred-together bodies. To become themselves, to become sisters to one another and sisters of their own, they'd had to give up being the Bonner girls, las gringas bonitas. The being that moved and breathed together, that stole boys and cats and roses and anything else they wanted.

Miel turned her back to the stained glass coffin, her forearm hot and sore but calming.

Sam stopped her, his hand on her back.

Miel's eyes paused on her own collarbone.

A wave of copper spilled over her shoulders. Her hair had turned the color of scarlet oak leaves, as deep red as Ivy's. It looked like a curtain of autumn.

Miel squinted toward the trees, picking out a dark fall of hair.

Ivy looked over her shoulder, the copper that once marked her now as dark as Aracely's eyes. The brown, almost black, made Ivy's face look pale as a cream pumpkin. Miel could almost pick out the two points of her eyes, now both bluer and grayer. But Ivy was too far off for her to be sure, and a rain of yellow leaves fell between them.

Miel pinched a lock of her own hair between her fingers. It could have been her hours locked in that stained glass where they locked each other. Or the moment when she realized she was as intertwined with Aracely as Ivy was with her sisters. Either way, the Bonner girls had left her a little of what made them.

But that wasn't where Sam's eyes landed now.

She lifted her chin, looking where he was looking.

Far off, in the direction of the Bonners' farm, the glitter of broken glass was rising above the trees. Miel and Sam watched it drifting into the sky.

The glass pumpkins, in all those violets and greens and blues, had shattered like the stained glass coffin. And the little shards were floating up, like snow the sky was taking back. They were studding the stars with their jeweled light. A deep autumn of glass constellations, like the summer of Aracely's arrival among those hundred thousand golden wings.

All these broken pieces, becoming a hundred thousand unmapped stars.

bay of love

☽

*T*here were whispers about it, about all of it. The glass rising into the sky like new-cut stars. The way Ivy's hair had
darkened to almost black. How Miel's had turned so red that, when
her skin was lighter in winter, at a distance, she could almost pass
for one of the Bonner sisters.

How Chloe had left, and no one knew yet if she was staying with
her aunt for good, both of them caring for her baby, or if she would
bring her daughter—Clara—back with her. How the rest of the
Bonner girls might or might not be coming back to school.

Not long after that night, Ivy sent Miel a cutting of her own hair,
along with the pressed flowers of the roses she'd taken. The orange
one, turned a little tan at the edges. The deep purple one they'd
sliced away in the dark. The yellow one streaked in its own red and
the dried wine stains of Miel's blood.

Miel had shivered a little opening the envelope, seeing those flowers between wax paper, and the lock of hair that looked so much like her own it took her a minute to remember hers was now red.

This was the closest to an apology Miel would ever get. This was Ivy's acknowledgment that she and her sisters had spent so long drawing life from the act of taking what did not belong to them.

That was the part that found its way into the whispers of this town. Those pressed roses and that lock of hair became woven into the story they told.

But there was something before that, that didn't.

The night after the sky had taken all the stained glass, Miel asked Sam for a moon he didn't mind never seeing again. He'd known what she meant, and gave her one so light gray it looked silver. Like the moon in those library atlases.

Miel and Aracely brought it outside, held it up, waited for the sky to take it.

Their mother would have a light to see by no matter whether the moon above them was a sickle or a bright coin. She could leave her broken heart with them. If she let it go, if she let it streak down to the earth like a fallen star, her spirit would be so light, so un-weighted, she would float to places so beautiful they could not be told in stories.

The wind came, and took the moon, the air filling it like a sail. It drifted away, pale and translucent as a slice of jicama. When the trees moved, leaves covered it, and its light flickered like a star.

Miel didn't hear her mother's voice on the wind. Neither did Aracely. Later, Aracely said that was a good thing. She said it meant that, like all the stained glass—Aracely had seen it that night too, speckling the dark—their mother had drifted free of this world. She was untethered by gravity or worry over her children, and the water didn't pull on her anymore.

Miel and Aracely stood with the cut grass brushing their bare feet, watching the moon until its light turned as small and faint as a firefly.

Then it was just them, on that patch of their yard, two sisters lifting their hands to the sky.

sea of nectar

☽

For so long, talking about Samira, acknowledging her as someone who no longer lived in him, had felt dangerous as running his fingers along a sharp edge. It had been Miel eating a slick of honey off a knife. It was an heirloom blade his mother would not leave out, fearing Sam was still a child who might cut himself.

But now he was Samir, and Samira was that friend he almost thought he imagined. And she would be a little more imaginary once he and his mother finished changing his name. He wanted to neither forget she existed nor live inside her.

She was someone he could not be.

He would need to consider everything he'd ignored. How hard he had to work to keep his voice at the pitch he wanted, how it was low enough that no one in person gave him a second look but still high enough that he avoided the phone whenever he could. The way he bled, at the same time each month as Miel, when the moon was a wisp of light so thin it was almost new. How he would have to figure out if these things bothered him because he didn't want anyone else to know about the effort it took, or simply because they were.

But for now, he knew this, that his name was Samir, and that he wanted every piece of paper declaring who he was to say it.

They could call him Moon if they wanted. They could still call him Sam. But when he said his name, he would be Samir, the sum of the blood his mother had given him and the man he was becoming. When he met a stranger and introduced himself, he would be Samir.

But he didn't have to tell Miel what to call him. She knew. She knew him.

She was outside, waiting for him in the space between their houses. And his hand was on the knob of his bedroom door, but his fingers would not turn it.

He couldn't settle on why they wouldn't do it. All he had to do step into the hall, go downstairs and outside, and she'd be there. This wasn't even the first time he was seeing her today. That afternoon he'd brought her to the Shanholts' farm, where he was working now. He'd set a wooden-handled pollination brush against her palm, the bristles pale as wheat, and shown her the rhythm of sweeping the bristles over the anther of one pumpkin flower and then spreading the pollen onto another. He'd knelt next to her. The hem of her skirt, damp and picking up a fine coating of dust, had brushed his jeans.

Still, he could not move from this space in front of his bedroom door. Not even for the girl tracing the path of light left by his moons.

He may have known the surface of the moon, memorized the names of the lunar *maria*, but Miel had done more than that with him. She'd learned him, but left room for the way he was still learning himself. She knew the shape of him, every place that was shadow and every place that reflected light, without deciding he was hers to name.

His hand drew back, to his own body.

He let his hands move, not thinking enough to stop them. They stripped off his jacket, his shirt, his undershirt, his binder, until he was naked from the waist up.

Then they put all of them back on him, every piece except one.

This time, when his fingers found the doorknob, they turned it.

To anyone else, anyone not looking closely, he would have been the same. A boy in the dark, a jacket thrown on over his shirt.

But Miel noticed. As soon as she saw him, she noticed. He'd left his jacket open, and she could see the shape of his chest through his shirt.

Her eyes flashed down his body before she drew them back up.

He laughed. He'd expected that, her startling a little when she realized he'd come outside without his binder on under his clothes. In front of anyone else, he always wore the binder, then an undershirt, then another shirt over it. Now it was just the shirt and the undershirt, covering him but showing her more of the shape of him than he'd ever let her see.

But he hadn't expected the look that came with it, her mouth open a little more.

He'd worried that any girl who ever saw him like this would look at him like a pinned insect. He'd worried that, with clothes on, he was the brown underside of a butterfly, blending in with branches and bark, but that, naked, the reality of his body would be as startling as the bright blue-green of its inner wings.

That look though. It told him Miel was interested, not fascinated. To her, he was not a specimen.

He was someone she wanted.

He could give his body, as it was, to the one girl who understood it was not the whole of him. That there was a story told not just in the contours of his chest and what he had or did not have pressing against the center seam of his jeans. The rest of him was in what he chose. His haircut. His clothes.

His name.

Miel wasn't looking around, searching the dark. There was no one else out there in the space between their houses, lit by a string of his moons. She knew that. It wasn't about them being seen. But there was still doubt in her face when she looked at his shirt, not embarrassed, but protective.

He wondered if that was the look he had when he saw a rose opening on her wrist, that feeling of wanting to guard it. He would have felt that now if anyone else was around, Miel's newest rose showing at the edge of her sleeve. The shell of the outer petals, cream-white as a moon, held a center as dark as her lipstick. The half-open blossom let off a scent that was less perfume and more oak and moss.

Light from the moons he'd hung out here brightened her hair, bleaching it from dark red to the color of rose apples. The white sliver of the moon in the sky traced her hands.

She had given Ivy Bonner something Ivy had never had, a part of her that was her own, that none of her sisters could lay claim to. Ivy's hair seemed black against the same pale coloring she shared with her sisters, and the soft brown of Miel's skin made that red look less like fire and more like blood oranges.

Ivy would always be a Bonner girl, and she and Miel would always have a spider-silk-thin thread between them that he only half understood. She still hadn't told him everything that had happened.

But these were things he needed to give her time to say. She'd given him years to tell her his name.

He pushed a lock of hair out of her face, a ribbon the color of apricot honey.

She caught him looking at it. "Does it bother you?"

He looked down at his chest, unbound under his shirt and his undershirt. "Does this?"

"It never did," she said. "But you don't have to do this. Not for me. Not for anyone."

"I know," he said. "And you're not anyone."

Miel slid one hand into the back pocket of his jeans. A flinch went through his back and hips, but he didn't pull away. She put her other hand between his shoulder blades, and the petals of her rose brushed the back of his neck.

She kept a little space between them, enough to keep the warmth of his body from meeting hers. She was following rules they had never set in words but that they'd held to, that there were parts of him he did not want to be reminded of.

But right now he wanted to claim all of himself.

When he got dressed for school, he'd put the binder back on before he put on anything else. He didn't want anyone looking at him and deciding for him what he was.

Tonight, though, he wanted to feel every part of his own body, and know it could not name him. It could not force him into a life that had never been his.

"If you're not ready," Miel said.

He took her hand and set it on the edge of his shirt, letting her fingers grasp the hem. "I am."

lake of hope

)

For so long she'd been so afraid of everything that grew in the pumpkin fields that she'd never understood the small miracle Sam's hands had held. His hands and his brushes turned paper and paint into moons, and his hands and the pollination brush turned the possibility of things growing into the truth of them growing. It made blossoms that opened for one day become flesh and seeds and so many colors.

With the warmth of his palm on the back of her hand, she'd learned it, this craft of taking a glint of possibility and helping it become the thing waiting inside it.

Aracely had taught Miel that so many things worth fearing—the water, the dark—brought with them things worth wanting. The river kept this town's fields growing and alive. The dark gave them the stars and the sudden warmth of certain fall nights.

But there were some things only a boy named Samir could teach her, because he had lived them with her. And this was the one she held onto now, as they stood in the wild land between their houses: that they would both become what they could not yet imagine, and that they would still be what they once were. The girl from the water tower, a rose growing from her wrist, and the boy on the wooden ladder, hanging the moon close enough for them to find.

Author's Note

)

*I*t wasn't long after we met, when we fell in love as teens, that I wondered if my not-yet-husband might be transgender. I wondered when I saw him wince at being included in the terms *ladies* or *girls.* I wondered when I caught his hopefulness at being called *young man,* and his devastation when a closer survey of his body in a T-shirt and jeans elicited an apology, an *oh, I'm so sorry, young lady.*

If I understood him in a way he didn't yet understand himself, he did the same for me. He knew my childhood nightmares of la llorona, the mythical spirit-woman who had drowned her children and now wailed through the night, looking to steal mestiza daughters like me from our parents. I had no idea I would later reimagine the legend of la llorona in a book about a girl who fears pumpkins and a boy who paints moons. All I knew as a child was that my fear of her was evidence that I'd been born between two worlds. And in his unease with the gender he'd been assigned at birth, my not-yet-husband knew a little about that feeling.

We're young enough, and all of this happened recently enough, that we heard the word *transgender* as we moved from our teens into our twenties. But neither of us could say it yet. Saying it would have marked a point my husband couldn't turn back from.

It was during this time that I learned of bacha posh, a cultural practice in parts of Afghanistan and Pakistan in which families who have daughters but no sons dress a daughter as a boy. This daughter then acts as a son to the family. As an adult, a bacha posh traditionally returns to living as a girl, now a woman.

It's understandable that often a bacha posh has difficulty adjusting to her role as an adult woman after years of living as a boy. From the other side of the world, it's easy to pretend this discomfort is just a product of the culture she lives in. But what daughter, in any part of the world, could learn the language of being a boy and not feel unsettled stepping back into her role as a young woman?

That space, between the lives boys and girls are expected to inhabit, came into sharper focus when my husband did come out as transgender, and as he transitioned to living in a way that better reflected his gender identity.

As teens, we feel the growing weight of questions we've held in our hands since we were children. For my husband, that question was how he wanted to live and what name he wanted to be called. For me, it was whether I could see myself as something more than a daughter born in that space between worlds.

Something happened when we sat with those questions, together but quiet. The boy I married became the man he'd never thought he was allowed to be. And I came to understand that the night held not only la llorona but the moon and all those stars.

This is the thing I learned from loving a transgender boy who took years to say his own name: that waiting with someone, existing in that quiet, wondering space with them when they need it, is worth all the words we have in us.